FINDING HARMONY

ROSEVILLE ROMANCES

Book One: Picture Imperfect
Book Two: Finding Harmony

FINDING HARMONY

by

Alyssa Roat   Hope Bolinger

Finding Harmony
Published by Mountain Brook Ink
White Salmon, WA U.S.A.

The website addresses shown in this book are not intended in any way to be or imply an endorsement on the part of Mountain Brook Ink, nor do we vouch for their content.

This story is a work of fiction. All characters and events are the product of the author's imagination. Any resemblance to any person, living or dead, is coincidental.

© 2022 Alyssa Roat and Hope Bolinger
Published in association with Cyle Young of Cyle Young Literary Elite.
ISBN 978-1943959-78-5

The Team: Miralee Ferrell, Nikki Wright, Kristen Johnson, Cindy Jackson
Cover Design: Indie Cover Design, Lynnette Bonner Designer

Mountain Brook Ink is an inspirational publisher offering fiction you can believe in.
Printed in the United States of America

HOPE'S ACKNOWLEDGMENTS

Here we stand at the precipice of another book, and I have a million and one people to thank, and only one page (give or take) to do so.

First, I want to thank my Lord and Savior, Jesus Christ. Jesus, you deserve all honor and praise, and I know I don't give nearly enough when I worship you. Remind me about what worship really means and help me to put aside personal preferences.

Secondly, to Alyssa. For the number of phone calls I sent your way, the strict deadlines I put you under. Thank you for teaming up with me as we write another book—to laugh/cry about all the relatable struggles our characters go through—from cars without AC to recipes gone wrong.

To my family who is ever supportive in my writing endeavors, and who gave me a love of music.

To my encouragement squad: The Merlin Group (or whatever you're called when this book releases, it changes so often), Pizza Squad, Sonya, James, Carlee, and David. Thank you for telling me when it's okay to have boundaries for myself, and when to say no.

To my church, especially to the worship team, for pouring your hearts out to God on a weekly basis.

To all music teachers and ensemble leaders, who instilled a love for music in us. Looking at you: Connie, Mrs. Moore, Dr. Kwan, and so many others.

To Miralee and Tessa, who believed in us and this book. We know it's a gamble to take on us younger folks, so thank you for bearing with our millions of ideas and characters.

To our cover revealers, reviewers, endorsers, and everyone who got the word out about our books. Without you, we would be absolutely nowhere.

And to the readers. Your notes of encouragement have gotten us through the toughest of days. Thank you for journeying with us on another story.

ALYSSA'S ACKNOWLEDGMENTS

How delightful to be sitting here continuing the stories of our Roseville characters, exploring another aspect of the arts. And it wouldn't be possible without so many people.

Who else to start this off but Hope? Hope who says, "Hey, what if we did this?" when I don't even think to try. (Like writing romance.) And then it turns out to be a great idea. We have so much fun chatting and plotting these stories, coming up with relatable problems for our fellow twenty-somethings. Thank you for being the best co-author a gal could ask for. You've got the hustle, the heart, and the humor.

To my family, always cheering me on, championing my books, and loving me unconditionally. And telling me not to burn myself out, like certain characters.

To the musical influences in my life, from my mom for putting me into lessons, to my wonderful piano teacher as a teen, Mrs. Dowdle, to Dr. Collins at TU who let me write odes to bread in Music Comp, and to the rest of the Taylor University music department faculty, including Dr. Kwan and the Taylor Ringers. To Jesus, who put music in my heart.

To "the squads," be that the Henchfolks, the prowrites, the Pizza Squad, the Soodleppoodlert, the Noblesville Peeps, for cheering us on and telling me when to take a chill pill and have fun. To Juli and Steph, my sisters.

To Miralee and Nikki, my MBI family.

And to our book community and our readers, who delight us by sharing our stories far and wide and clamoring for the sequels. You're why we do what we do. Thank you!

HOPE'S DEDICATION

*To Ian and Libby, more family to love, and more
people who share in the insatiable love of music.*

ALYSSA'S DEDICATION

*To Linda Dowdle, who taught me the language of music.
You always told me God would use the music for
things I couldn't imagine, and you were right.*

Chapter One

OLIVIA WILSON CLOSED HER EYES, LETTING the music flow through her arms, her wrists, her fingers, and into the keys.

The full sound of the grand piano reverberating through the sanctuary rolled over her, filling her heart and pouring more music out through her hands.

She hit an A flat and winced. Slightly off. That was the third out-of-tune note she'd hit. Definitely time for the piano tuner to come take a look.

Her buzzing phone interrupted the rich harmonies. She sighed and glanced at the caller ID before picking up with a smile. "Hey, Caroline."

Her roommate immediately started speaking, words coming as fast as an auctioneer. "Liv! Helping Hope has an event going on in one hour, and I'm not technically going but I'm supposed to pick up the cupcakes and bring them by, but my car won't start and the icing is starting to melt and…"

Liv pressed two fingers over her lips, containing a laugh. "You need me to come pick you up?"

"Yes, please. I'm at Charlie's Confections. Andy's doing a mural or something on the other side of town and I could try to jump my car but I think that might take too long and—"

"I got you, girl. I'll be there in ten minutes."

Liv hung up, shaking her head. Everything was always a crisis with Caroline. Thank goodness Caroline's boyfriend, Andy, had an easygoing manner that helped keep her grounded.

Liv looked back at the piano and sighed. She would have preferred to spend a bit more time enjoying the full grand, unlike the uprights she usually got to play. The elderly woman who played on Sunday mornings had asked Liv to check if it was out of tune.

"It sounds a little out of sorts," she'd said with a chuckle. "I heard that you teach my grandkids and thought maybe you could give a listen. I can play hymns just fine, but I don't have any of that fancy training."

Liv had already taught two piano lessons to homeschooled children today, and she had a shift at the coffee shop later, but she couldn't help saying yes to the sweet woman. The congregation deserved to enjoy a tuned piano, and Liv would be out of town tomorrow for her usual first-Saturday-of-the-month visit to her dad. So, she'd squeezed it in.

It looked like she needed to squeeze in a roommate rescue as well.

She grabbed her purse, slung it over her shoulder, and headed down the aisle, her lightweight maxi skirt fluttering behind her while her sandals flip flopped. She nodded to the church secretary on her way out the door.

Outside, the summer sun paired with humidity created a dense atmosphere that reminded Liv of an ill-fated tomato soup she'd tried to make a few days ago. Never again. Squinting, she dug for her sunglasses in her purse, found them on top of her head, and slipped them on.

She climbed into her old sky-blue Volkswagen Beetle, nearly the same color as Caroline's car, though more faded over the years. Each time she turned the key in the ignition, she wondered if today would be the day the Bug finally went kaput, but so far it still puttered along.

She left one window down—the AC hadn't worked in over a year—and tapped her fingers to a song on the local radio station while the breeze from the moving vehicle slapped tendrils of dark hair out of her messy bun and into her face.

The song ended and a tinny voice spoke through the static of the old radio. "Calling all music aficionados! It's the fourth annual Roseville Indie Music Festival."

Liv reached over and turned up the volume knob.

"Do you think you have what it takes to be the next big artist? Come on down to the Damask County Fairgrounds and…"

A turn coming up snagged Liv's attention. She turned on her blinker, merged lanes, then tuned back in to what the radio host was saying.

"Your song could play on 92.5 FM, The Beat! Head down to the county fairgrounds."

An ad for car insurance followed the announcement. A Roseville music festival? Liv had missed most of the details, but some of her students might be interested in attending. She ran through the list of kids of all ages whom she taught piano or voice lessons. Asher seemed to like indie music, or maybe Mia...Claire only had an ear for the classics.

Her smile thinking of her students melted into a frown. The list grew smaller every day. Fewer parents seemed willing to pay for private tutors anymore.

She pulled into the parking lot of Charlie's Confections. As she stepped out of the car, a woman in slacks, heels, and a tight bun hurried out of the shop toward her.

"Liv!" Caroline threw her arms around her roommate. "Thank goodness. I had to take the cupcakes back into the shop so they would quit melting. The event is at The Vine."

The Vine? Liv had sung with the worship band at the enormous church a few times. She tilted her head. "Why there? Why not at the Hope Club?"

Caroline worked for Helping Hope Publishing, a nonprofit publishing house that specialized in helping kids. The Hope Club was the local boys and girls club run by the organization.

Caroline shook her head, tugging Liv toward the shop. "No way. This is a *donor* event. Super fancy. Too fancy even for me. I'm just the cupcake girl. They have a big conference room rented or something."

Liv suppressed another smile. In her no-nonsense business attire, Caroline looked nothing like a "cupcake girl." Caroline could switch on her professional charm in an instant—when she wasn't panicking about life.

The bell at the door jingled and cool air washed over Liv inside the shop. She only had a few seconds to bask in the cool air and the scent of fresh baked goods before Caroline was hefting what looked like five dozen intricately frosted cupcakes in distinctive blue and white Charlie's boxes. Caroline nodded to the round-faced man behind the counter. "Thanks, Charlie."

He watched Caroline with a furrowed brow. "Careful with those."

Liv swiped two boxes off the top of Caroline's stack and backed into the door to open it. "Let's get these to the event before something happens to them."

After situating the cupcakes safely in the car with Caroline hovering over them like a mother hen with frosted chicks, Liv eased out of the parking lot, avoiding potholes.

Caroline wiped her brow. "Still no AC in the Bug, huh?"

"Sorry about that." Liv reached for the switches on her door. "I can roll down another window."

"I'm just grateful you came to get me." Caroline waved Liv off and rolled down the window herself.

Liv glanced at the clock. Still an hour until her shift. No worries. "Of course."

"No, really. I owe you iced coffee or something. Want to hit up She Brews after this?"

Liv laughed. "I work there in an hour."

"Perfect. We can hang out and relax for a while before you start."

Liv bit her lip. She'd been hoping to do a bit of lesson planning before work. "What about you?" She glanced at her roommate, still guarding the cupcakes protectively from any rogue bumps or potholes. "Don't you have to go back to work?"

Caroline smirked. "Nope. All the important people are at the event, so they gave us the rest of the day off."

Liv wanted to feel proud of her roommate. Just a few months ago, Caroline never would have treated a day off like, well, a day off. She would have been in the office anyway, doing who knew what. But

Caroline had learned a lot from her mom's burnout and the events of the past few months.

Instead, a small part of Liv wished Caroline did have something else to do. But she wouldn't crush this progress in Caroline's battle against workaholism. Her lessons could wait.

"Sounds like a plan. Let's just hope Griffith isn't working today."

Caroline snorted. "I pity the person who tries one of his concoctions."

Liv had learned that the hard way.

She tried to relax. *Don't worry about the lesson prep. You can do them after work. When you send Miss Evie the link to the songs you recommended. And transpose the hymn for Cherilynn into E Major.*

How did she become an unofficial music consultant for what felt like every small neighborhood church in town? At least she didn't sing at The Vine anymore.

It may be the slightest bit possible that you've agreed to do just the tiniest bit too much.

Elijah Peterson let another person go in front of him in the line at the coffee shop. Up at the front counter of She Brews, the prime Joe-on-the-go spot in Roseville, a stocky man with a buzz cut and too loud a voice called out an order for "Sarah" for a lavender macchiato.

Elijah's nose wrinkled. Sure, he'd had his fair share of cooking fails back at his apartment—hence why his roommate Andy signed him up for a cooking class this evening—but the brewista slash local playwright, Griffith, got too experimental with the flavors sometimes.

He felt a body hover behind him. Elijah spun around. Make that two bodies. A couple with their fingers laced together in a tight grip nodded at him.

"You go ahead." Elijah motioned for them to move ahead of him in the queue.

The boyfriend of the couple—his left hand didn't appear to have a ring—shook his head. "I've seen you let five people step in front of you. We're not in a rush."

Elijah nodded and tugged a strand of long black hair behind his ear. Andy had poked fun at him for rocking the "worship leader" look, a.k.a., the need to get a haircut soon. But from what Elijah could tell from YouTube videos of the previous worship leader at The Vine Community Chapel, the church where he now worked, he'd gotten just about everything right—the long hair, often tied up in a bun, the skinny jeans, the trimmed beard.

After barista Griffith fulfilled an order for a teenager who wanted a blended drink the color of hot pink cotton candy, Elijah approached the counter. He breathed in the strong scent of coffee beans and scanned the menu for the third time for a drink.

Griffith grinned as he straightened his red apron. "Want me to surprise you again today?"

Elijah's teeth crashed onto his bottom lip. The past few times he'd come here Griffith had whipped up a few "concoctions" for him. They either left a weird, sour taste on his tongue, or if they happened to make it to Elijah's stomach, caused his abdomen to sear in pain.

But when he saw the hopeful glint in Griffith's eye, a man who lived for creating the next best "flavor" and who complained during their pickup games of basketball about how every customer ordered the same five drinks, he dropped his shoulders. Relented.

"Sure, Griffith. What do you got for me today?"

Griffith squeaked the lid off of a marker to write Elijah's name on a plastic cup. "An iced lavender matcha with a couple of pumps of vanilla syrup."

Oh, goodness, that sounded horrendous. "I'll bet it's amazing." Elijah winced. He strolled to the end of the counter and waited for Griffith to call his name.

As Griffith dumped a scoopful of ice into Elijah's cup, the door to the store dinged. In walked a towering man with ice blond hair that screamed a Scandinavian descent. Mason Smith, head pastor of Vine

Community Chapel, nodded at Elijah and then selected a table near the door. Right then, Griffith slid the drink onto the counter, and Elijah scooped the cold beverage into his hands.

Here went nothing.

He swallowed hard and strode to the table. Perhaps this time in their weekly Friday coffee meeting, Pastor Smith would have something positive to say.

It would be the first time in their history since Elijah took over the worship leader position in the spring. But like his constant agreement to try Griffith's drinks, perhaps miracles could happen.

The long red straw to the drink slipped into his mouth when he reached the table. A mouthful of sickening sweet juice that somehow tasted of grass smothered his tongue. Yikes. So much for that.

Elijah slid into the seat and noted how the plastic chair dug into his leg.

"Morning, Lij." Pastor Smith leaned against the windowpane near the table. Summer sunlight dazzled his brilliant blue eyes.

Okay, his boss had begun the conversation with Elijah's nickname, a decent start.

Smith dug into his pocket and procured a phone. Elijah's shoulders dropped. Great, the part of the meeting he hated, the emails. "Sorry to head off the meeting this way." True, they often started everything by talking about the latest Wolverines baseball game before they got to…the complaints. The many, many gripes from church members. "But I double-booked myself this afternoon with a couple doing premarital counseling. This shouldn't take long."

Elijah wore his best it's-okay-I-love-getting-lambasted-by-the-congregation smile.

"To be honest." Smith rubbed the corners of his eyes and placed his phone on the table. "I may just have the church secretary forward these to you. They've been filling up my inbox, and I keep losing important emails about counseling and funerals in the shuffle."

"Sure, no problem." The words lodged in Elijah's throat like the blended drink Griffith made him last week with caramel and grape. He shuddered. Never again.

"Most of the disgruntled messages are about Sarah. Her harmonies are a little experimental."

The worship team of the large church often had three of its female singers on rotation. Alexandra had to put her time on hold because since May, she'd been taking care of her mom at home. And Sarah...well, Sarah liked to do Mariah Carey types of runs, where the notes would bobble in her throat. Except, unlike Mariah, Sarah seldom found the right key.

They did have one other vocalist who knew harmony and the keyboard like she'd come out of the womb singing and playing piano at the same time. But ever since last Easter, part-time jobs and freelance gigs had swallowed her whole. He hadn't heard from her since.

Pastor Smith tapped the table with his large palm. Then he scooped his phone into his hand. "Go ahead and look over the emails the secretary forwards you today. Try to change the worship set by Sunday based on their feedback."

"No problem."

Problem indeed. The band had already practiced this week, and Elijah had spent Monday through Wednesday trying to address the complaint of an elderly woman who said he made her stand too long during worship. He'd vowed to have three songs at the beginning of service and two after the sermon to accommodate.

Much as he would love to be honest with Pastor Smith, he *had* just gotten the job months before. Something told him that if he put too much on the pastor that he'd have to scroll through employment listings on Indeed again.

But who knew what else he'd have to fix now?

Smith meant well, of course. From what Elijah could tell, a number of congregation members had left the church when the previous worship leader retired. "People do that," Pastor Smith had told him back in May. "Withhold giving or leave a church entirely when their favorite worship leader or pastor goes away."

A buzz from Smith's phone vibrated in his hand. He pressed the device to his ear, gave a half-hearted wave to Elijah, and disappeared out of the shop. A heavy sigh deflated Elijah. He realized, moments later, that he'd splashed bright-green liquid onto his pants. Must've gotten a splotch of Griffith's drink on his jeans when he sat.

He hopped off his seat and headed toward the restrooms at the other end of the shop. Giggles from a table with teenagers and blended drinks prickled his ears on the way. When he reached the door to the men's room, he halted when he saw a bright orange sheet attached to the Community Announcements corkboard. Business cards and posters for various local businesses littered the notice board situated between the two restrooms.

Once his retinas recovered from the blazing orange, he read.

Roseville Fourth Annual Indie Music Festival

What: Performers from the city of Roseville and surrounding areas play an original song with the hopes of being chosen to be the next big musical sensation.

Where: Damask County Fairgrounds

Prizes: 1st place - $20,000, a deal with Diatonic Records, and your song will be played on local hit radio stations such as 92.5 FM, The Beat

Before he could read the second and third place prizes, his eyes scanned over the prize dollar amount again. Twenty grand? He made that over the span of a year. And even though worship leading was supposed to be "part-time," with all the changes Pastor Smith had him do, he ended up working way more.

But with that amount of money…wow, he could do a lot with that.

His heart sank when he read the "When" section. How could he ever pull together a song in less than a month? And who would he play with? The worship band, maybe? He doubted they had the time to compose lyrics or chords.

"Sorry, excuse me." A girl with black hair and bangles that clanked on her arms tapped his shoulder. Those gorgeous dark brown eyes trapped him for a moment, like a chorus to a song that wouldn't let him go. Scarlet covered her cheeks and she motioned to the restroom.

He didn't realize he'd been blocking the entrance. "Whoops, my bad!" Elijah stepped to the side, and recognition dawned. The third girl on the worship set rotation, the one who could find the harmony. "Olivia, right?"

She moved a bracelet up and down her arm in a motion he assumed she did often and without conscious thought. "Liv, actually."

"You have one of the most beautiful voices I've ever heard." And beautiful eyes too, but he didn't add this part. "It's too late to add you to the set this week, but any way we could work you back into the worship rotation of singers at church?" He held back a "please." Something about her woodsy perfume clouded his senses, and he couldn't get all the words out.

Having Liv on the worship set could save them. Maybe the congregation would hear her vocals and forget about their aching feet or Sarah's attempts and failures to find the right notes.

Liv chewed on her lip and dropped the armlet onto her wrist with a clank. "I'd love to, believe me." She winced. "But I just don't have enough time." With that, she ducked into the women's restroom and disappeared.

Chapter Two

OLIVIA HUNG UP HER APRON IN the back and grabbed her purse. She took a deep breath, held it, and exhaled while relaxing her shoulders.

Coffee shop shift—done. Next stop, home, some dinner, and lesson plans.

"Bye, Liv, take care." Griffith flapped a dish towel at her in goodbye, his stage voice projecting across the shop.

She waved back as she pushed through the jingling shop door and headed for her car. She shot off a text to Caroline to tell her she was on her way home.

Her phone buzzed when she slid behind the wheel of her car.

Caroline: Great! I have takeout Chinese ready for you. And some special news ;)

Something about that winky face made Liv nervous.

At home, the fried scent of orange chicken and chow mein wafted through the apartment as soon as Liv opened the door. She heard Caroline humming in the other room as she put down her purse and took off her shoes.

Caroline came bobbing out of her bedroom with a small ball of fluff in her hands, singing, "Who's the cutest hamster in the whole wide world? It's *Raaaaabbiiiiit.*"

Liv snorted. "Great song."

"Thanks. Rabbit likes it." Caroline tucked her dwarf hamster into the breast pocket of her blouse and handed him a slice of carrot. "Come eat. You don't have much time."

Liv headed for the kitchen. "What are we doing? Does it have to do with the special news?"

"Not we. *You.*" Caroline clasped her hands together in excitement. "I signed you up for cooking classes."

Liv blinked. Her mind sputtered, struggling to compute. "Cooking classes?" she repeated.

Caroline grabbed a flyer off the table and handed it to Liv. "I saw this on one of the tables at She Brews. I called and got you one of the last available slots."

Liv scanned the flyer. "Boris's Cooking for Beginners," she read. The culinary class would be held at the community center. She glanced up at Caroline. "Twice a week for six weeks?" That was a lot of sessions.

"Yup. And for such a good price. Boris even gave me a discount." Caroline beamed. "I know how much you like to cook. And how it...sometimes...doesn't turn out the way you plan."

"You mean like the cabbage catastrophe?" Liv's lips twitched.

Caroline laughed. "Exactly."

Liv was a terrible cook, and she'd be the first to admit it. A cooking class could be fun and helpful. But twice a week? And... She glanced at the flyer. "Uh. Does that say the first class is tonight?"

"Right. That's why you need to hustle. You have about half an hour until class starts." Caroline picked up a box of noodles and thrust the container at Liv.

Lesson plans, song recommendations, transposing hymns. Liv accepted the carton while her brain whirred with all the tasks she had yet to accomplish. *I don't have time for cooking classes. I hardly have time for my other obligations.* Should she say no?

"Surprise!" Caroline grinned. "I can't wait to try all your new dishes. I know you're not a fan of all my kale and quinoa."

Liv bit her lip. Thanks to Caroline's strict mother, Caroline's culinary talents tended toward the super-healthy, which Liv often found synonymous with super-tasteless and super-cardboard-y. For both their sakes, someone in this apartment really needed to know how to cook decently.

"My coworker Zinnia is going too. She was talking about it at work this morning, and she was worried she would be the only adult. I told her you would be going, so at least she'd have you."

Zinnia, the coworker Caroline never got along with. Great.

But now someone else expected Liv to be there too.

Her mind wandered to tomorrow, when she would go to see her dad. She imagined if she could make him a home-cooked meal. What if she brought a casserole or lasagna or something to the table? She could treat her father to something other than sandwiches. He probably hadn't had someone make him a true meal in the fifteen years since Liv's mom passed away. Liv certainly hadn't.

Though he swore he loved Liv's sandwiches.

"That sounds great." Liv plopped into a chair at the kitchen table. "Thanks for signing me up, Caroline."

Caroline bounced. "Of course. I'm going to put Rabbit away and join you."

Liv dug into the chow mein, trying to convince herself she'd made the right decision. *Just two nights a week. And only for a little over a month. That's not bad, right?*

Caroline returned, slid into a seat, and grabbed the orange chicken, daintily lifting a piece with chopsticks. Liv set down her plastic fork and grabbed the other pair of chopsticks on the table. She leaned over and stabbed a piece of chicken with a single stick, popping it in her mouth like a kebab.

"Heathen," Caroline muttered, chuckling. Her expression turned sly. "There's another person in the cooking class you'll know."

Liv slurped up a noodle. "Who?"

"I guess you'll find out." She sat straight-backed, dabbing an invisible crumb from her lip with a napkin that she placed back in her lap. Always poised and proper. Liv knew Caroline felt self-conscious about appearances, but as far as Liv was concerned, Caroline always acted the part of a high-class professional—when she wasn't singing to a hamster.

Liv rolled her eyes. "Okay, be cryptic." She held out a hand. "Switch."

Caroline handed over the orange chicken, and Liv passed her the chow mein.

Caroline twisted the noodles with her chopsticks. "Are you doing anything fun this weekend?"

"Just seeing my dad."

"I thought you were singing with the worship band at The Vine these days." Caroline relinquished her chopsticks in favor of a fork.

"Well, I did a few times. But not anymore." Liv stabbed at the chicken.

"You liked that a lot, right? You should do it again."

"I don't really have time." With all of her jobs and obligations, she hardly found time to sleep, let alone commit to another activity and set of practices. She did miss singing with a band, though, worshipping together...

Caroline frowned. "I don't see you doing much of anything for fun anymore. You seemed super passionate about leading worship."

"I enjoy working with kids and teaching them."

"Sure, but that's work. You have to do things purely for fun sometimes."

Maybe if you didn't randomly sign me up for things like cooking classes, I'd have more time. Liv bit her tongue before the uncharitable sentiment came out of her mouth. She knew Caroline meant well. "I'll think about it."

"Good." Caroline nodded at the carton. "You almost done? You're going to be late."

Liv shoved one last piece of chicken in her mouth and stood. "I'll see you later."

"I'm ready to be dazzled by your new knowledge."

Once on the road in her Bug, Liv glanced at the clock. The community center was ten minutes away, and the class started in five. She would be late. She winced at the thought of walking in front of a crowd of students while some fancy chef with a poofy hat gave her a condescending look.

She pulled into the parking lot and rushed through the halls of the community center, scanning for a sign for the class. There, on one of the doors. Cartoon onions and carrots flew around bold letters declaring "Cooking with Boris."

Liv took a deep breath and rushed through the door.

Inside, students, mostly adults—Zinnia hadn't needed to worry—chatted at counter stations. It didn't appear the class had started yet.

She scanned the room, looking for the familiar face Caroline had hinted about. She saw Zinnia, and beside her...oh.

Elijah. The worship leader from The Vine.

She'd been surprised when she ran into him at the coffee shop to see he'd grown facial hair in the months since she'd last sung with the band. She didn't usually like beards, but his complemented his shoulder-length dark hair well. The look reminded her of Prince Caspian in the movie *The Voyage of the Dawn Treader.*

Not that Prince Caspian was her biggest childhood crush or anything.

How did Caroline figure it out? Liv hadn't said anything. After all, she hardly knew the guitar-playing, dark-eyed worship leader with the wide grin and hair that looked silkier than her own.

At that moment, Elijah seemed to spot her. His eyes brightened and he waved. "Liv. Want to partner up?"

Ah, Caroline. You've gotten me into more trouble than I realized.

Elijah didn't know what to expect when it came to that evening's cooking class. But a balding man at the front of the classroom chuckling and playing with knives didn't top the list.

To Elijah's horror, the man spotted him a moment later and introduced himself as the instructor.

"Boris Antonov." With a thick finger of the hand not holding a knife, he tapped his name tag. Elijah couldn't detect Boris's precise accent. He placed the gravel-filled sound somewhere in Eastern Europe.

Boris giggled. "Welcome to Cooking for Beginners." He waved a knife at Elijah's nose, an inch too close for comfort. "We going to have so much fun, eh?"

Andy, what did you get me into?

By reflex, Elijah stepped back, and his calves bumped something. He turned on his heel to find a cooking area behind him. The counter with carrots placed on a cutting board reminded him of the stations from the show *The Great British Bake Off* that Andy made him watch in May.

Andy claimed he enjoyed watching people from the United Kingdom stress about the orange flavorings they put in scones...but his roommate dropped one hint too many that Elijah should pay attention to the cooking technique. Elijah had a feeling this had to do with the botched Mother's Day cupcakes he made when he mixed up baking soda and baking powder.

Maybe Boris is just a little eccentric.

The brochure had mentioned that Boris had graduated from the Culinary Institute of America and worked at world-class restaurants around the globe. Why he retired and decided to teach this class, Elijah couldn't say.

"First time cooking, eh?" Boris asked as he rubbed his knife back and forth on a smooth stone placed at the cooking station in the front of the room. Elijah spun around and placed his hands on the counter behind him. Marble cooled his palms, which had grown sweaty.

As much as he would've loved to escape the conversation, and the room, something kept his sneakers rooted to the linoleum floor.

"Yeah." A nervous laugh squeaked in Elijah's throat. "Excited to learn."

Boris grabbed an orange bell pepper at his station and placed it on the singular bald spot amidst his sea of peppery hair. "You think this makes a good hat?"

"Do we have a specific station we're supposed to go to?"

"Choose anywhere you like."

By now, dozens of students had filtered in and found a spot to stand. A mere three places remained.

A voice, female and sharp, called from the door.

Elijah craned his neck at the door. He would recognize those severe, plucked eyebrows and long-taloned nails anywhere—Zinnia.

Zinnia and Elijah had only met on one occasion. This past spring, Andy needed to secure one thousand pre-orders of a picture book he and Caroline worked on together to save Caroline's job and the publishing branch at Helping Hope. Elijah chipped in with decorating, bringing guests, and helping the event to run smoothly. All of Helping Hope's employees arrived, which included Zinnia.

Although the two of them exchanged an amiable conversation over a veggie dip tray, Elijah had heard plenty of stories from Andy about how Zinnia attempted to take over the picture book project and made Caroline's life miserable at her job.

People do change.

Andy had, after all, reversed many of his procrastination habits within the span of a few months. Why couldn't Zinnia morph for the better?

With a clank, Boris set his knife on his table. He reached for a sheath cover to protect the blade from other students whose noses he'd point it at. "Go wherever you like, but you will have a partner." He winked at Elijah. "Want to stand next to pretty lady, eh?"

No, Elijah very much did not. He grimaced and clasped his hand around his forearm.

Unlike Andy, he showed up ten minutes early to everything—a habit ingrained into him since the days of his youth. Best to make light conversation with Zinnia.

"So, umm, Zinnia, what have you been up to lately?"

She tugged her blonde hair behind her ear. A dangly earring with a tassel went all the way down to her neck. "Summers are slow at Helping Hope. Been trying out for some local indie movie gigs, but."

She paused and sucked her teeth. Then she blew out a breath. "No luck."

A pang of sympathy filled Elijah's gut. He remembered auditioning for talent shows and top bands in high school and missing the cut by a fraction.

Zinnia blinked away a glaze in her eyes and forced a smile. "It's fine. It's probably a silly dream. Most people in their late twenties don't have a chance against all the younger, prettier stars."

Huh, he could relate. Members of his musical family had landed gigs in Italian opera houses and as professors of musical composition in universities by their mid-twenties. And at twenty-seven, what did he have to show for himself? A worship leader position that made the same amount of money as a retail worker, and instead of standing ovations, he got angry emails.

"It's fine." Zinnia chewed on her bottom lip. Then she rolled a large carrot on her cutting board back and forth between her palms. "I've volunteered to help with the community theater this summer, so I'll get my artistic fix then."

Right before Elijah could suggest he and Zinnia partner up for the next few classes—since he didn't have many options left—a woman rushed in the door. Above her, a clock's long hand had drifted five minutes past the starting time of the class.

Boris didn't appear to mind. At the front of the classroom, he tried various vegetables on his head to see which ones would cover the bald patch best.

Elijah's gaze roved back to the door. Hey, he'd recognize the bangles on those arms anywhere.

"Liv." He waved and then jabbed his thumb over his shoulder at the remaining station. "Want to partner up?"

Much as he enjoyed the conversation with Zinnia, he also didn't trust her. Not yet.

Liv's eyelids narrowed for a second. Not in an angry way, more like confusion had filled her for a moment. Then her eyebrows unlinked and she nodded. "Sounds good."

They met at the back of the classroom near a window. Although evening had approached, the sun bled pink into the sky. He had the perfect view—and a beautiful woman by his side helped—a lot.

"All right, class." Boris clapped his hands and stepped behind his station. "Today we gonna work on knife skills." He removed the cover from the large blade he'd pointed at Elijah earlier. "First, we'll practice the motion of cutting the carrot in front of you. Rock the knife back and forth."

Boris see-sawed his hand.

"Don't cut the vegetable. Just practice the motion. You try."

Elijah and Liv unsheathed their utensils and moved their wrists up and down.

"So." Elijah kept his eyes glued to the knife to make sure it didn't come anywhere near Liv. "You can't cook to save your life either?"

Liv snorted. "Caroline made me sign up for this. After my cabbage concoction disaster from the spring, she ducks and covers whenever I'm near the kitchen." She paused. "Don't ask."

Elijah clamped his lips shut. How did she know what he was going to ask? "Well, if it helps, Andy made me do this too. He can't even look at mayonnaise the same way after my attempt at devilled eggs."

Boris wound his way around the tables and shouted compliments at the students who rocked their knives the best.

"I don't mind it though." Liv's bangles made music as her wrist moved up and down. "I think it could be good to learn tips on spices and tricks of the kitchen trade. I'm a firm believer that spices are like harmony. Just enough, and the dish sings. Too much, and you can only taste the paprika."

Sarah could use a lesson when it came to seasonings. Liv, on the other hand...Liv knew how to pepper and sprinkle every musical recipe.

"Well, at least you're good at musical spices." Elijah frowned. That came out weird. "I know you said no, but we could use a culinary master such as yourself on the team."

Liv didn't speak for a few moments. Instead, all Elijah could hear was Boris telling Zinnia that she would "be a carrot-cutting master in no time" and that "all vegetables will fear the name of Zinnia."

Then Liv cleared her throat and set down her knife on the counter. Elijah did the same, and they both massaged their wrists.

"To be honest, Elijah, I do really miss it. Worship team, I mean. I don't know if I could make it a regular part of my schedule. But I may be able to do a few Sundays."

His heart buoyed like a balloon in his chest. "That's great!" He rubbed his thumb on a sore spot from the knife rocking. "What made you change your mind?"

Her lips twitched. She opened her mouth and then closed it again. Finally, she said, "Let's just say, I feel like spicing things up."

Chapter Three

TREES ROLLED BY, AND THE STIFF breeze from the highway billowed through the Bug from the window Liv had cracked open a few inches.

She pushed flopping strands of hair out of her face before reaching for the knob of the radio. She cranked up the volume, singing along to one of her favorite worship songs.

Vibrant green leaves waving in the trees sparkled with golden morning sunlight. Traffic remained light on a Saturday, and Liv hadn't encountered any aggressive drivers yet today.

Fifteen more minutes to her childhood home gave her plenty of time to think about her cooking class the night before. After "how to cut a vegetable 101," Boris introduced them to the exciting worlds of dicing and peeling until Liv's right hand and arm ached.

"Cooking is like sport," Boris had declared. "Practice. Build strength." He winked at Liv. "Grow big muscles, make the men want to wife."

Liv didn't think Boris quite understood typical American beauty standards, but she'd smiled and nodded.

Elijah seemed to take the weirdness of the class in stride, taking a note from Boris and placing half a bell pepper on his head as a hat. Elijah had confided that his roommate signed him up for the class too, but he seemed happy to make the best of it.

Dad was like that. Always making the best of things.

Liv frowned, putting on her blinker to make a turn onto a smaller road. Dad had called her this morning, warning that she might want to come a different time.

"My back isn't doing so hot today, Livy," he had said. She could hear the wince in his voice. "I don't know if I'll be able to move around a lot. I might not be much fun."

"Aw, no competitive pole vaulting?" Liv teased. "It's fine, Dad. We can hang out. I'll bring a book if you need to nap."

He chuckled. "Oh sure, like I'll be the only one napping."

"What, that's what afternoons are for. I'll see you in an hour and a half."

Now, driving along the wooded country road leading home, Liv tapped her fingers on the steering wheel. Despite their lighthearted banter, she worried. Dad didn't usually say much about his pain. *It must be particularly bad.* Which meant even more reason she wanted to be there to check on him.

Liv had been on winter break a mere two days before the start of her second semester of college when she got the terrible call. Her father, a contractor, had fallen three stories at a construction site. Words like "fractures" and "spinal cord" crashed over her like tidal waves. She hardly remembered her drive to the hospital, but when she had arrived, they didn't let her see him, as he was in emergency surgery.

The next few weeks felt like an unending nightmare of procedures, late nights in the hospital, and fighting with the college over being refunded for the semester. She refused to leave her father's side.

And then the medical bills had stacked up.

And she never went back to school.

Liv pulled into the long drive leading toward her childhood home. The squat, forest green house nestled between the trees, a pond sparkling behind it. Wildflowers grew around the foundation, swaying against the weather-beaten siding. It wasn't much, but this place had always been home.

Gravel crunched under her tires as she rolled to a stop and parked in front of the porch. Stepping out of the Bug, she adjusted the waistband of her flowy cotton pants and redid her bun, her bracelets clacking on her arms and jingling against her dangling earrings. With a simple tank top tucked into her colorful patterned pants, Liv felt the need to accessorize up top to balance out the bright oranges and yellows of the bottom half of her outfit. No doubt Dad would make a teasing remark about wearing half her jewelry box at once.

But she also knew he would notice her sporting at least five pieces he had given her.

She strode across the porch and knocked on the door before throwing it open. "Knock knock!"

"What's that?" a deep voice called back. "Are there varmints in my house again?"

Liv followed the sound toward the back of the house, letting the screen door bounce back into place. "Gotta be careful about leaving the door unlocked. You never know what sort of creatures will get in."

She headed through the kitchen and into the sunken den. Dad sat in his recliner, a glass of Arnold Palmer in his hand, another full glass sweating on a coaster on the end table next to a plate of shortbread cookies.

He grinned at her, slight laugh lines forming. "So far, I've liked all the critters that have gotten in. Hey, Livy."

"Hi, Dad." She bounced across the faded rug and planted a kiss on his forehead, right beneath the sweep of his salt-and-pepper hair. She tried to hide her evaluating gaze as she took in the extra rigid back brace he wore and the tightness around his eyes. He also hadn't even tried to stand to hug her. It was a bad day. "You've let other critters in?"

"Eh, you know Susan down the road likes to be nosy and pop in during her morning walk." He gestured at the second glass of lemonade and iced tea mixture sitting on the end table. "She made a whole pitcher for me yesterday. I poured you a glass."

Liv raised her eyebrows while plopping onto the couch. "A whole pitcher of your favorite drink? Something you want to tell me?"

He took a gulp of his beverage. "I don't know what you're talking about."

Liv snorted. "If you say so." She sipped from her own glass, appreciating the balance of sweet and sour and the lingering tang that indicated fresh lemons had been used. "Just interesting that a sweet, very single lady seems to be popping by to be 'nosy' so often. She's at least a twenty-minute walk down the road, isn't she?"

"Susan likes walking." Liv gave him a look, and he added, "A lot." He set down his glass, smirking. "Enough about your boring old man. What's going on with you?"

Liv shook her head, amused, but allowed him to turn the topic of conversation away from Susan. The woman had moved to the area a couple years ago after retiring. She'd been widowed for twenty years, even longer than Dad. Liv couldn't help but think God might be up to something.

Liv regaled her father with tales of her roommate, her students, and interesting coffee shop customers. She carefully avoided mention of her dwindling student list. When she got to her new cooking class from the night before and Boris's romance advice, Dad roared with laughter, then grunted in pain and put a hand to his back.

Liv winced. "Do you know why it's particularly bad today?"

He eased back in his seat, shooting her a half-teasing glare. "Don't you get started on me with the mother hen act. I didn't do anything stupid recently, if that's what you're asking."

"I seem to recall that last time, once I kept asking questions, it came out that someone had been moving furniture to vacuum." Trying to keep the conversation light-hearted, Liv tapped her finger to her lips in exaggerated thought.

"Yeah, yeah." His lips twitched as he tried to suppress a smile and keep up the peeved act. "Don't worry, the PT nagged me plenty about that one."

Liv popped a shortbread biscuit in her mouth. "How's physical therapy going?"

Dad hesitated. "Ah. I haven't been in a while."

"Oh? Why's that?"

"I don't think I need it anymore." His eyes shifted away.

Liv looked down at the back brace, then back to his face. "Yeah?"

He took a deep breath and blew it out. "I don't know how to tell you this, Livy. The medical bills...the settlement ran out a while ago.

I...they're advising me to sell the house."

Time seemed to slow, dust motes freezing in the beams of sunlight streaming through the window. Liv clutched her stomach as if she'd been punched. "The house?" she whispered.

"Well, the house itself isn't worth a whole lot, but the property..." Dad raked a hand through his hair. "We have a few acres. Plenty of renovators are looking for places with land around here. The area's gotten a lot more popular."

Liv focused on her breathing. "You and Mom bought this house when you got married. I grew up here. We've lived here—*you've* lived here—for almost thirty years."

"I know." He sighed. He opened his mouth as if to say more, closed it. Instead he repeated, "I know."

The green house in the woods had been Liv's retreat, her place of safety, even after she grew up and moved out. The rope swing still swayed next to the pond. Her initials remained carved in a tree. Each scratch, each dent and stain in this house, had a story, whether it was a pancake she accidentally stuck to the ceiling at twelve, or the time she and Dad pretended to joust in the living room with brooms and scraped paint off the wall.

Most importantly, Mom had lived here. Liv's memories were fuzzy, but most were associated with this house, whether it was sitting on Mom's lap watching the sun sparkle on the pond, or sitting in rocking chairs on the porch licking popsicles, or Mom bundling her up before she and Dad ran out to sled down the driveway in winter.

Liv reached over and took his hand. "We'll figure something out." She gave it a squeeze. "We will not lose our home."

Elijah paused the YouTube video and rubbed the corners of his eyes.

He'd watched three hours straight of worship videos from The Vine from before the previous worship leader Chris Bethel had quit.

Their church often liked to "stream" services to homes all around the Roseville area for agoraphobes and bedridden church attendees who still wanted to watch a sermon by Pastor and listen to the music beforehand.

Elijah leaned back into his family room chair. Sunlight streamed through the window and illuminated Peaches and Sammy. The two dogs, a corgi and golden retriever, played tug-o-war with a buffalo squeaky toy. A few seconds later, Sammy, the larger of the two, relented and let Peaches "win" the game.

Sammy panted and padded over to Elijah's seat. Thinking himself a lap dog, as he always did, he jumped up and plopped down onto Elijah's lap.

"Oof." Elijah grunted from the impact of a seventy-pound dog now squishing his abdomen. Then he scritched Sammy's ears. "You're probably right, buddy. I need to step away from the computer for a while."

Instead of going for a walk on this beautiful Saturday morning, Elijah had gotten up at seven to figure out how to accommodate all the emails that the church secretary forwarded him the other day. Most of them had a slightly disgruntled tone. But one of them might as well have been written in all capital letters, because Elijah felt as though the sender had shouted at him through the screen.

Elijah Peterson,

To say your music has been lacking would be generous. As a former director of the church choir, I should know the ins and outs of leading a melodic experience that brings glory to God and keeps the congregation happy. Our previous worship leader Chris Bethel seemed to grasp this concept.

Their church had a traditional service held on Saturdays for the church folks who preferred hymns and more liturgical elements. Why this man didn't choose to go to that service, Elijah couldn't say.

I have been very clear with the head pastor that if I do not see an improvement, then I will withhold tithing. As I single-handedly fund the drama club ministry, the handbell choir, and the Christmas Pageant the church holds every year—need I remind you, the number one event that brings in new members of the congregation—I do hope that you and Pastor Smith will take my messages far more seriously than you have before.

Regards,
Don Wadsworth

Pastor Smith had issued a warning to Elijah about Don when Elijah first joined the worship team. How the man with perfect pitch and two decades of conducting premiere symphonic bands in Michigan wouldn't stand for a sour note.

But he hadn't expected this.

Hence why he'd spent the morning researching previous videos of Bethel. Analyzing, filling up index cards with notes...anything he could do to find the magic formula to save church funding and his job.

Elijah rested his neck against the seat back and gazed outside. Near a tree that was stationed outside his window, a college-aged boy strummed his acoustic guitar. A group of girls had huddled around him in the grass and stared, mesmerized.

Goodness, I miss that.

Back in college, Elijah would spend hours in the lobby of his dorm plucking out notes on his old hand-me-down Dreadnought until his fingers developed calluses from the friction of the strings. He didn't care. Music and melody would drown him in a sea of tranquility until he forgot about the stress of term papers, roommate fights, and the disappointed looks on his parents' faces when he announced he'd pursue a business degree instead of landing a big musical gig like all his siblings had.

Now, fun had evaporated from the whole experience. How he dreaded Sundays.

"Does Sammy still think he's a small dog?"

Elijah hadn't even heard Andy step into the family room.

Andy combed his fingers through his dark hair. No use, the bedhead was strong with this one. Then his roommate tucked his wrinkled shirt into his shorts.

Summer had tanned Andy's skin to a nice caramel color.

"You look like you're in a rush." Elijah grunted as Sammy catapulted off of his stomach and toward Andy. It didn't matter that the two roommates had gotten the dog together when they first moved into the apartment. Sammy knew which one of them gave more treats.

"Date with Caroline. Didn't realize how much time had passed."

Elijah's lips twitched and his eyebrows raised. Even though Andy did show up to many things on time, he still hadn't quite kicked his procrastination habits.

"Sorry to do this, Lij." Andy dug into his pockets and fished out a pair of car keys. "But any chance you can take Peaches and Sammy out for me?"

O-U-T—the forbidden word caused both dogs to jump up and down and bark. Their nails clicked against the hard floor. This and F-O-O-D and T-R-E-A-T always had to be spelled out. Otherwise it would send the canines into a frenzy. Already, Peaches spun circles in the never-ending race to bite her tail.

Elijah stared back at the computer. He'd still not made complete progress with the worship set for tomorrow, especially with new emails pouring in even that morning. And the dogs liked to take their time outside. Often Peaches would spend fifteen minutes alone sniffing the same bush they passed every day.

He sighed. "Sure, Andy. No problem. You go have fun on your date."

Andy had already reached the door before Elijah finished the sentence. A single wave of the arm, and then Andy disappeared.

Peaches slumped to the floor a moment later, exhausted.

"Okay." Elijah chuckled. "Let's get your leashes." He strode to a basket where they kept the dogs' harnesses and toys. Once he dug out the purple one for Peaches and the red one for Sammy, he motioned them over. Right before he could put Peaches's harness on her, his phone buzzed on the couch.

He considered for a moment letting it go to voicemail. *But it could be Pastor Smith.* Did he really want to risk making his boss any more frustrated?

"Won't be more than a minute." He lifted a finger to indicate the number one and then booped Peaches's nose. She licked off his fingerprint.

By the third ring, he reached the couch and read the name on the screen.

Jonah Peterson.

His brother? The phone indicated Jonah wanted to do a FaceTime call. Elijah slid open the call and saw his own face on the screen. Ugh, bedhead had attacked his follicles as well, it appeared. He did his best to comb some tangles as he sat on the couch. "What's up, Jonah?"

"Thought we'd check in." Jonah grinned and then flipped the camera screen so Elijah could see the people behind him. His whole family, all with dark hair—with the exception of his opera singer sister Miriam who had to sport a redheaded 'do for Gianni Schicci—waved.

Had he missed a family gathering or something? True, he didn't get many chances to check the family group chat about happenings. Too many church emails had evaporated his time.

Jonah turned the screen back to himself and collapsed onto something. Maybe a bean bag? That would make sense considering squishy purple fabric surrounded his brother.

"We figured we hadn't heard back from you on the family vacation, so we're including you in the planning meeting."

Family vacation? Ice froze his veins.

Did Jonah mean the trip his family took to Hilton Head every year?

Had it already arrived?

"You know." Jonah rolled his eyes and cocked his head in a "you can't have forgotten about our annual family bonding time" look. "The one we are going on in ten days?"

Elijah could swear he wrote the date in a planner somewhere. He didn't have many chances to clean the apartment and find the calendar in which he marked it. Not with him taking care of church tasks all the time.

"Oh, ten days." Realization hit Elijah's abdomen like a seventy-pound dog. "I-I'm not sure if I can take off."

Not with the angry feedback from the congregation. If Elijah left on a trip, he might as well turn in a resignation too.

"What?" Although she was off screen, Miriam's sharp mezzo-soprano voice carried through the phone like a slap. "Elijah, I had to practically beg my director to let my understudy go in my place for a week. Summer is the prime time for people to attend the opera."

"Also, do you know how hard it is to get a Wednesday to Wednesday rental at Hilton Head?" another voice chimed this in. Probably his father, from the sound of the bass gruff. "We scheduled mostly weekdays since your little worship leader gig makes you work on weekends."

Elijah chewed so hard on his lip that his skin throbbed. How could he explain to them that he didn't get days off? That even during the weekdays, the pastor made him play for staff worship times, for the youth group, for men's retreats. Even though Pastor Smith took off on Mondays, Elijah couldn't. Let alone a whole week in South Carolina.

"I'm sorry, guys." Elijah sighed. "I really wish I could go. Believe me."

"That's just great, Elijah." Miriam muttered, as much as an opera singer could do that. "Thanks a lot."

With that, the phone call ended. Jonah must've spotted a nonverbal signal from Miriam to hang up.

Elijah sunk into the couch until the fabric absorbed half of him. "I can't make anyone happy."

Chapter Four

LIV SHUFFLED SIDEWAYS INTO A PEW, exchanging polite smiles with the strangers around her.

Usually when she attended The Vine, she went to the Saturday night service, but she'd stayed later than usual with Dad, so here she was on a Sunday morning, surrounded by churchgoers she didn't know.

The seats sloped down toward the stage, where Elijah and his crew set up their instruments and music stands. Conversation buzzed through the large sanctuary, bouncing off high ceilings.

Liv had come fifteen minutes early to take in the surroundings. If she was going to start singing again, she wanted to experience Sunday service from the pews. She usually opted to go with Caroline to a smaller church with an organist rather than a worship band, but Liv thought she should get to know the congregation if she planned to lead them in worship.

Unless this was a bad idea. Taking on more responsibilities, when really she needed extra work hours to help pay off medical bills.

She lifted her face toward the stained glass behind the stage and closed her eyes. *Lord, what should I do? We can't lose our house. But I don't know what we can do.*

At Liv's insistence, her father had allowed her to take a look at the finances. The situation wasn't good. Dad's part-time online consulting business didn't do nearly enough to offset the medical debt, and Liv's meager paychecks barely paid her own rent.

"Dad, you have to keep going to physical therapy," Liv had told him.

He shook his head. "Can't afford it, Livy."

"No." She took his hand. "You can't do anything if you're in too much pain to get out of bed. Your health is most important. We'll figure this out."

She opened her eyes, gazing again at the stained glass. *What should I do, Lord?* She could move back in with her father, but that wouldn't help. Her sources of income were here, in Roseville. She didn't have job opportunities there.

The popular Christian music emanating from the loudspeakers trailed off and the band onstage struck a few opening chords. Elijah leaned into the microphone. "Good morning, church. Come join us in worship."

More congregants streamed in from the foyer, taking their places in the pews. The crowd was much larger on a Sunday morning than on Saturday night, easily the largest congregation in Roseville. Liv remembered how her palms had grown sweaty the first time she sang on stage in front of this crowd. It had been with the previous worship pastor, before he...moved? Retired? She realized she didn't know.

"We have a special treat for you today," Elijah said. "The children's choir is giving a preview of the selection they're working on for Kids' Takeover Day."

"Oh, I love it when children sing," a woman said behind Liv, clapping her hands together. "Those angelic little voices."

A herd of children milled onto the stage, loosely corralled into rows by a few elderly Sunday school ladies. A woman with poofy gray hair stood in front of them. Once the mass of children had compacted into a manageable size, the woman lifted her hands and began waving her arms in what Liv assumed was meant to be conducting.

The woman behind Liv may have praised the angelic voices of children. Liv had heard some beautiful children's choirs in her time as well.

This choir bore no resemblance.

Children in the first row climbed up and down the steps. One had a finger so far up his nose Liv worried for the safety of his brain. Older children in the back scowled, muttering or mouthing what could hardly be called lyrics. A few girls belted out screeching soprano notes that had no business in the song at all, while another seemed to be dancing to a tune all her own. And...that little girl had her skirt up over her head, showing off her bloomers to the congregation.

Liv passed a hand over her face. She couldn't watch this.

At last, the cacophony died down. A few enthusiastic parents clapped wildly while the rest of the congregation offered a confused smattering of applause.

Elijah blinked for a moment, then stepped up to the microphone. "Thank you, Vine kids! While we wait for the kids to head off to their classes, let's hear from Pastor Smith for our announcements."

As the pastor ran through the events and outreaches the church should be aware of, Liv's thoughts turned back to Dad and the house. Could she take more shifts at the coffee shop? Were her rates for private lessons too high? Would she get more business with lower prices?

The band started up again, and Liv tuned back in.

The contemporary worship song started off strong, until a few beats in the blonde with the tambourine seemed to lose the key and the beat. Liv heard the voices of people around her falter, trying to follow the melody. Elijah sang louder, but he couldn't quite drown out the unruly blonde.

It felt like someone raked their fingernails down a chalkboard inside Liv's chest. She took a deep breath, focusing on her own singing rather than the chaos onstage.

None of that matters. They were making a joyful noise to the Lord. Worship didn't hinge on the prowess of the singers or musicians, the artistry of the arrangements, or even the cleverness of the lyrics. It was about communing with God and praising the Savior.

Liv's mind wandered to a distant memory. Dust motes filtered through beams of sunlight illuminating worn wooden pews in a small country church. A young Liv clutched her mother's hand while a broad-shouldered alto belted out hymns at the front of the sanctuary.

Child Liv winced. "She's not a very good singer," she complained.

Her mother squeezed her hand and leaned down to whisper, "I know, Livy. But look at her face. Look how much she's smiling."

Mom's soft face broke into a matching smile. "She's worshipping the Lord. And to Him, it's a beautiful sound." Mom poked Liv's chest. "It's about what's in here."

Mom never criticized anyone's attempts at music. She would offer instruction if asked, but she far preferred to encourage. Most of Liv's memories of her mother included a cheerful soundtrack of humming, singing, or playing in the background.

"You were meant to be famous," Dad would tell Mom. "Your name should be in playbills across the world."

Mom would take his hands, press them to her heart. "The spotlight is lonely. I would rather be here."

Liv coughed away a tightness in her chest.

Behind her, someone grumbled, "I swear they get worse every Sunday."

Liv whipped her head around and skewered the pointy-nosed woman with a reproachful look. "They're doing their best."

The woman's eyes widened. "Humph." She sniffed and looked away.

Liv faced forward once more, her cheeks burning. What had come over her? The urge to defend Elijah and his band had rushed out into an uncharitable look right in the middle of church.

Sorry, Lord.

The band launched into another song, this one so new Liv had only heard it on the radio once or twice. Even still, she could tell the blonde was off with her overly enthusiastic tambourine. Liv resolved that once the service was over, she would find Elijah and encourage him.

From the grumbles she heard around her, he would need it.

A man, scarlet-faced and fists balled, marched to the front of the sanctuary. Elijah had a *great* feeling about this.

"You." The man jabbed a finger at Elijah. On his suit, a name tag showed itself next to a khaki lapel. Don Wadsworth, etched in crimson permanent marker, threatened to burn Elijah's retinas.

Oh boy, angry email man. Elijah tore out the earpiece he wore for worship. During their songs in the service, music would play through it along with a steady beat to make sure everyone in the band stayed together.

Dryness clawed its way up his esophagus.

Elijah cleared his throat and tried to stretch his lips as wide as they could go into a smile. "Hi, Mr. Wadsworth? What can I do for you?" The headphone rested on his shoulder, attached to a cord.

Don brushed away the greeting with a quick wave of the arm. Then he paused next to the front pews, stepped inside, and pressed his hands against the backs of them. "Pastor Smith hasn't been forwarding my emails to you, has he?" He breathed out of his mouth, like he'd just completed a 5k race.

"Umm." Elijah glanced over his shoulder at his band mates for help. Busy with collecting their sheet music from their stands, they didn't take notice. *Inhale, exhale,* Elijah turned back to Don and tried to stare at the man's forehead, to avoid those bloodshot eyes. "I—"

"Of course he hasn't." Don cut him off and snatched a bulletin in the pew beside him. He flicked through the pages. "That would be why you didn't play any hymns in today's service."

Hymns? The choir often sang the classics of "Be Thou My Vision" and "Come Thou Fount" and any other tune with a "thou" in the traditional service on Saturday. *Maybe I should suggest he go to that one.* Something told Elijah that Don would shake his fist at him if he did.

"To be honest, sir." Elijah placed the guitar pick nestled between his fingers onto his music stand. "We've gotten a lot of emails with various suggestions from the congregation members. We're doing our best to make sure everyone has an enjoyable experience."

He tried to accommodate all the Sarah complaints by having no harmony parts whatsoever in today's service. And he sang the majority of the verses by himself, giving Sarah a tambourine to clap against her hip.

To his chagrin, Sarah got off-beat two measures in and wiggled the jangles by accident during a solemn moment of prayer.

Don fanned his face with the bulletin. "Frankly, I don't care what the other congregation members have to say. They don't give as much as I do." Don thrust the papers onto the pew. Even against the soft red cushioning, the impact and "clap" noise sounded all the way to the stage. "And get them to crank up the AC. I'm not paying them to broil me like a potluck dish."

Do I even know the facilities staff who could take care of that? The large church had dozens, if not hundreds, of staff members.

Don's sleek black shoes squeaked when he turned out of the pew and trooped to the back of the sanctuary.

Blue stage lights that surrounded them burned Elijah's neck. He'd have a lot to do for next week's worship set. Shakiness filled him from the confrontation. Kneeling, he tried to focus on unplugging his acoustic guitar from his amp.

"And I didn't think anyone could be crazier than Boris."

A soft voice, feminine, drew his gaze back to the sanctuary. At the base of the stage, Liv beamed at him. She tucked a flyaway hair back into her ponytail, in a somewhat shy motion. Today she wore a loose bohemian-style dress with a blue floral pattern.

"Occupational hazard." Elijah's knees cracked when he rose to stand. "I didn't know you came here regularly."

She drummed her fingertips on the black-painted platform. "I go to the service on Saturdays. That man didn't handle things well, but a lot of us do like hymns. It couldn't hurt to slip one or two into your next set."

"Maybe you can help me out with that. Sarah won't sing anything that was published earlier than the 2000s."

Sarah had already evacuated the stage. Right after the last song, she muttered something about meeting up with a friend at a local diner. So she left behind her sheet music and earpiece for the band to clean up.

"Do you have any sheet music? Maybe a hymnal?" Liv headed toward the steps that led to the stage.

"Liv, we're in a church that has all the latest gadgets and projects all the lyrics on big screens. I don't think a hymnal has touched this place in over twenty years."

"I'll do my best, then. I do think I have four or five pieces memorized. Classical training does have its perks." Liv reached the keyboard and turned the knob for the power on switch.

They didn't use this instrument today—as Sarah could, at best, plunk out Hot Cross Buns—but they left the electric piano on stage due to its heavy nature. Pastor Smith only asked them to carry it to storage when weddings, funerals, and Vacation Bible School took place.

Liv's lips curved when she placed her fingers on the white keys.

Her shoulders dropped, eyes shut, and she lifted her chin to the heavens. Then the music took over.

Elijah recognized the melody five seconds in, "It Is Well with My Soul." But this time, the notes took on light, on life. Her fingers moved up and down the octaves like she'd played this song every day of her life. She added melismas and harmonies that didn't exist in the original sheet music. Liv replayed certain lines over and over again like they'd carried her spirit somewhere far, far away, and she could not help but repeat them.

Crescendos of the final chorus filled the sanctuary so much that those members who stayed behind to fellowship stopped, stared at the stage, and drank in the music.

When she hit the final chord, leaning into the piano and pressing all her fingers into the perfect combination of notes, sadness filled Elijah's veins. How he wanted that to last forever.

A hush fell over the sanctuary.

Then conversation over church coffee in Styrofoam cups echoed once again.

Tongue numb, Elijah managed to slip out one word. "Wow."

Liv shrugged. A bashful scarlet covered her cheeks. "Or just something like that. Nothing too crazy." She switched off the keyboard. The electric hum of the instrument died.

Did she not hear the song she played? What's with the sudden humility? "You're really good. I'm surprised you don't play professionally." He bet she could even beat his brother who held first chair in the Detroit Symphony Orchestra. Granted his brother did play French horn, but still. He stood by that.

Darkness shrouded her eyes. She clasped her arm and kept her gaze glued to the stage floor. "Yeah. Maybe someday." Color and life had disappeared from her voice.

What had he said?

"Guys, you need to check out this flier."

Derek, their drummer, waved an orange flier when he emerged from his transparent shield that surrounded his drums. Their bass player, Charlize, said they often kept Derek in his "plexiglass cage" for good reason. Not only because without the acoustic shield, the crash of his cymbals would make up the sole sound of music the congregation would hear...but Derek had issues.

He wore baggy pants, greased his hair so much that the tendrils stuck to his temples like gorilla glue...and he had a tendency to flirt with anything feminine in the church that didn't have a ring on her left finger.

Charlize dragged her fingers through her dark pixie cut and groaned. "Derek, if you are trying to call local businesses to ask them if they have eligible bachelorettes, we don't want to know. You're the reason we can't have a community announcements board." Charlize placed her shiny red bass guitar into its case. She shut the lid with a slam.

"Ha ha. No." Derek brandished the orange sheet of paper higher above his head. "I saw this flier at She Brews when I went to grab my usual lavender matcha with two pumps of vanilla."

Ah, that answered the question for where Griffith got his inspiration for drinks.

"It's an indie music competition. Twenty thousand dollars. Maybe

Elijah could finally afford a nice guitar, and a pedal board that doesn't die every other service."

Pedal boards, devices that engineered the sound of a guitar, cost a minimum of five thousand dollars. Hence why he got a used one at a sketch store that wafted a weird smell.

Derek slapped the bright orange sheet onto Charlize's guitar case before she could grab the handle.

"I was in She Brews the other day and saw the poster—*without* stealing it, mind you." Charlize wrinkled her nose at the flier. Her silver nose ring glinted in the sapphire stage lights. "Deadline's coming up quick, though. Doubt we could pull together something in that time."

"It's twenty thousand dollars, Charlize."

"Don't care, Derek. We're not going to make fools of ourselves by not coming prepared. Lord knows plenty of these bands probably have practiced all year for this."

"Elijah has some lyrics, doesn't he?" Derek's eyes widened like a wild animal.

Elijah scrunched his eyes. "I mean, I have a few songs I've worked on over the years, but nothing solid."

"Great." Derek scooped up the flier and kissed the paper for good measure. "Pull us together something for our next practice on Thursday. And you." He winked at Liv. "After hearing that glorious hymn, you might want to give a whack at it as well. That way we can have options when we reconvene. I'd be more than delighted to offer you a spot in our indie band." He rolled his tongue in a Spanish R.

Anger sizzled underneath Elijah's skin when Derek grinned at Liv. Elijah rolled his fist and clenched his teeth.

Before either Liv or Elijah could protest, Derek folded the poster into his pocket and zoomed out of the sanctuary.

Chapter Five

LIV SCROLLED THROUGH HER ELECTRONIC MUSIC files. Her laptop whirred, overtaxed by the amount of tabs she had open at once.

She hadn't intended to take Derek's words to heart. The greasy drummer didn't often have helpful things to say, in her limited experience with The Vine's band. But as she drove home, his words began to percolate.

Twenty grand. A year's wages for someone like her.

She'd done the math in her head as best she could. That was enough to help her dad—to save the house.

When she got home, Caroline had left a note saying she was out with Andy, which meant Liv had the apartment to herself. Well, except for Rabbit. The hamster sat in her lap and she fed it seeds while frowning at her computer in her room.

Was the competition a sign from God? She'd been praying for answers, but she hadn't expected them to come like this.

Liv bit her lip. She'd only had one semester of formal training. Most of the scores she'd written had been on her own, outside of class. She had no idea if they were any good.

She clicked on a file, a piano trio in d minor. Her sheet music software spun before the notes displayed on the screen, a three-part piece for viola, cello, and piano. The time counter read about four minutes—a decent length for a normal song.

She remembered this piece from her junior year in high school. At the time, the teacher of her informal music composition extracurricular had assigned them to write two compositions for their final performance—each no more than five minutes long, for no more than three "normal" instruments.

Liv had silently grumbled when she learned the oboe didn't count as a normal instrument.

She'd felt stifled in that class, held back by the other students who couldn't seem to remember the circle of fifths, limited to writing pieces for one instrument at a time. Symphonies floated through her head, orchestral pieces with her favorite instruments like oboes, French horns, violas, and thundering timpani. Of course, those enormous drums weren't available for her small class.

So for her final performance, she'd settled on this section of a much larger symphony rattling around in her brain, boiled down to three voices.

She hit play on the software.

The playback was tinny, not nearly as good as the expensive software they had in the music labs at college, but the program sufficed for inputting music onto the staff in a far more legible manner than she could with her messy handwritten notes.

The piece started off softly, the viola singing with a sense of longing, nostalgia, then a mournful tone that arced into a lament. The cello vibrated beneath, full, moody, while the piano intertwined with the viola, sometimes in tandem, sometimes weaving above and below as a complex counterpoint.

Liv loved this piece. When Dad heard it performed for the first time, he'd teared up. "You were born with music in your soul, Livy. Just like your mother."

However, the problem remained—there were no lyrics.

She knew what the instruments were saying, what they sang into her heart. The viola lamenting death and begging for another way, the cello the rumbling storm, the piano mourning the inevitability of sacrifice.

Yes, high school Liv was dramatic. But to be fair, the passage represented the death of Christ. It had been part of her admittedly far too ambitious plan to write a symphony that musically represented the Bible from Creation to Revelation.

She began to write down what the viola seemed to be saying.

My son, my son,
How I loved Thee.
How I watched Thee
Grow wise and strong.

A bit archaic, but maybe she could clean up the lyrics later. She searched for the next spot of dialogue the instruments sang to her.

Angels sang about Thee
But now to the grave
Thou dost fall.

She turned to the lyrics for the piano, which she imagined being sung by God the Father. She wrote them out until she reached the ascending climax of all three instruments, as Mary looked away from the cross to weep and the Father turned His face from His Son so that the world might be saved.

Yet I must turn my face away.

She stared at the words. It would take two lead singers, one male, one female, with at least some operatic training and experience in complex interweaving harmonies. And she would like the cello part to be voiced by a men's choir...

In other words, not a worship band.

She plopped her head on her desk. That had always been her problem. Too complicated, too ambitious, too visionary. And she'd always hated lyrics. She preferred the instruments to do the talking, in a way that bypassed the brain and drove straight to the soul.

Not to mention, she was pretty sure this was a secular competition for popular music. *Calm down there, Handel.*

She powered on her midi keyboard. Usually she wished she had a real piano in front of her, but this had to suffice, since her neighbors wouldn't appreciate the resonating of a grand piano echoing through the walls and ceilings. Not to mention the lack of space and money. However, at times like this, when she wanted to quickly compose, it was helpful to have a keyboard that connected to her computer.

What did pop sound like? She plunked out some simple chords and added a jazzy beat with a mixer. She bobbed her head along, dancing in her chair, much to Rabbit's chagrin as the hamster bounced in her lap. She added in more beats and sounds electronically, mimicking a bass and some drums.

That sounds pretty good. But what about words?

I like to dance,
Dance, dance, yeah.
Dancing makes me happy.
Dance, dance, yeah.

She snorted and set the beat going again. What did people like to hear about? Love, right? That was a usual topic? She spun in her chair, singing to herself,

"*Love is great,*
Yay, love,
Who doesn't like love?
Woohoo!
Kissy kissy, smoochy smoochy..."

"Uh...Liv?"

She stopped spinning to see Caroline standing in the doorway, her lips pressed together in an attempt to hold in a laugh. "What are you doing?" Caroline asked.

Liv must not have heard the front door while engrossed in her music. She burst into giggles. "I'm trying to write a song, but I stink at it, so I was doing some...free-verse singing?"

Caroline's grin broke through. "I think you have a winner."

"Thanks." Liv took off her headphones. "How was your date?"

"It was more of a casual hangout. We mostly talked about ideas for future books in our picture book series, to be honest." Caroline cupped her elbows, her eyes sparkling. "We have a lot of ideas. And I love watching Andy sketch out his concepts."

Liv smiled at her roommate's dreamy expression. Two artistic souls—a perfect match.

"So." Caroline focused on Liv. "What's this about writing a song?"

Liv's smile faded into a frown. "There's this music competition I vaguely considered entering, but I don't know what to even begin writing a song about. The music is easy. But words..." She perked up. "You're a writer. Any tips?"

"I don't know." Caroline leaned against the doorframe. "I've never tried to write a song. With books, I guess you find a story you want to tell, and then you tell it."

Liv tapped two keys on the keyboard, a dissonant beat. "I usually tell the story through the music itself." She lifted her fingers. "I guess I'll think about it."

Rabbit chittered in her lap, and Liv handed the hamster to Caroline. Her roommate nuzzled the little ball of fuzz. "Your music is amazing. Maybe you could team up with someone who writes lyrics?" She stroked the hamster thoughtfully. "Some creative projects are better as a team. I'm better at more complicated plots, like novels, but I've grown to love picture books too. With Andy, we come up with the concepts together, then I create the words, and he creates the pictures. I don't know much about songwriting, but maybe it's similar."

Teaming up with someone. Her thoughts drifted to Elijah and the band at The Vine. Anything she wrote would need a band to play it anyway. Maybe she could find some lyrical help there.

Maybe a pop song was like a children's book—deceptively easy on the outside, difficult once you tried to do it well.

"Thanks, Caroline. I'll give it a shot." She shut her laptop.

Next time she saw Elijah, she'd ask him about songwriting.

Elijah strummed his strings and grimaced. Being a worship leader had its downsides—including playing the same chords used in worship songs—C, F, and G.

And if they felt like spicing it up, Christian musicians threw in an A Major or E Major for kicks.

He set the guitar down on his apartment floor and stared at the smattering of papers that surrounded him. On his nearby bed, Sammy burritoed himself in a Mexican handwoven blanket Elijah had bought on a mission trip to Guadalajara.

Silly dog. Sammy had a habit of snuggling with his owners and with bedspreads during the summer months, despite his thick golden coat.

Elijah's wrist daubed the sweat that brimmed on his upper lip. His gaze roved to the thermostat in his room. Why did Andy like to keep the apartment at seventy-five degrees in the summer? He would turn down the temperature, except, he didn't want to upset his roommate…the same reason he didn't want to bring any of the Don problems to Pastor Smith.

He shook his head and craned his neck back to the pages full of lyrics. *Focus, Elijah.*

Three hours had evaporated before he narrowed down his selection for their Thursday practice. A breakup song he'd penned for a girl who stood him up for a taco date in college, a funeral dirge for his grandmother who passed nine years before, and a tune he wrote as soon as he got the worship-leading job at the church.

Two fingers pinched his shirt, and he moved the fabric back and forth to fan himself. It had to be at least two degrees cooler outside.

He considered cracking open the window at the other end of his room. He should down the AC, but would that result in higher utility bills? Could he and Andy afford to shell out more money with Elijah's previous salary slashed in half?

Sunlight glimmered through the pane, and through the dust motes, he watched a mother sparrow return with a worm for her peeping babies.

Outside could offer a refreshing change of pace.

Mind made up, he bundled the papers into his arms and wandered out the door of his apartment. When he reached the ground floor and swung open the doors, summery scents from a nearby breeze held him at the entrance to the apartment for a moment.

The air smelled of sunshine and freshly mowed grass and the sizzle of steak.

Men in cargo shorts flipped meats on nearby grills that the apartment allowed its tenants to use. Smoke billowed toward a brilliant cerulean sky. At the edge of the street, two children held up glass pitchers full of pink lemonade. Their wooden sign asked for a donation of one dollar.

Elijah dug into his pockets of his shorts and procured four shiny quarters.

He moseyed over to the stand and plunked the change into a tin can they had set near the "Donations" sign. A girl in a tutu grinned at him with a gap between her teeth. She heaved the pitcher and splashed the rosy liquid into a transparent cup.

"Thank you very much, miss." Elijah saluted her with two fingers and grabbed the drink. Ice clicked against the plastic. He ambled to his favorite tree nearby the blue postal box for the apartment. He kneeled, and his spine fit into the long groove on the cottonwood. He tipped the cup back and drained the contents.

Kids had done well, he thought. Perhaps added a teaspoon too much of sugar.

He leaned forward and placed the three pages on the ground. Wind threatened to send them tumbling toward the street, so Elijah found a handful of rocks at the base of the tree and used those as paperweights.

"Okay." He sloped over the breakup song first. "Let's narrow this down."

Don't Want to Tac-o 'Bout It
I asked you out to tacos,
But you just walked, oh,
Out of my life
Oh, oh,
Out of my life

His lips sagged. How did this one make the final cut? Imagined laughter and ridicule from his bandmates pummeled his temples. Who knew the amount of Mexican-food-themed jokes they would launch at him if he presented this to them? And he guessed Derek would probably put a taco on his music stand every Sunday from now until Elijah left the church.

No go on the breakup song, time for the funeral dirge.

Gently Singing into the Night
You raged against the darkness
You never ceased the fight
You raged against the fear
Of the coming night

Yes, you raged against the fear
Of the dying of the light

Tightness filled his chest. The first verse was the only thing his siblings hadn't touched. Scarlet ink bled onto all parts of the paper. His eyes scoured them over and over again until he disappeared into the memory.

He was back in his childhood home. Now in a black suit and a nine-year-ago haircut that didn't stretch past his ears. Tears blotted the edges of the page.

The matriarch of the family, Grandma Violetta Peterson, had passed away. These past eighteen years she'd trained him on his scales, had his family sing at every Christmas concert at her church, set aside money to pay for Elijah's music lessons in college.

And now, after raging against the light for a week, and after she had a chance to say goodbye to all of her many children, she passed away in a hospital bed from cystic fibrosis.

His family had four days to pull together a song. Elijah wrote one based on Grandma's favorite poem, "Do not go gentle into that good night" by Dylan Thomas. Two days in, on the afternoon of calling hours, he finished.

Cotton fabric on his suit cuffs absorbed his tears. He sniffed and then marched the lyrics into the family room. "It's done."

Elijah brandished the paper and then set the page on a cherry wood table in the middle of the room. His family, all bedecked in black garb, hesitated to say anything for a moment. Blotched faces from nonstop crying stared at him. A grandfather clock ticked in a corner of the room next to the fireplace and mantle filled with photographs of his family members in various operas and symphonic bands.

Then Miriam rose from a large velvet chair and strode to the song. Chiffon swished from her dress. She plucked the page and squinted at it.

Her tongue tsked. "It was a nice effort, Bud."

Fire flamed Elijah's cheeks from the condescending "Bud." Being the youngest, he received this epithet from his siblings on multiple occasions.

"But A/B A/B rhyme scheme? You could've at least varied this up with A/B C/D. And do you even have any ideas what notes you're going to couple with these lyrics?"

His shoulders slumped until it felt like his two-sizes-too-big suit would slip right off. Should've clasped the golden buttons on the front together.

Miriam wrinkled her slender nose. "I think the second verse may be salvageable. Anyone have a pen?"

Five minutes later, the family members each had scoured the sheet with red marks so much that the song looked like a victim of a slasher movie. They left alone the first verse, seeing no use for it in a funeral service that would—no doubt—have a large church full of hundreds of attendees.

Miriam met Elijah's glance when he stared at the bloodied page, crestfallen.

"Tip for the future, Bud. In anything artistic, you have to be open to criticism. Music is a people-pleasing business. Not something you can do for fun. At least, you can't make any good money that way."

She clasped his shoulder and then carried the music sheet to the piano in the other room to create some notes for the new Frankenstein-ed piece.

Laughter from a group of children waving bubble wands pulled Elijah from the memory.

Moisture had filled his eyes. He blinked away the mist and turned away from the song dedicated to his grandma. No way he could use that, not with all the hurt attached to the work.

He'd tried to do whatever he could to accommodate people after that incident. But even so, something about seeing the scarlet edits caused him to want to drop the paper into an incinerator.

"I guess that leaves the third song." The one he wrote as he received the email from Pastor Smith that he acquired the worship leader job, right after he'd lost his position at an insurance firm.

Limbo
Am I falling,
Floating?
Am I waiting,
Or finally arriving?

Am I chosen,
Forsaken?
When I'm in limbo, you're still holding me
When I'm in limbo, you're still holding on to me.

Upon receiving the news of the worship leading position, Elijah felt a swirl of excitement and fear. Would his family see this "gig" as something lesser than all their accomplishments? What if the church hated something new?

But for once, when he penned those lyrics, he could smother Miriam's voice that had plagued him since his grandmother's funeral. This time, he'd written something that was his, something that he loved, and something his sister's red pen couldn't touch.

Now for the notes.

He'd pictured harmony parts at the beginning, mixed with chord clusters to give the audience a sense of incompleteness and yearning. Of the uncertainty he never could seem to escape. But how could he translate that to paper?

Birdsong interrupted his thoughts.

And he was floating again, lost in the music. Elijah listened for several moments before recalling where he last felt like notes had tugged him away from limbo—when Liv played in church.

He grinned at a bright red cardinal who perched on a nearby branch. "Let's hope she had better luck with pulling something together."

Chapter Six

"NOT LOON, *LUNE*." LIV LAUGHED AS seven-year-old Rowan shook his bottom, a.k.a. "tail feathers," making hooting bird noises.

Rowan rattled off facts while circling Liv's chair next to the piano. "Loons are aquatic birds. They look like ducks, but they're not. Loons swim underwater to catch fish." He hopped from foot to foot, flapping his feathers at his sister on the piano bench.

Ten-year-old Claire sighed and crossed her arms. She kicked her feet, which still hovered over the pedals if she didn't scoot down far enough on the bench. "Rowan, it's my lesson time. You already had yours. Go bug Mikayla."

Rowan gave one last long, keening loon call, then ran off.

Liv snorted and shook her head. "Anyway. You were saying you want to play Debussy, but not Reverie or Clair de Lune."

"No way." Claire wrinkled her nose. "You know what my brothers and sisters would say?" She adopted a singsong chant. "Loony Claire, Loony Claire, Loony Claire playing Clair de Lune."

"I wish I could disagree." Liv leaned forward in the chair, enjoying the cool air wafting through the Etmanns' sunny living room. Though the summer sun shone through a full wall of windows, stonework along the massive fireplace remained in shadow, aiding the AC billowing from a vent above a slowly spinning fan hanging from the vaulted ceiling.

With seven children aged sixteen to four, the Etmanns were Liv's best clients. Four girls, and then three boys, all enrolled except for the oldest and the preschooler.

Claire was the youngest girl, and though Liv would never tell her sisters, she showed the most natural talent.

Claire shuffled through the sheet music. "How about Children's Corner?"

"All six movements?"

"Right. It probably only ends up being like half an hour altogether." Claire scooted closer to the piano. "Look, I've been working on 'Serenade for the Doll' already." She launched into a jaunty, sweet bit of staccato, playing until she hit a snag several seconds in.

Liv bit back a smile. It wouldn't be her first choice, but she wanted the young musician to come to a decision on her recital piece for herself. Claire was the sort who would work hard on things she was passionate about—and not so much on anything she was forced to do.

"I think that would be great. But if it ends up being too much, you can select two or three of the movements to perform instead of all six."

Claire gave her a look. Liv laughed.

For the next twenty minutes, the two hovered over the piano, playing and marking problem notes on the sheet music. Liv circled important timing, phrasing, and dynamics to watch out for.

When their time ended, Claire hopped down from the bench, white-blonde braids bouncing. "My mom told me to go get her when we're done. She's cleaning the boys' room."

Claire danced away humming. Liv organized the books and sheet music, packing her own binders and books back into her bag.

Since she evidently stunk at songwriting, she needed some more sources of income to help with the house. Maybe she would ask Jen, the matron of the Etmann clan, if anyone in the homeschool community was looking for music lessons—or tutors, or babysitters, or just about any job at this point.

"Liv." A warm voice drifted toward her.

Liv turned as a woman in her late thirties with honey-colored hair floated across the floor, slight and willowy just like Claire. Liv didn't know how she still appeared so youthful after all these kids. Caroline would say Jennifer Etmann looked like a friendly woodland fae. "Hi, Jen."

Jen beamed. "I heard so much beautiful music coming from this side of the house all afternoon. Well." She paused and laughed. "Not as much during Rowan's turn."

Liv chuckled. "He's definitely making progress."

"Come on." Jen beckoned Liv after her through a doorway. "Emily and Mikayla made way too many chocolate chip cookies yesterday, so you better help us eat some before the boys make themselves sick."

Liv followed Jen to a spacious kitchen with beautiful natural wood and stainless-steel appliances. The sink alone was big enough to fit a small child—Rowan or his younger brother Tom had probably been rinsed of flour and cookie dough there a time or two.

Her heart squeezed, imagining wrangling her own brood of children in a big house like this. *Someday, maybe.* Liv didn't have a chance to have siblings, but if she ever had kids, she wanted a lot of them.

Liv sat at the counter for her usual post-lessons chat with Jen. Jen seemed to enjoy the adult conversation, and Liv had no complaints about the delicious snacks Jen's two oldest girls, both aspiring bakers, created. It passed a bit of time before Liv headed to her Monday shift at the coffee shop, and often provided a much-needed sugar boost before jumping into work.

Jen slid Liv a plate piled with cookies, and Liv snagged one. "Thanks." She took a bite and closed her eyes as gooey chocolate and chewy cookie dissolved in her mouth. "Delicious. How are you, lately?"

Jen moved to the fridge and poured two glasses of milk, handing one to Liv. Her usual buoyant expression faltered. "We're doing well, as usual." She hesitated. "Joe got a new job offer."

Jen named the enormous tech company, and Liv's eyes widened. Joe, a software engineer, already did quite well for himself, but a job like this... "Wow. That's amazing!"

"It's a huge blessing, and he really likes the company." Jen fiddled with her glass. "The problem is...they want him in office."

A sense of foreboding settled in Liv's stomach. "Where's that?"

"California."

Liv stared at her cookie, trying to muster words. "You're moving?"

"Joe's sister and brother-in-law and their kids are out there, and it would be closer to my parents in Washington as well." Jen sighed. "It's a godsend, but I'm really going to miss everyone here in Roseville." She patted Liv's hand. "Including you."

Liv swallowed a lump in her throat. The cookie now tasted like ash. "When are you leaving?"

"It's a process, but we're hoping to all be moved out there within a month."

A month. So much for asking Jen about extra work—now Liv needed *replacement* work. And it would take a lot to make up for five lessons a week.

"I'm happy for you all." She forced a smile. "I'm sure the kids will love being closer to their cousins—and the beach."

Relief spread across Jen's face. She must have been worried how Liv would react, but Liv was determined to keep it positive, for the sake of Jen and the kids. "Trust me," Jen said, "the kids are already planning their mega sandcastles."

Liv chatted with Jen for another fifteen minutes about the excitement and stresses of moving, some updates on the kids' progress in lessons, then said her goodbyes. She didn't have the heart to bring up other jobs—she didn't want to make Jen feel more guilty than she already did.

Behind the wheel, Liv took a shuddering breath. *What's going on, Lord? Why this, and why now?*

She turned the key in the ignition and backed out of the Etmanns' driveway. Once on the road, her phone buzzed in her purse. At a stop sign, she pulled it out and glanced down. It was the lady from the small church down the road from her apartment.

Cherilynn: Hi, there, Liv! You did such a good job on that hymn this weekend. I was wondering if you would be able to transpose another hymn for us? The ladies of the choir really appreciated your work in lowering the key for them last time.

Liv set the phone down and took a deep breath. She'd only expected to do one hymn. It hadn't taken long, but it was still yet another thing on the mental to-do list.

For a moment, she wondered if she should teach Cherilynn how to do it herself instead, but she quickly thought better of the idea. The sweet older lady already detested downloading and sending PDFs, let alone working a music software.

It's fine. It doesn't take long.

At the next stoplight, she pulled out her phone.

Liv: No problem! Can you email me the hymn? Same email address as last time :)

She set down the phone and switched her foot to the gas as the light turned green. After her shift at the coffee shop, and after making dinner, and working on lesson plans, and checking the community job boards again, she would transpose that hymn.

Hopefully no one would ask anything else of her this evening.

Because she just didn't seem to know how to say no.

Elijah knew he'd made a mistake that Monday morning when he checked his phone next to his bed as soon as he got up.

A slew of frantic texts and emails from Pastor Smith filled the whole screen.

He palmed his face and pulled down on the skin like taffy until his hand reached his chin. Then he stared at his tattered Bible on his nightstand and jabbed a finger at the worn leather cover. "I should've looked at you first thing."

Trying his best to keep his heart rate down, which now throbbed in his temples, he skimmed the messages.

Pastor Smith: Looks like Don has a posse of disgruntled congregation members.

Pastor Smith: Now he thinks you played too many hymns last Sunday, and he's gotten all the younger people riled up. Even though the previous Sunday he claimed you didn't play ENOUGH hymns.

Pastor Smith: I'll do what I can to calm them down, but any way you can do some modern stuff this next Sunday?

Pastor Smith: I looked at this week's giving, and it was the most abysmal we've ever seen.

Pastor Smith said tithing went down in the summer months because everyone had gone on vacation. But with Don stirring up a group of haggled-looking men at the back of the church yesterday, Elijah didn't doubt they would blame the worship leader for the deficit.

Elijah's door swung open with a creak. Andy stepped in with a tray full of donuts. A glass of orange juice placed at the center jiggled.

"Made you a surprise, roomie." Andy placed the tray on the stand next to the Bible. "Well, by 'made' I mean stopped by 'Ah Nuts' and ordered a baker's dozen."

Ah Nuts, a local donut shop, served some of Elijah's favorite breakfast pastries. He grabbed a napkin off a tray, plucked an oval-shaped treat, and bit into a maple cream stick. Buttercream frosting filled his mouth.

"Ah, yeah." Elijah swallowed. "That's the good stuff."

Andy sank into a beanbag chair in the corner of Elijah's room and bit into something with pink frosting and sprinkles. "You walked into the apartment last night looking like a zombie. I figured you could use a pick-me-up."

"Thanks. I needed this. Especially after—"

Elijah set the donut down on the napkin and motioned to his phone.

Andy squinted at him. "Pastor sending you more emails?"

"Enough to fill a book. Here." Elijah tossed him the device. "See for yourself."

The sweet maple frosting coated Elijah's tongue as Andy scrolled through the texts. Then his roommate set the phone on the floor and slumped into the squishy chair.

"Lij, isn't there something about church discipline? Don's clearly trying to cause a stir where there doesn't need to be one."

Elijah shrugged, placed his treat back on the tray, and shoved off his covers. They'd started to warm his legs too much. "Technically, yes, following biblical standards, Don should be confronted. But Pastor Smith's a bit of a pushover. We both are." He scooped the juice glass into his hands and swigged.

Yikes, the citrus did not mix well with the vanilla sweet cream filling.

"That's a shame." Andy rose and motioned to the breakfast tray. "Feel free to eat whatever. I'll take care of the leftovers."

With a wink, he handed Elijah's phone back and disappeared through the door. The device buzzed moments later.

Groan. Elijah peered at the new text.

Pastor Smith: The ladies who are running the VBS skits need you to move the keyboard off stage, so they can rehearse. When can you get to church?

VBS, already? Man, he should've paid more attention to Pastor Smith's morning announcements.

He pulled himself out of bed and yanked on a blue t-shirt and khaki shorts. On his way out to the car, he allowed himself to take in a few deep breaths of the warm summer air before sitting on a sweltering leather seat on the way to church. His AC had broken a few weeks back, and he didn't have a chance to get it checked yet.

When he arrived, he fixed his hair that had been tousled from his windows-down ride. He raced up the concrete steps that led to the entrance and into the sanctuary.

Cool air refreshed his skin.

"Watch the decorations." A gangly woman hanging fake moss on the walls wagged a finger at him. He realized, seconds later, that he'd opened the door too fast. A red shield with a lion on it had almost collapsed from the force of his entry.

Heat filled his cheeks. "Sorry."

"You here to move the piano?" Moss Lady turned back to the wall and planted greenery all around some paper lamp posts.

"Yes, ma'am." Elijah tiptoed over five garlands that littered the main aisle of the sanctuary. Then he ambled to the stage where children and adults in medieval costumes held scripts. "It looks like Narnia took over this place."

A young woman on the stage who wore a long denim skirt, tightly wound bun, and a modest plaid top approached him. "Technically, due to copyright, we're not allowed to say this VBS is Narnia themed."

"There is a literal wardrobe on stage."

"We call it the 'Cabinet of Wonders' in our skits. Again, copyright issues." She paused and stared him up and down. "But someone would make a great Prince Caspian—ahem, I mean, 'Prince Raspian'—if he wanted to participate in the skit we have for next Wednesday."

He grinned. Where had he seen this girl before? Oh, right, Hadassah. He'd set her up on a date with Andy a while back.

"No thanks, Hadassah, just here to move the piano." The keyboard blocked a group of children who acted out a battle scene with foam swords.

She shrugged. "Suit yourself. Heaven knows we can use more volunteers."

Elijah knew the feeling. Even working at a church that had more than two thousand attendees, he struggled to get more than three female singers on rotation for their worship band. He'd heard of other churches their size that had as many as eight instrumentalists on a Sunday. How they managed that, he could never guess.

If he had time, he would volunteer for VBS. But Pastor Smith already had him scheduled to play for the youth group on Wednesday. And he had to rework the set to include more "modern" songs now. With a grunt, he heaved the keyboard and walked it through a dark backstage and toward the storage closet.

He returned minutes later, panting. Boy, he did not like having to move that thing.

Moss Lady motioned him over with a curled index finger. "Help hold up this shield while I hot glue it to the wall."

"But I—" He was already behind on his Monday tasks.

"Quickly, before I burn my finger."

His sandals squeaked as he raced over. He held the shield above his head, and Moss Lady, now on a ladder, glued the top edges of the aegis to the bricks. Elijah's arms wobbled from having lifted the heavy instrument moments before.

He distracted himself and took in the surroundings. Two women placed fake snow and pine trees on the sides of the pews. A teenager, by the looks of it, strung up regal curtains, all in shades of dark purple and red.

"Man, you guys go all out." Elijah blew a low whistle.

Moss Lady snorted. "You think this is something? You should've seen it last year."

"How so?" He adjusted his footing to give his arms some rest.

"Well, it was before Don made a big stink about his kid being in the skit. He wants his little boy to do community choirs only. Just like his mom. You can imagine the conniption Don threw when his boy not only signed up for our skit team, but also landed a part in the community theater play."

She descended the ladder and reached for another shield. Elijah's muscles ached, but he lifted up the decoration without complaint. Moss Lady stepped up the rungs again.

"I had a musical family." Elijah leaned against the wall for support. "But I don't think my grandma ever *forced* me to do any of that. Why's he so insistent?"

A dark cloud filled Moss Lady's eyes, and she rested her glue gun nozzle against a large brick.

"Don lost his wife to a respiratory disease last year, and he doesn't seem to have recovered since. Music was her thing. She used to sing harmony with the last worship leader, you know."

No, he didn't.

That made sense, however. After Elijah's grandmother had died, his family had become obsessed with the musical legacies of their children. Hence why they met him with glazed expressions and a dull "oh, nice" when he told them he'd landed his first job at an insurance company.

Moss Lady hmphed and placed her glue gun on the top rung on the ladder. Time for a break at last. "Anyway, that's why we don't have the funding to put on the show we did last year. Since Don decided not to give toward the VBS this year."

"Well, at least the kids will still enjoy it? Whether you go full-out with smoke machines or muster together what you have. That's all that matters, right?"

She didn't reply.

Chapter Seven

LIV PASSED A HOT PEPPERMINT MOCHA to a girl with long blonde hair. A strange choice for a summer afternoon, but she'd seen weirder.

Especially when Griffith got creative.

"Here you go." She offered a bright customer-service smile.

The girl mumbled a "thank you" and shuffled away toward a seat in an overstuffed chair.

Liv surveyed the empty queue and let out a sigh of relief. "Looks like we get a break for a while," she said, glancing toward her pink-haired coworker.

Her fellow barista, Reina, harrumphed, shaking choppy pink locks out of her eyes. "About time. It felt like the morning rush hour at four in the afternoon. No one's going to be able to sleep tonight with all that caffeine this late in the day."

Liv grabbed a cloth and started wiping down the counters. Her feet ached, and her stomach grumbled. She'd forgotten to eat lunch today. Whoops. "It's not that late."

"No caffeine after two. That's what I always told my kids." Reina threw a blender in the sink and turned the water on.

Liv watched Reina in admiration. The woman had to be at least in her mid-fifties, slaying it in pink hair, playing in an indie punk rock band on Fridays, and visiting her two-year-old granddaughter on the weekends. Liv could only hope to be that cool as a grandma.

"Is your band playing in the Roseville Indie Music Festival?" Liv asked.

"Of course!" Reina raised her voice over the din of dishes clattering in the sink. Although, Reina's voice usually carried anyway. Probably a result of years spent in front of a blaring speaker, screaming into a microphone. "We've participated all four years, ever since it started."

Liv paused her cleaning. "Did you ever win?"

Reina snorted. "Nah. We're not exactly everyone's cup of tea." She grinned over her shoulder. "It's all for fun. Some of the bands are in it to win, but a lot of us just enjoy the camaraderie."

"Yeah." Liv grabbed a towel to soak up a spill. Ordinarily, she'd think that sounded like the best way to approach the festival. But with the medical bills and the house looming over her head…

"You're a musician, right?" Reina's head tilted. "Are you entering?"

Liv scanned the coffee shop for customers in need. Finding no escape from the question that was plaguing her own mind, she sighed. "I don't know." She glanced at the clock, a teapot with numbers and spoons for hands. The minute hand inched toward the twelve as the hour spoon hovered near the five. "It's about time for me to head out. I need to grab some dinner before cooking class. Can I help you with anything before I leave?"

Reina waved her off. "Go, and enjoy that cooking class. Maybe you'll snag a man who can cook while you're there. That's why I married Tim. Completely tone-deaf, that man, but his five-cheese bacon and apple macaroni…" She closed her eyes and hummed. "Attraction is fine, but good eating is forever."

Liv laughed. "I'm pretty sure the only one of us any good at cooking is Boris, and, well, he likes to wear peppers on his head."

After hanging up her apron and saying goodbye to Reina, Liv headed to her Bug to zip home for a meal. Soon enough, with dinner in her belly and a post-class to-do list rattling in her brain, Liv stepped into the classroom to find that pepper-hat-wearing man not wearing produce on his head but juggling raw eggs.

One of the poultry projectiles flew through the air and crashed on the counter in front of Boris with a smack, splattering yolk across his workspace. "Sometimes you lose one, ah?" Boris continued tossing eggs with his meaty hands. He slipped into a singsong. "Crack an egg, we got more. Crack an egg, don't walk out door."

Liv turned her attention from Boris's rhyming prowess to scan the room for Elijah.

The long-haired worship leader stood frowning down at a carton of eggs on his counter with an expression too troubled to be the result of classic kitchen ingredients.

Liv sidled up beside him at the workstation and peered at the carton. "They look okay to me."

Elijah blinked and looked up. His brow smoothed when he saw her, and he broke into a smile. "Hey. I didn't see you come in."

Worry still lingered in his eyes. Were the congregants giving him grief again? Maybe the pastor gave him a talking-to about Rogue Tambourine Lady.

"You could say I'm egg-cellent at sneaking." Liv smirked.

He groaned. "Not you too. Boris has been at it ever since I got here."

As if to prove his point, Boris shouted at students as they walked in, "Take a place. We egg-splore wonders of eggs today."

Liv bit her lip, holding in a chuckle. "Oh, no."

"Oh, yes." A hint of the shadow in Elijah's eyes lightened. "I didn't eggs-agerate."

Before Liv could give the pun the groan it deserved, Boris clacked a whisk against a bowl to get the class's attention. "Lesson one. We crack eggs. Not too hard, not too soft. Crack on side of bowl. Never!" He pointed a whisk at them, glaring. "*Never* crack directly into recipe. Maybe egg rotten, ah? Maybe you drop in shell. Always separate bowl." His serious expression didn't falter as he met Zinnia's eyes on the other end of the room. "Cracking eggs into recipe is too risky."

Elijah leaned over to Liv and whispered, "Doesn't he mean too *whisk*-y?"

Liv's chest trembled with suppressed laughter. She made the mistake of glancing at Elijah and broke down entirely at his twitching lips as he tried to control his expression. Elijah's snort melted into a guffaw, and Liv burst into giggles.

Boris turned a puzzled gaze in their direction. "Bad egg not joke. Ruin whole recipe. Unhappy customer. Unhappy chef."

Liv and Elijah nodded dutifully.

Boris held up a frying pan. "Good. We crack eggs, we make omelet. Maybe next week make quiche." He pointed at them. "Chop vegetables. From last lesson, ah? You learn, you build."

As Elijah painstakingly cracked eggs into a bowl, Liv began chopping up the provided bell peppers to go in the omelet.

Liv stole glances at Elijah. Something was still wrong. "Did you work on any projects for the music festival?"

He grimaced. "A few, but nothing I'm ready to bring to the band." A shell slipped out of his hand and splashed into the bowl of yolk. His nose wrinkled as he fished it out. "You?"

She sighed and reached for the onion. "I tried, but I can't come up with lyrics for the life of me."

"I get it. I had some ideas for lyrics, but I'm not sure what kind of music to layer under it, you know?" Elijah wiped his eggy fingers on a paper towel.

"I guess I never really studied lyrics. They feel almost more like writing than music. Which is more Caroline's thing." Liv blinked and sniffed, her eyes watering from the onion. "In college, they never asked me to write lyrics. It was always instrumental—and they were more concerned about correct use of theory than about whether people would enjoy it."

Elijah's head tilted. "I remember you saying you were classically trained, but I didn't know you had a degree in music."

"I don't." She set aside the unused half of the onion and started dicing. "I only got a semester in." She hesitated. "My dad was in a work accident, and he needed me, so I dropped out. I was going to go back, but I never did."

She braced herself for condolences, or some sort of patronizing "it's okay, a lot of people don't go to college" or "college isn't for everyone."

Instead, he grabbed the whisk and began beating the eggs. "What was your major?"

She could feel her cheeks redden. "This is kind of embarrassing considering I couldn't write a song, but...it was music composition."

"That's not embarrassing." He shook his head and set down the whisk. "I come from a musical family. My sister's an opera star, my brother's first chair...and I'm a part-time worship leader with a congregation I can't seem to please."

Liv scowled and put a hand on her hip. "You're leading people in worship. You help people grow closer to God. That's not embarrassing at all." She realized she was waving the knife and put it down before she sliced off someone's nose. "My mom always said that music is God's language. It doesn't matter your age, where you come from, if you even speak the same language. Music speaks to us all. As a worship leader, you're doing something special."

His mouth hung open.

Her face heated. Now he probably thought she was weird. "Er, sorry." She picked up her knife again. "I, uh, get a little passionate about music."

His jaw snapped shut. "Don't be sorry. That was just...I never thought of it in that way before." He added milk to the eggs, glancing at her with an almost shy expression before looking down again. "Thanks, Liv."

Her stomach fluttered at the slight, sweet smile hanging around the corners of his mouth and lighting his eyes. *I'd like to see his face do that more often.*

Her cheeks really began to burn at the thought. *Stop it. No falling for that worship-leader charisma.* "So, uh, maybe we could work together on writing that song?"

Elijah beamed. "Yeah, for sure. You can join us for practice on Thursday."

"Ah, eggs-actly right!" Boris's voice boomed in front of them, and Liv jumped. Boris stood on the opposite side of the counter, grinning at

Elijah and Liv. "Cooking make hearts grow close, ah? Now, we cook. I show you how. Come to stove."

Liv smiled at Elijah. "Thursday sounds good."

Elijah escorted Liv back to her car after cooking class. They snickered over Boris's various names he attributed to the eggs they cooked today.

Liv pinched her nose when she reached the driver's door. "What did he call your omelet again?"

"I can't remember if it was Egg-ward or Megg."

They dissolved into a fit of laughter. With an index finger, Liv swiped away moisture from the corners of her eyes. "Anyway, see you on Thursday, I guess."

Two days from now. He waved and dug into his pockets for his keys. *Beep, beep* sounded from his car when he probed the unlock button. When he reached the door, he had to pull with extra force. The hinges had rusted over during Michigan's notorious winters and liked to get stuck.

Clammy humidity stuck to his skin when he dove into the driver's seat. He fanned himself and glanced at the street lamps in the parking lot to the Community Center. Mosquitos swirled around the beams.

By habit, he reached into his other pocket for his phone and pulled out the device. A text from Pastor Smith burned his retinas.

Pastor Smith: Almost forgot. The usual tech team is out for Sunday. We're sending a new volunteer to you on Thursday, but it's going to take some time for him to get adjusted. Expect practice to go extra long.

He slumped back into his seat. Skin stuck to the leather.

"Great." He'd already wanted to run the band through some of the lyrics he composed the other day to see if they had any ideas for music to accompany it. And he'd *planned* to do that during practice.

But with the usual tech guy, Jason, missing, this would put them way behind.

Memories flickered of the last time they'd trained someone new. The team spent over an hour doing "tests" into the microphones on stage before they had reached a volume that the back row could hear but that wouldn't blow out the eardrums of the front pew sitters.

Thumbs sweaty, he wiped his hands on his pants before clicking out of the text message and opening the group chat he had with the worship team members who played every Sunday—Derek and Charlize.

Elijah: Hey, guys. I guess we're going to be spending most of our time helping the new tech guy at practice on Thursday. Any chance we could meet earlier in the day to get the ball rolling on the indie song?

He would've suggested tomorrow. But Charlize took cosmetology classes on that day at a local beauty school. They must've been on a unit about eye makeup, because she'd gone extreme with the eyeliner wings during last week's practice.

And Elijah did *not* want to be left alone with Derek for longer than needed.

Without waiting for a response, he tossed the phone onto the passenger seat and dug his keys into the ignition. Two seconds of engine sputtering later, the car whirred to life. He rolled down the window. A moist summer breeze licked his hair and face on the way home.

When he got back to the apartment, he could smell the paint fumes from the hallway. Andy must've chosen a more potent colorant tonight than the usual watercolor.

Elijah swung open the door to the apartment. As expected, Andy had shielded himself with an easel and canvas. His roommate had a paintbrush stuck between his teeth as he stared at the work.

The door slam alerted Andy to Elijah's presence.

"Hey, roomie. How did the cooking class go?"

"Really great." Elijah found a towel in the kitchen and soaked up the perspiration on his face. He went to his room to toss the cloth in his hamper and replaced it when he returned. "Any chance you have leftovers? I'm starving."

Andy narrowed his eyes at the painting. "I thought you just went to a *cooking* class. Doesn't that involve eating?"

"Didn't have the heart to eat any anthropomorphized eggs named Megg and Egg-ward."

"What?"

"Never mind."

Andy swirled his brush into a water cup and motioned to the fridge. "Have leftover food from my date with Caroline tonight. I don't know how someone could ruin Chinese by bringing her own kale, but she did. Knock yourself out."

"Thanks."

Elijah swung open the refrigerator door and found a takeout container with brown sauce smudged on the top. He dumped the contents onto a plate and set them in the microwave for one minute.

He pulled out his phone and noticed a few new messages from his band mates. Sadness soured his insides.

Charlize: Sorry, this week is pretty booked. My teacher has us working on this awful group project. She says it's to prepare us for doing wedding makeup. Sometimes you work in groups for that sort of thing.
Charlize: Teamwork and makeup never go well together. You end up with one eye with purple eyeshadow and the other with blue. Anyway, I was planning to spend most of Thursday on perfecting my technique. That's the only day our classmates can meet outside of class.
Derek: I'm out all of Thursday, except for worship practice. I have a paintball battle with my family, and after last time, let's just say, justice needs to be served to a certain sibling named Samson.
Derek: I'll splatter paint on his leg just for you, Charlize ;)
Charlize: Eww. In what way was that supposed to be romantic?
Derek: I am free Wednesday, though. Wanna hang, Lij? Just us bros?

The microwave beeped loud enough to drown out Elijah's groan. Steam billowed off the plate when he pulled the dinner out.

So much for getting that twenty-thousand dollars. After hanging up VBS decorations—his sore arm still hadn't recovered—he thought about how the twenty grand could help the church. Maybe if he won the prize amount, he could pay Pastor Smith back for all the funds Don withdrew.

And, hopefully, keep his job secure.

After what happened with the insurance place, he couldn't be too sure about anything.

Nevertheless, he had to try.

This time Elijah rattled off a text to his last resort, Liv.

She'd tried her hand at songwriting. Perhaps they could meet ahead of time and synergize what they came up with.

Elijah carried the hot dish to the main room's couch and observed Andy add a streak of orange to a painting of a sunset. Elijah's fork impaled a chunk of orange chicken with a piece of dampened kale stuck to the breading.

"You painting something for a new picture book?"

Andy's successful launch of the last one promised future book deals with Caroline.

Droplets of dark blue paint speckled the tarp underneath the easel. The river Andy had etched at the bottom of the canvas had gotten a little runny.

"I am not." Andy wiped his forehead with the back of his hand. Streaks of white smeared his skin.

"A new client?" Elijah could, in no way, keep track of the number of freelance gigs Andy took on.

"This is just for me."

"Do you have time for that?"

Andy shrugged. "I make time." He set his brush back in the red plastic cup of water and parked next to Elijah. Elijah plopped a warm piece of broccoli into his mouth to blot out the bitter bite of the kale.

The two dogs emerged from Andy's room. Their noses pulled them toward the plate of food.

Andy reached forward to block them from reaching Elijah. "Lij, do you remember how I used to get really upset at my art teachers in college? And how I asked you a million times if I could quit my major?"

Elijah squeezed his eyes shut and drifted into the memory. Then he nodded.

"The reason wasn't because I hated class or what they had to say." Andy raised his eyebrows. "It became about the grades. How my work couldn't be something I enjoyed, but rather, a thing that either got me an A, a B, or an F."

On one occasion, Andy had punched a hole through a canvas when the professor deemed his painting of evergreens not worth more than a D.

"Same thing happened when I started freelancing." Andy scratched Sammy's ear. The dog grunted, tail wagging. "It would be about how much money the artwork would get. I forgot how to *enjoy* creating. It became a burden."

Elijah stuck his gaze back on Andy's painting. Beautiful streaks of orange and scarlet bled into an indigo sky. This felt different than the artwork he saw Andy working on for commission or freelance work. It was more free, unhindered.

Andy grabbed the dogs' collars and led them toward their leashes. No doubt they were heading on their nighttime walk.

"Sometimes, Lij, you gotta do something because you love it."

Metallic hooks clicked onto the dogs' collars. Within seconds, they vanished behind the apartment door, leaving Elijah alone with his kale-infested chicken. His phone buzzed. He set his plate down on his legs. By now the dish had cooled enough not to burn. Then he fished out his device and read the new messages that had just come in.

Liv: Sorry, I can't make any decisions until I see my shifts at She Brews tomorrow. My manager doesn't really release our weekly schedule until the last minute.

Liv: But I hope it goes well. Tell the band members I said, "Hi!"

Liv: Oh, and tell Megg that I'm sorry you didn't eat her. It would've been weird with Boris staring at you the whole time, waiting for you to consume your eggs like a maniac.

Despite the less-than-positive news, Elijah fought a smile. Something must've been in the water at Caroline's apartment, because he felt drawn to this woman. Just as Andy had with Liv's roommate a few months back.

Chapter Eight

"AND SUSAN'S COMING OVER FOR DINNER TONIGHT—"

"What?" Liv interrupted. Her eyebrows shot toward the sky, along with the rising late morning temperatures. She settled her loose earbud back in her ear as she pulled into the parking lot at She Brews. "You invited her over for dinner? That sounds serious."

Dad cleared his throat on the other end of the line. "Well, I don't know about *invited…*"

Liv claimed a parking spot near the back, out of the way of customers, and spoke into the mic on the headphone cord connected to her phone. "Oh? She's just going to show up? Without an invite? But you know about it?"

She grinned at her father's hemming and hawing. "Well," he sputtered. "We were just talking. About food. And she mentioned missing having someone to taste test her new recipes. And our kitchen's a lot bigger than hers…" He seemed to grasp at straws. "And her grandson will be there too. She's babysitting him for the evening. He's five. I'm sure we'll have some, ah, manly bonding time."

Liv laughed. "Fine, Dad, I'll stop teasing. Have fun on your not-date with Susan." She unbuckled her seatbelt and threw open the car door. "I have to go into work, but I'll talk to you later."

"Love you, Livy. Behave yourself."

"Look who's talking. Love you."

As she hung up and headed for the door, her smile faded. She wished teasing Dad about Susan had been the only part of their conversation. But in the twenty minutes between driving from her last piano lesson to She Brews, her midweek chat with Dad had brought up stressors she didn't want to face. "Should have waited to call until tonight," she muttered.

She shook off thoughts of Dad's news. She would deal with it later. And hopefully Susan would help keep his mind off things.

A smile tugged the edge of her lips at the thought. Having a home-cooked meal, playing with a spunky kid, spending time with a woman who clearly adored him—all things Dad hadn't experienced in far too long. *Susan, if you break his heart, I'll unfortunately have to sic my roommate on you. She's an author, with plenty of twisted ideas in her brain.* Like the time Caroline thought she and Andy should write a children's book about a creepy old lady who ate kids or something. Luckily, Caroline's boss vetoed that.

The bell chimed above the door as Liv stepped into She Brews, blinking while her eyes adjusted from the blasting summer sun.

Across the bar, Griffith raised a hand and waved. "Hey, Liv."

Liv returned the gesture. She went to put away her things, don her apron, and wash her hands while Griffith finished up with a customer.

She scanned the schedule tacked to the wall in the back room, searching for her name. Good, more shifts—she needed the money.

Feet scuffed next to her as Griffith tap-danced over, holding a hand towel horizontally like a cane. "Oh yeah, forgot to look at that when I came in." He squinted at the board, then groaned, slapping a hand to his forehead. "Oh, no. I forgot to tell them. I can't work tomorrow evening. I have a rehearsal."

Liv felt his pain. She Brews needed employees to mark out any times they would be unavailable at least two weeks in advance, but sometimes it was hard to remember.

Griffith wrung the towel. "And it's an important one, too. Aw, man, how am I going to get someone to cover on such short notice?"

She glanced at the schedule for Thursday evening—a closing shift. And she was opening the shop on Friday, with Griffith. She Brews opened at five-thirty a.m. every weekday to serve the caffeine-dependent populace on their way to work. Closing Thursday evening could easily take her until after ten-thirty, and she had to arrive before five on Friday to get things ready to open. All employees knew to avoid the dreaded "clopen" at all costs. But the look of distress on Griffith's face...

"I can take your shift," she heard herself say.

His eyes brightened. "Really? I mean, you don't have to do that. I can call around."

"Don't worry about it. You're not going to get someone to come in that late of notice. Reina doesn't do the late evening shift, and Jordy's out of town." She forced a bright smile. "I got this."

"You're a lifesaver." He clasped a hand over his heart as if he was about to recite a soliloquy. "I'll make it up to you someday." With that, he whipped off his apron. "I gotta go. I'm teaching a drama class for kids in like...well, five minutes." He saluted. "Thanks again, Liv."

She kept her smile until Griffith had done the grapevine out the door, then let her features sag into a frown. Extra shifts meant extra money, but she was going to be exhausted come her Friday afternoon lesson. Maybe she would sleep in Thursday morning.

The door jingled open, and Liv snatched up her customer service smile once more. "Welcome to She Brews."

The brunette smiled back shyly, then stood a few feet away from the queue, contemplating the menu written on the chalkboard above Liv's head. Liv paid attention to the customer with half an ear while restocking straws and considering her schedule.

Oh, no, I can't sleep in tomorrow morning. She'd told Elijah she would join him and the band Thursday morning to work on ideas for the festival. And Elijah had asked her to meet early to work on the project, since the team had to do some sort of tech thing later.

She still hadn't given him a response.

"Okay, I think I'm ready." The brunette stepped up to the counter. Her long hair hung to her waist. "Sorry for making you wait."

"No problem. What can I get for you?" Liv poised herself at the register.

She clasped her hands together, shoulders seeming to turn in. Such a small, timid creature. She laughed nervously. "Usually I come in when Griffith is here, and he comes up with something for me. I guess I just missed him."

Liv's eyebrows rose. "Do you have a favorite he makes?" *Is there one of his concoctions that isn't disgusting?*

"It's hard to choose one, but I think I'll go with a lavender matcha latte today. If that's okay?"

Are you *okay?* "Of course. What size?"

"Medium, please."

As Liv rang her up, the matcha-loving girl tilted her head. "Do you go to The Vine?"

"Sometimes. I kind of bounce back and forth between there and a smaller church." She took the woman's card and swiped it.

"Ah, I've seen you sing there before. I'm Hadassah. You're Olivia, right?"

"Yeah." Liv blinked as she handed back the card. People remembered her singing? "Nice to meet you."

"If you like the stage, I'm running the skits at VBS next week. I could use a couple more volunteers."

Liv pulled out the lavender and matcha powder. "Oh, I don't like the stage much. Just the music." And she could not take on any more responsibilities.

"Fair enough." Hadassah gave an easy smile, her shoulders lifting. "I don't like the stage, necessarily, but I love theater. It's probably the same feeling."

Conversation waned as Liv created the drink and then handed it off to Hadassah. After the theater-lover left, Liv served a steady trickle of customers that picked up as more people began to get off work.

The stream of orders kept her mind occupied and away from worrisome topics. Usually she had a partner at this hour, but the other girl had called in sick, so she had even more to do.

Somehow, her mind found time to wander back to her conversation with Dad anyway.

"What do you mean the PT says there's not much more they can do?" Liv had demanded. "They're giving up?"

"No, not exactly. They don't think PT can get me much further." Dad hesitated. "They say I have a tethered cord from the scar tissue. It's usually a pediatric issue, but...well, sometimes surgeries have unexpected complications. I guess I was one of those cases."

Liv had squeezed the steering wheel. "Can't they have you do stretches or something? To make it better?"

He sighed, the sound wearier than she'd heard in years. "It's my spinal cord, Livy. Not a muscle." He hesitated again. "They say they could fix it with surgery."

She bit her lip. "Okay. When is it? I can take off work to be with you—"

"No." He cut her off. "I don't need the surgery. I'll be fine. It's just an...explanation. For why things aren't getting better."

"Things *should* be getting better. Which is why you need this."

"I don't have the money, Livy."

"We'll find the money." She clenched her jaw.

"How about we talk about this another time? Tell me about your kiddos today."

She'd let him change the subject, but she hadn't quit thinking about the conversation since.

As Liv slid an iced macchiato in front of a customer, she made up her mind.

She would text Elijah. She would meet as early as he needed to. And she would win that prize money.

Elijah arrived at the Vine Youth Center with his guitar neck in one hand and amp in the other. He heaved the amp onto the stage at the end of a large room.

After an unfortunate Nerf battle incident a few months back, the church decided to purchase a warehouse nearby for all youth group events. From time to time, Elijah still found foam Nerf darts on the Vine church's mainstage from the supposed epic battle that had taken place right before Elijah onboarded.

"Thanks for coming early."

A squat woman in glasses approached him. He hadn't quite learned the names of everyone yet, but no one could forget Brooklyn, the bubbly youth leader. She beamed at him, cheeks obscuring half of her eyes. "I think the high schoolers will get here in a few minutes."

Not that Elijah hadn't played at the youth group before, but they often had Brooklyn lead them in a few songs.

Vine, wanting to appear more edgy and professional, decided that Brooklyn on her out-of-tune ukelele wouldn't cut it. So, in June they sent in Elijah to play one or two Wednesdays a month.

Elijah gripped a cord to his amp and plugged it into the wall. "Any new members join since I last played?"

When had he last come here? Three weeks ago?

An air conditioner unit above him groaned. Cool air rushed onto his neck.

"We have a new girl who I think has been forced to come by her parents." Brooklyn adjusted a crooked lamp near a couch seating area. "She doesn't really participate in the games, so I don't think you'll get much conversation out of her."

Fat chance. If Brooklyn couldn't crack a smile on someone's face, no one could.

Elijah set his guitar on a stand and took in the room. "Ah, you guys have re-decorated."

In June, the whole building smelled of dust, and Brooklyn had managed to hang a few lanterns and paper fan decorations—to spruce up the slate-hued cinder block.

These past three weeks, she'd slapped bright green and blue paint onto the walls and threw in enough lamps and furniture at the edges of the room to upstage a lightshow at a home goods store. Brooklyn and Elijah ambled to a snack table in the back. Elijah dug his fist into a bowl of cheesy chips and slapped them onto a paper plate. He wiped the cheesy residue off on a napkin.

"What's the plan for tonight, Brook?" His tongue probed his teeth. Powder had coated them when he bit into a snack.

"Pastor Smith is being really anal about everything being precise. Mind you, Don doesn't have a high-school aged kid. But I guess Smith wants us to get a head start for when Don's son leaves middle school."

Brooklyn frowned. Then she plucked a celery stick and swirled its head in a glob of dip.

Elijah swallowed. "What does that mean for me?"

The celery stick snapped under her teeth. "Pretend it's a rock and roll show. Crank up the amp to eleven. I don't know." She shrugged. "My music expertise stops after a few chords on a uke."

He craned his neck to the stage and the corners of his lips sank. Although, yes, teens did like loud music, wouldn't that make it somewhat awkward? Him on a stage alone, pretending to be some melodic sensation?

Before he could protest, laughter sounded from the door. A group of teens in ripped jeans bolted for the snack table.

Sidestepping to safety, Elijah watched them pile their plates to maximum capacity.

One, a girl with braces, waved at him before joining her friends on a couch. Elijah ambled to the stage and flipped through the lyrics on a music stand.

When he'd chosen the songs back at his apartment, he'd been engulfed in a memory from his teenage years. Eighteen and at a lock-in, he dedicated his life to Christ...three days after his grandmother's funeral. He'd hoped he could recreate the same experience tonight. One youth leader, corralling the teens into a circle, and everyone singing together old worship songs.

But now...

While teens filtered through the doors and toward couches, Elijah noticed one girl slink into a corner. She pressed her legs to her chest and balanced a plate on her knees. Curly red hair obscured her face. She must've been the teen Brooklyn talked about.

Brooklyn asked Elijah to help her set up a net for an activity on the center of the room's bright orange carpet.

Fifteen minutes passed, and the youth had all but demolished the contents found within plastic bowls on the snack table. Brooklyn called them over to play a game of "blanket volleyball."

"We'll divide you into two teams. Each gets a blanket that you all hold. The objective is to get the ball over the net. We'll play to fifteen points."

Brooklyn had Elijah stand on a ladder to serve as referee.

When he reached the top rung, he noticed the one girl hadn't moved from her spot. He tried to focus on the game.

During his time at the lock-in all those years ago, he'd refused to talk with anyone. No one would understand. They didn't just lose someone close to them. They didn't have their siblings mar the lyrics written for the funeral.

But when worship came…something broke inside his chest. Shrapnel from the weight he'd heaved for days clawed at him. Until he lifted his hands, until he prayed with the youth leader afterward. Then came bliss.

Blanket volleyball concluded with an upset. One team with a spaceship-printed tie blanket creamed the other with a 15–3 win.

"Great work, Team Spaceship. You win this family-sized package of Sour Patch Kids." Brooklyn held the neon-green bag above her head. A tall teen snatched it from her clutches, and Team Spaceship devoured the contents within seconds.

Brooklyn motioned for Elijah to hop on stage and "do his thing."

He leapt up the steps and swung his guitar strap over his shoulders. "Who's ready to worship?" he asked in his stadium announcer voice. Feedback from the microphone pierced the air. Everyone reached to cover their ears.

They were off to a *great* start.

As he strummed his strings as hard as possible, so much that he thought his pick would snap in half, he noticed the girl in the back corner hadn't budged. No matter how high he cranked his amp, no amount of sound waves could move her from her position.

The song finished with a loud chord that Elijah swore shook the building.

Teens that huddled around the stage pumped their fists in the air and cheered.

Sourness filled Elijah's stomach. This didn't feel right. Often, when he played in his apartment, he felt the Spirit carry him away, soul floating like a balloon. Now, his soul had popped and sagged all over the crevices of his skeleton.

This wasn't worship.

"Guys." His lips trembled inches away from the mic Brooklyn had placed on the stage earlier in the day. "This feels a little awkward. Me up here. You down here. We're all part of the same body, worshipping the same God. This doesn't make sense for me to be playing like this."

He winced when Brooklyn raised an eyebrow. Her usual glowing complexion had faded.

Yes, he would have to go against Pastor Smith's orders. Sorry, Brook.

"Actually, would you all mind forming a circle?" Elijah made a round motion with his index finger. The girl in the corner raised her head. She set down her plate on the floor but didn't move. All the other teens created a blobbish shape.

Elijah unplugged his guitar from the amp and stepped off the stage. He joined the if-you-could-call-it-a-circle and glided his pick on his strings.

He started with the song that had moved his spirit first at that lock-in, "Heart of Worship." His eyes squeezed shut and his voice got lost in the dozens of others that joined in. One tune bled into another. From "Christ Alone" to "O Come to the Altar," they went from one chorus to the next like a dancer shifting between moves with grace and ease. Every once in a while, they would have a moment's pause, where Elijah strummed the same key.

Then a youth grouper started another song, and they set off again.

During a longer moment of silence, Elijah's eyes flew open. The girl from the corner had joined the circle. Tears streaked her freckled cheeks.

Elijah dropped his hands, and the G chord hung in the air. Seconds passed before the teens lowered their arms and stared at him, expectant.

"Thanks for worshipping together, guys." Elijah clutched his pick in his fist. "With seeing a worship team on stage, it's easy to forget that we're all singing together."

As Brooklyn carried her Bible on stage to read some Scripture, Elijah noticed the freckled girl had returned to her corner, sobbing. He edged over and halted when they were five feet apart. Minding the distance between adult and adolescent, he knelt. "You doing okay?"

She nodded, fingers shielding her eyes. "I haven't done worship like that before. It's like the words in the music were...alive." She lifted her hands and smudged the water off her cheeks. "It never feels like that at my church."

"I understand the feeling." For the first time in a long time, the lyrics had taken on a fire. Something Elijah had not experienced ever since he joined The Vine.

Chapter Nine

EXHAUSTION DRAGGED AT LIV'S FEET AS she tromped up the stairs to her apartment. Her keys rattled in the lock, then she pushed the door open to the unmistakable smell of—

Kale. Cooked kale.

She'd mentioned to Caroline a few times about turning on the vent over the stove when cooking the pungent greens, but Caroline never seemed to remember. And Liv didn't want to say anything that would make Caroline feel self-conscious about her favorite vegetable.

But the apartment reeked of Liv's *least* favorite vegetable.

"Hey, Liv." Caroline poked her head out of the kitchen. "Can you help me with this stir fry? I forgot to set the rice going."

All Liv wanted to do was crash on the couch after five hours straight on her feet at She Brews. But her roommate was being nice, making dinner for both of them. Even if it was a meal Liv didn't particularly enjoy. *I'm just grumpy after a long day and bad news.* She set down her bag and headed toward the kitchen.

She stopped as she turned the corner and saw their table. Above it, some sort of stringy yarn monstrosity hung on the wall. "What's that?"

Caroline glanced over her shoulder while stirring the veggies sizzling in a pan. "Oh, that. It's macrame. I just bought it. My mom said it's in right now."

Liv had seen pretty macrame. This...it looked more like a cat shredded a ball of yarn. "Oh."

She couldn't come up with anything nice to comment about it, so she headed to the sink to wash her hands. *Please don't ask, please don't ask, please don't ask...*

"What do you think?" Caroline asked.

Great. "Where did you get it?" Liv deflected.

"A thrift store downtown. We're doing a fifties-themed event for a Helping Hope fundraiser, so I was looking for old things."

"That sounds like fun." She mustered up her usual smile. "You'll have to show me your outfit."

After putting brown rice in a pot—she did know how to do that much—Liv tapped out a text to Elijah.

Liv: Hey, I'm available tomorrow morning, if you still want to meet and work on songs. When and where?

During dinner, Caroline chattered about book projects, and Liv answered questions about her kids, and how work went. Liv tried to engage, but part of her wished she could spend a peaceful meal alone, with something tastier than kale chicken and bland brown rice.

Caroline set her fork down and cocked her head. "Are you okay, Liv? You're pretty quiet today."

A pang of guilt twanged through her stomach. This was Caroline, her friend, who cared about her. She didn't need to hold it all in. Pretending everything was fine to the parents of her kids, to the people at work, even to Dad, trying to keep him from worrying... Not to mention the fact that she'd made the mistake of doing some medical research on her phone after work, and realized things were only going to get worse until Dad had his surgery.

But she felt too tired to even begin to unpack what was going on right now. "I'm just really tired."

Caroline's expression softened. "Hey, why don't you turn in early? Don't worry about the dishes. I've got them."

"But what about 'I cook, you clean'?" Liv protested. That had been their rule from the start.

Caroline waved her off. "It's fine. Maybe relax in a hot shower or something, then go to bed. You look half-dead."

Liv fought against tears pricking the back of her eyes. *You're tired. Everything will feel fine in the morning.* "Thanks, girl."

As she brushed her teeth, her phone vibrated on the counter.

Elijah: I'm still all for doing this. It needs to be pretty early, though, and the church doesn't open doors until nine. Can we head to a practice room at the community college or something?

A practice room. Liv remembered those days. They would be open at all hours for music students desperately cramming in extra practice time. She had friends who would even stay overnight, catching a couple hours of sleep under a piano bench before rousing to scribble out the answers to more theory homework in a half-delusional state. She rinsed out her mouth and put her toothbrush away before replying.

Liv: That works! How about seven, since your worship team practice is at nine? That should give us at least an hour and a half to play around with ideas.
Elijah: Perfect, I'll see you then.

Liv barely kept her eyes open to set her alarm before she collapsed onto her pillow and entered a dreamless sleep.

The next morning found her power walking down the hall of the music department. She glanced up at one of the clocks, which read 7:01. From one end of the hall, she could hear a soprano doing warmups, and at the other end, a violin hit a sour note and stopped abruptly, probably for the student to scratch a note onto the sheet music.

Elijah had texted that he was in room five. She found the correct door and peeked in the window.

Elijah hunched over a sheet of staff paper on the piano's lid, frowning and tapping a pencil against his chin. His hair was slightly tousled, as if he'd brushed it that far-too-early morning but hadn't put much other effort into it. The locks still looked soft and silky. Liv wanted to touch it.

Stop it. She knocked.

He looked up and grinned a big golden retriever smile. He bounded over and opened the door. "Hey."

"Hey." She tucked a loose piece of hair behind her ear, suddenly wishing she'd put a little more effort into her own appearance. "How's the songwriting going?"

He grimaced. "I don't know. I have some ideas for lyrics, but the instrumental side of things…You?"

"I guess that's why we're teaming up. I have the opposite problem. Can I see your ideas?"

"Sure."

He stepped aside, and Liv entered the practice room. He led the way toward the piano bench.

His hands trembled as he handed her one of the many sheets of paper strewn over the piano and bench. Was he nervous? She looked down at the page and prayed the lyrics wouldn't be horrible. She didn't know what she'd tell the poor guy if they were.

Her eyes scanned the words, accompanied by a single-voice melody line. Then stopped. Scanned them slower.

When I'm in limbo, you're still holding me.

Tension formed behind her eyes. She swallowed. The lyrics were beautiful, capturing the essence of feeling suspended in the waiting, in the trying, in the unknown.

Like how she felt right now.

"This is beautiful, Elijah."

"Really?" The line between his brows faded.

"Really. I just…" She cleared the papers off the piano lid and set them on a music stand. Then she sat down and opened the lid.

Her fingers rested on the keys for a moment, then she took a deep breath and began to play.

Slowly at first, and then more confidently, she felt out a sweet melody, a bit haunting, a bit warm, a bit nostalgic.

"They inspire me," she explained. "They make me feel something kind of like this."

Elijah sank into a chair next to the piano. "Wow. Is that a piece you've played before?"

Liv shook her head. "They're some pretty simple chords, honestly. They don't do it justice. I'd have to play around more. And I don't know if this is even close to what you were thinking."

He gazed at the keys wide-eyed. "I don't know what I was thinking, but this is better."

She shifted. "It needs more." She played the melody line with one hand. "I sense multiple voices. The melody needs a counterpoint, not just accompanying chords."

"Counterpoint?" He smiled sheepishly. "Remind me what that means. I'm bad with the technical terms."

"It's the combination of more than one melodic line that can function independently but combine to form harmony." She played one melody with one hand, then a different one with the other. Then she played them together. "The classical masters were known for having multiple voices that could each function as a song all their own, but together created an even more beautiful harmony."

"Yeah." He sat forward in his seat. "Exactly. All of us in limbo, separate but together."

"And when we come together…" Their eyes met. "Our melody lines become an even more beautiful harmony."

He grinned. "Let's find that harmony."

Elijah and Liv fiddled with various chords and melody lines for the next half an hour.

Suddenly Liv froze and stared at the page with his original lyrics. She felt around the piano for something, and then, moments later, brandished a pen.

"Do you mind if I do a slight edit?"

Elijah clenched his fist. Nerves braced themselves. Of course. He should've known this perfect practice would go sideways. Just like

Miriam had all those years before, Liv would scour the lyrics with scarlet slashes.

Liv appeared to read his face, and hers softened.

"Really, Lij, the lyrics are amazing. I was tearing up the first time I read them. But." She hesitated. "It's the title."

"What's wrong with 'Limbo'?"

She chewed on her lip and set down the pen on the piano stand. A clock positioned above the door ticked in the silence. "You know, the limbo. Where your elementary class goes roller skating, and a man in a Walrus mustache has everyone line up. And you arch your back to go underneath a bar. And if you hit it, you're out."

Liv curved her spine, demonstrating.

Elijah's eyebrows pulled together. Seconds later, they sprang apart.

Oh, the limbo dance. Of course, he'd done a similar exercise. He palmed his forehead. "Oh my goodness, I feel so stupid now."

Liv's nose wrinkled when she giggled. "Don't worry at all. I have some far more cringy titles I've come up with for songs. You should've seen my middle school days when I was obsessed with boybands." She shuddered. "Oh, the painful memories."

They laughed. Elijah pressed his elbow against the keys to rest his chin on his hands. Low thunderous notes rumbled as he did so. Liv picked up the pen again and stared at the music.

And Elijah…well, he admired the view.

Light filled her eyes five clock ticks later. "Why don't you call it 'Finding Harmony'?"

She tapped her chipped fingernail on the second verse.

Are you listening?
Waiting?
Do our chords clash
Or will they finally meet?

Are you singing
Over me?

When I'm in limbo, you're still holding me
When I'm in limbo, finding harmony.

"Think about it." She pressed the silver tip of the pen to her lips. "Sometimes when the melody lines interact, they create dissonance or tension. The chords they formed when we were just playing resolved into consonance when we reached the 'when I'm in limbo' part. The whole song is about finding that final harmonious chord."

Elijah remembered how when Liv hit the chord clusters of notes, he wanted her to resolve them with a sweet chord. When she had at last, relief washed over him.

"The whole song is about finding harmony."

Liv shrugged. "I suppose that's what life is about too. Hearing God sing over you amidst the noise and clashing chords." Mist coated her eyes and she blinked it away. Her shoulders bounced up two inches and she set the pen down on the stand again. "But it's whatever you want. No worries if you want to keep it at Limbo. Limbo is great."

What a shift. So palpable, that Elijah felt he could slice the tension with a violin bow. Something told him that Liv didn't speak up all that often when she wanted something fixed or changed.

"No, I appreciate the suggestion, Liv. Let's change the title to Finding Harmony."

Brightness filled Liv. Her lips twitched and she gazed out the window of the practice classroom. Two college students outside flicked a frisbee back and forth. They must've come here for summer classes.

Elijah clicked the pen and drew a slash through the title "Limbo," replacing it with the new name.

"I like what we've come up with." He slid the writing utensil behind a booklet filled with sheet music of classical songs. Discomfort throbbed in his legs. He adjusted his seating on the hard bench. "We definitely have something we can show to the band members—maybe even at practice if training the new tech guys goes well."

"For sure." Her voice cracked. Liv clasped her arm. Today she'd worn braided bracelets, opposed to her usual bangles.

Elijah's mouth drooped. "What's wrong?"

"Nothing, it's just…I've had a lot of fun with this. But because I listen to mostly classical stuff, I don't know what 'indie music' sounds like." She threw up air quotes. "Is this even on par with what we'll be competing against?"

They could get it to the proper length, sure, with two verses and a bridge. But what about song quality?

Hmm, the thought hadn't occurred to Elijah yet.

Pull out his phone, and he could show anyone tons of playlists filled with "indie" songs. But each had a different flavor, different spices. Some loved a techno flair as a nod to the 80s, and others enjoyed a rough, dry sound of an acoustic guitar and little else. Would the judges at the festival look for paprika or oregano? Bands that pulled out all the stops or who took a minimalist approach?

"Well." Elijah dug his palms into the corners of the bench and leaned back. "Indie music is basically any band that doesn't sign on with a record label—which is ironic considering the prize of the festival. But I don't suppose it could hurt to see videos of who won last year."

They set the sheet music and booklets on the floor to make room for Elijah's phone screen.

Squeaks from a clarinet came from a nearby practice room. Elijah placed his device on the center of the piano stand, and Liv scooted closer to him to, he assumed, get a better position to view the screen. Electricity tingled in his fingertips. Her hand was inches away from his. He resisted the urge to clasp it.

He pulled up YouTube and searched the name of the festival. "Roseville Third Annual Indie Music Festival Winner Performance" appeared in the top listings. Elijah clicked on the video, and they watched.

A boy band with matching haircuts strummed electric guitars.

One with a tattoo sleeve on his arms grabbed the microphone. "Yeah, yeah." The drummer in the plexiglass cage thrummed the same *bum bum BUM buh bum bum BUM* the whole time.

Elijah didn't count the words in the song, but if he could hazard a guess, they may have used a total of fifteen. Tattoo sleeve dude repeated the line, "Yeah, yeah, summer days. Yeah, yeah. Summer time" so often, Elijah wanted to chuck his phone out the classroom window.

The lyrics said nothing. The song sounded like a copy of anything found on the radio.

And to make things worse, the leader concluded with, "All right, Roseville. We're Ed, Ned, and Ted, and we want to thank you. Goodnight." It was very clearly daytime in the video. The sun hadn't even reached the tree line in its descent.

Both Elijah and Liv sank when the screen went dark.

"Well that was." Liv searched the ceiling for a word. "Interesting."

Elijah palmed his neck. "The song really, you know, makes you appreciate summer."

Clarinet shrieks ceased, and they sat in silence for a few seconds.

"That was horrible, wasn't it?" Elijah asked.

Liv nodded. "I wasn't going to say anything, but." She sighed. "Our song sounds nothing like that. If that's what the judges are looking for, do you think we're already disqualified?"

"I don't know. It's an indie music festival, but that song sounded like everything indie music is against—selling out, sounding the same as everyone else. Some artists don't even write their own songs and beats, and that's exactly what this sounded like."

"No, really?"

He proceeded to explain how many famous artists bought lyrics or even song "beats" from others.

"It's why indie artists take pride when they make it big. Because they feel like they did it all on their own."

Liv crossed her arms and pursed her lips. "Maybe we should try to make a version of our song that sounds more like that. Just in case. I'd hate to go up on stage and make fools of ourselves, you know."

Elijah hesitated.

How many hours had he ranted to Andy about his frustrations with the music world? With artists who had brilliant albums in the beginning of their career, but by the end, he couldn't pick them apart in a lineup.

With twenty thousand on the line, the thought hadn't occurred to Elijah yet. Could he afford to stick to principle?

And what would they do, splitting that prize money four ways, *if* they won?

"It's worth a try." Liv placed her fingers on the keys and played an upbeat tune. Elijah had to hand it to her, for someone who listened to very little pop music, she caught onto the formula fast.

The notes bounced, but still somehow dead and lacking the life of Liv's previous versions of the song. It sounded catchy, it sounded like a winner—it sounded like at least nine out of the Top 40.

She concluded with a drumroll of notes and then slid her fingers across the keys on the piano. Then she clasped her hands in her lap and wouldn't meet his eyes.

"Well?"

"That version could definitely win the festival." He reached forward and pulled out the cover for the piano keys. Then he slammed the lid shut. "And that's what I'm afraid of."

Chapter Ten

Liv hummed the tune to "Finding Harmony" in the car on her way to her piano lesson, desperately trying to stay awake.

After her brainstorming session with Elijah, she'd joined the band to practice for Sunday service, but there had been no time to even show them the song after tech finished. Then she'd headed off to another lesson, then to She Brews. After last night's late closing, she woke up early this morning to open. And now, after a quick lunch, she was on her way to another lesson.

She tuned the radio to a hard rock station and cranked up the sound. *Stay awake, stay awake, stay awake.*

When she pulled into the driveaway, she breathed a sigh of relief and turned down the volume. She swigged the last of her double-shot espresso from She Brews and forced herself out of the Bug and up the sidewalk to the front door. She rang the bell.

The door swung open and Cathy, a broad-shouldered woman with an even broader smile, greeted her. "Hi, Liv! Come on in." She ushered Liv into the front room. "Ignore the mess. VBS is next week, you know." She ran a hand through her dark hair and gave a breathless laugh. "Can't believe it's only three days away."

Giant sheets of butcher paper, scissors, glue, markers, streamers, paint, and fake foliage littered the floor. As the children's director at The Vine, VBS marked one of the busiest times of year for Cathy.

"How's it all going?" Liv asked, following Cathy through the kitchen to the living room.

"I can't wait for this year's theme." Cathy's steady attention and warm voice always made Liv feel like she was being cared for by a mother. Probably why Cathy was such a good children's director—she made kids feel treasured. "And I love getting to see all the kiddos have so much fun learning about our Lord."

Liv sensed there was more to the story. "But?"

Cathy sighed. "But I'm not getting the volunteers I need this year. We have barely enough for the kids signed up right now, but a lot of parents don't register their kids until the Sunday right before—or just show up on the first day." She shook her head. "We might have to turn people away if we don't get more helpers. We have to stay in a legal ratio."

Liv's eyes widened. She'd heard the calls for volunteers on Sunday mornings, but she hadn't known the situation was this bad.

"Garrett, Miss Liv's here!" Cathy called.

Liv ran through her schedule at She Brews and with lessons in her mind. VBS ran until noon. She didn't have any shifts until at least one in the afternoon next week. She had two morning lessons, but she was pretty sure those families wouldn't mind pushing them back a couple hours.

"Sign me up," Liv blurted.

Cathy cocked her head at Liv as eight-year-old Garrett came bounding into the room. "What's that?"

"Sign me up for VBS," Liv repeated. "Anywhere you need me."

Cathy burst into a wide grin and threw her arms around Liv. "Oh, thank you!" She pulled back. "I know you're very busy…"

"For the kids." Liv smiled. "VBS is the highlight of the summer for a lot of them. We can't let them down."

Cathy wiped her eyes. "For the kiddos." She placed a hand on Garrett's head. "You ready for your lesson, bud?"

Garrett's enthusiasm didn't match his accuracy, but Liv always enjoyed instructing the piano-loving boy. His one goal in life was to master the instrument to the point that he could someday play the Imperial March from Star Wars.

After the lesson, Liv found Cathy sitting at a coffee table that overflowed with craft supplies, cutting out stacks and stacks of paper leaves. "For one of our object lessons," she explained. She shook out her hand that had been holding the scissors. "It sounds like Garrett had a great time. I don't have a musical bone in my body, but he has an ear for it."

"He has a lot of natural talent." Liv looked down at the leaves printed on a still-tall stack of paper. "Want some help cutting?"

"I'd love that." Cathy gestured to the corner. "There are more scissors in that box."

Liv grabbed a pair and perched on the edge of a loveseat across the coffee table from Cathy. The espresso must have kicked in, because even though her bed called to her for a nap, she didn't feel like she would fall asleep sitting up.

Thankfully, Boris had cancelled cooking class this evening, so she could turn in early. He sent out an email telling students he had a stomach bug that was *definitely not* food poisoning. He emphasized that point three times.

"Are you singing with the band anymore?" Cathy asked. "I haven't seen you up there in a while."

Liv cut around a stem. "Actually, I'll be singing this coming Sunday. Elijah and I have been working on some...stuff, so I've been hanging out with the band, and I figured I might as well."

She didn't want to mention the competition specifically—Cathy loved to talk, and anything she learned tended to spread to half the moms in the church within a week. Cathy would never share any malicious rumors or sensitive information, only fun facts, but Liv didn't really want the church to know she and the band were trying to write a song to win the festival. She didn't need that kind of pressure on top of what she already felt.

"Wonderful! I love hearing you sing." Cathy re-twisted her hair into the massive clip on the back of her head. She huffed a laugh. "You know, my oldest, Cheyenne, desperately wishes she could sing."

"Maybe she just needs practice. The voice is an instrument like any other." Her professors had drilled into their students that talent played a role, but practice and instruction were just as important.

"Oh, no, she's completely tone deaf. Has no interest in music. Just in a certain young worship leader." Cathy chuckled. "Half her girlfriends in the college group are crazy about him. Of course, I doubt he has any idea. Too old for all of them, anyway."

Something about the thought of a slew of girls batting their eyes at Elijah made Liv annoyed.

"Him and Brooklyn, though. Cheyenne said they spend a decent amount of time together, since he helps out with the youth."

Liv searched her brain for context for the name Brooklyn. Ah, yes. The youth leader. She was probably around their age. "Oh, she's single?"

"Unabashedly. Some of the older congregants weren't sure about her at first because of it, but I think most of them have come around. She does a great job with the youth, and the numbers have exploded."

So Brooklyn had originally faced antagonistic forces, just like Elijah. *I guess, with something as important as church leadership, people tend to have strong opinions about what's best.* But Brooklyn had overcome those who had doubts about her. Maybe soon, Elijah would too.

Her thoughts turned back to Brooklyn and Elijah. She'd never asked him about his love life—it wasn't exactly relevant to songwriting. Were he and Brooklyn seeing one another? "Do you think they like each other?"

Cathy shrugged. "Who knows? It wouldn't be unusual, though. You see a lot of young people in ministry pair up. It comes with working together all the time and having similar values and passions." She shook out her scissors hand again. Then her mouth formed an "o," and her eyes widened. "Wait, are you and Elijah seeing each other?"

Liv's heart gave a quick *thump-thump*. She and Elijah... He was sweet, smart, passionate about music and the Lord, with a big helping of natural charisma and good looks.

But she'd been down that path before.

Her one semester in college, she'd met an aspiring Christian musician, an unusual find in her secular university's program. His passion and drive drew her in, along with the way he gushed over her compositions and could talk about music for hours. They went on dates, exchanged her first kiss, and he even wrote and recorded a love song especially for her.

"This one isn't for the world to hear," he told her. "It's just for you."

She'd thought it the most romantic gesture he could have given her—until she heard a girl in another practice room playing the same tune.

It turned out, three other girls in the program besides Liv received that same "exclusive" song, and those glowing words about their compositions being the best he'd ever heard. The three of them found out, found each other, and exposed him as the jerk he was in the juiciest gossip the music program had had in years.

Liv never told the other three she had been one of "Connor's girls" too. The secret girl number four. She'd been too ashamed to have fallen for him, and soon, she'd gone home for good after Dad's accident.

But for a couple months with Connor, she'd imagined her romance was like what Mom and Dad had had. She thought maybe she could bring someone home to add to their little family of two.

She'd been wrong.

After that, she had learned not to let beautiful music blind her. She'd sworn she wouldn't let artistic passion obscure the truth from her again, or assume someone earnestly followed the Lord because they claimed to. Elijah made a great partner in songwriting, but she wasn't willing to risk anything else. Not for a long, long time.

Liv donned a casual smile for Cathy. "Oh, no. Just friends."

"Just checking." Cathy set down another leaf. "Anyway, I was thinking maybe for VBS, you could…"

But as Cathy moved on to other subjects, and Liv cut out several dozen more leaves, part of her wondered if there was a chance she and Elijah could someday be something more.

Thursday band practice had gone pretty much how Elijah had expected.

Ten minutes into the rehearsal, the tech trainee accidentally shut down the system. They spent half an hour waiting for everything to reboot.

Elijah and Liv didn't get a chance to run the band through the two versions of Finding Harmony they'd created earlier that afternoon, but Liv vowed to commit the melody to sheet music so the band had some tracks to listen to that week.

Now, on Saturday, Elijah braced himself on the family room couch for his mid-morning scroll through his emails. Pastor Smith preached on Saturdays and Sundays, but sometimes he would send Elijah a message in between services.

Sure enough, when his inbox loaded, a new message in bold blazed at the top of his laptop screen.

Hi, Elijah,

I just got word that our music volunteer for VBS had to cancel at the last minute. Supposedly a "family vacation" to Northern Michigan. I did see Don conversing with him last Sunday, so I have a feeling that there may be something else in play.

Because our music director dropped out for the event, I need you to take over. I'm having the church secretary send over some video files on the motions to the songs. Below I've also pasted some links to the lyrics. You don't have to accompany it with music—there are pre-recorded tracks we plan to use. But VBS songs do require some choreography, so brush up on your dance skills.

Elijah paused his skim and sucked his teeth. How did the pastor know he couldn't dance for beans? He continued reading.

Also, at noon after the service a videographer is stopping by. He plans to film during VBS for some promo. As you and I know, our church desperately needs some good PR.

He says his name is Ryan and that you two play pick-up basketball together in the winter and spring. Because you already have connected with him previously, I'd like you to swing by church later, give him a tour, and walk him through the VBS schedule. I'll also have the church secretary forward you that.

Hope you're having a blessed Saturday and that we can pull ourselves out of this summer slump soon.

In Him,
Pastor Smith

Elijah filled in an "or else" in his mind after the "summer slump soon" portion of the email. Pastor Smith would never outright say that he may have to cut the most recently hired worship leader—since the other one quit—if church attendance and tithing didn't pick up soon, but the pastor didn't do too well on harder topics. Even in his sermons, Pastor Smith's knees buckled whenever he spoke about wrath, sin, or judgment.

Those subjects, after all, caused numbers to drop.

He slammed the laptop shut and groaned into his fingers. Nutty-scented coffee alerted his senses. In the kitchen, Andy's Keurig groaned.

Andy caught Elijah's eye and leaned against a counter. "More work?"

After burning himself out last spring, Andy had vowed to take at least one day off a week. Saturdays. The roommates would often go on hikes or stop by local burger joints on Andy's day of rest. That was until

Pastor Smith gave Elijah tasks seven days a week.

"I guess I have to work VBS now. Three hours a day, five days this week."

Steamy liquid from the Keurig poured into a mug. Moments later, Andy emerged from the kitchen nursing a hand-painted cup. "You know, for a part-time job, he sure has you working a lot of full-time hours."

"For half the pay of a real job." Elijah sighed. "But what can I do? The guy threw me a lifeline last spring when I was out of work. And I keep causing his numbers to go down. If I don't do everything he asks me, he might as well hand the position to someone else."

That may not have been a bad thing...if they didn't have apartment rent to pay.

Andy set his cup on a coaster and scooped it up moments later when Sammy attempted to slurp the contents of the mug. The dog's long neck could traverse any table. "What all do you have to do?"

Elijah read him the email.

By the time he reached the "In Him," he noticed another message had entered his inbox. "VBS Motions and Schedule" proclaimed itself in bold letters, from the church secretary.

Andy blew on the rim of the cup. "From everything you've told me about The Vine, it sounds like you got an Ice and Everything Nice church."

Elijah's eyebrows drew together. "A what?"

"It's the opposite of a Fire and Brimstone church." Andy paused to drink half the coffee. *This guy could handle hot drinks.* "Basically, when a pastor is raised in a church where everything is about judgment, judgment, judgment, he decides he doesn't want to preach on that when he grows up. He preaches about love, love, love. They don't want to step on toes, because they had theirs stomped on when they were little."

"Well, love is nice." Elijah's stomach burned. *Man did that coffee smell heavenly.*

"Agreed. Love is great, but." Andy fished a quarter out of his shorts' pockets. He pinched the coin. "Love and wrath are two sides of the same thing, and you gotta preach both to share the whole Bible. The two don't clash, they harmonize. They sing the same story about a loving and holy God."

Elijah allowed the weight of that to sink in. Then he plunged further into the soft couch cushions. "Good luck telling Pastor Smith that. He's so afraid of losing more members."

With his cup drained, Elijah returned his mug to the coaster. Sammy sniffed the contents and tossed Andy a betrayed look.

"Well, Lij, I can't tell Pastor Smith how to do his job. But we can try to salvage whatever dance skills you have. Let's go over the videos."

"Together?" Elijah cracked a grin. This was about to be hilarious.

"Why, of course," Andy said in a brutal attempt at a British accent. "We do hang out on Saturdays, work or no work. It would be my pleasure to learn these dance moves with you."

They set up Elijah's laptop on the table in the center of the common area room and clicked play on the video. A woman in a red polo shirt with a too-bright a smile led them through the motions of the songs. Her voice reminded Elijah of a cheerleader's—far too peppy to be teaching dance moves to a children's song.

Peaches wove figure eights around their legs while they learned to turn their arms into wiggly worms.

"Man," Elijah said, halfway through learning one song. "These moves get complicated."

Andy chuckled. "They're for *children*, Elijah."

Two hours later, they managed to get down the choreography of three songs. In time for Elijah to head to church to show Ryan the ropes.

"I'll have to learn the other two songs during the week." Elijah closed his laptop and reached for his wallet and keys on the family room table. How would he fit that in with the worship set, preparing the song for the festival, and whatever other duties Pastor Smith sent him?

Sweat clung to Elijah on the drive over to church. Oh, right, he'd have to find time to get his car repaired too.

When he arrived, he spotted a figure with blocky glasses at the top of the concrete steps. Ryan had gotten here early. Elijah raced up the stairs and hugged his friend. Ryan arched his back, probably sensing the amount of perspiration on Elijah's clothing.

"Hey, Lij, thanks for showing me around." Ryan eased himself out of Elijah's arms and pushed his glasses up his nose. "I didn't used to make people give me tours, but long story short...after a client made me film something at a haunted house, I want to scope the place beforehand." He shuddered.

"No problem. Let's get into some AC." Elijah fanned himself with his shirt.

They explored large rooms and winding halls. Everything was decorated in fake stones, coats of arms, and "not" Narnia paraphernalia.

"So, Ryan." Elijah ducked under a hanging decorative vine. Yeesh, a kid would pull that thing by Monday, no doubt. "Do you have a crazy summer of film gigs?"

"Yeah. Tons of weddings this summer, and Griffith asked me to film his play he's putting on."

"Sounds busy."

"Actually, I really cut back this year."

Ryan clicked on and off a bulb in a children's classroom. To see how the lighting would show up on film, Elijah guessed.

"Cut back?"

"Yeah, last year I was editing and filming nonstop. Summer's a happening time for film projects, especially for people getting hitched. It wasn't until I ended up in the hospital that I decided to tell a lot of people no."

Hospital? Elijah seldom saw Ryan at a basketball practice without an inhaler plugged into his mouth. But did he have other health problems too?

Ryan flicked the light switch off again and ventured to the

classroom next door. "Yeah, it was hard at first. I kept telling myself that if I turned them down, then I wouldn't get any business. That didn't happen. Now I actually sleep eight hours a night and have cut down on microwave meals."

Something sparked inside Elijah's chest. Hope, maybe? It felt like helium, lifting up his head and shoulders all the way through the rest of the tour.

Chapter Eleven

Liv descended the stairs to the stage at The Vine, her knees wobbly. *Thank goodness that's over.*

She'd never felt nervous about leading worship before, but with the amount of complaints Elijah had been facing, she didn't want to be the reason for any more.

She had dressed a little nicer than usual and avoided bracelets that might clack and make noise through the microphone. She wore comfortable flats under her long skirt to lessen the possibility of tripping—not that she had ever tripped onstage before, but there was a first time for everything.

This is ridiculous. She sank into a seat in the front row of the church. *Leading worship should be about communing with God as a body, not about trying to appease everyone.*

Most of the congregants had left the sanctuary, though a few still loitered, chatting. Liv and the band had continued to play while people filtered out at the end of the service, but now that it was over, Christian pop filtered through the loudspeakers.

Derek the drummer plopped down a seat away from her, shaking greasy locks out of his eyes. "Looks like that guy Don isn't here to yell at us, so that's nice." He shrugged. "Maybe he's in the foyer working up a mob, though."

Liv pressed her lips together. As far as she could tell, nothing had gone wrong today. The lights might have been a bit much—the new tech guy had been gung-ho about the colored spotlights—-but that had nothing to do with the band.

"I think we have a good chance of surviving today." Liv offered Derek a friendly smile. "Everyone did well this morning."

He grinned and winked. "I always do."

Liv resisted the urge to roll her eyes.

"But I guess everyone else wasn't too bad either." He gave another awkward wink. Then he stood, stretched, and waved to the bassist. "Hey, Charlize, need help with that?"

Liv's thoughts turned elsewhere as Derek and Charlize began their usual dance of flirtatious comment and brutal comeback. Liv was beginning to think Derek enjoyed Charlize's disdain.

She mentally went through her to-do list for the day—preparing for lessons, more arrangements and transposing for the network of ladies who all had learned of her "amazing talent" of creating scores with music software so they didn't have to scratch them out by hand, a random babysitting gig tonight...hopefully the parents didn't stay out too late. She needed to get up at a decent time for VBS on Monday.

Liv had been assigned the title of "floater," which meant her job was to fill in wherever people were missing on a given day. According to Cathy, many volunteers couldn't commit to all five days, necessitating floaters.

"And of course, we'd love to have you help with the music," Cathy had said, passing her a CD. "Here are the songs. Your job will be more along the lines of corralling children, but you'll need to learn the motions, too. Nothing gets distracted kiddos back into the worship like dancing along with them."

Liv's arms were still a little sore from practicing last night. She might have to run through the choreography again today. Maybe she would inflict the moves on Caroline as well. Caroline couldn't help with VBS, since she worked during the day, but it wasn't fair for her to miss all the fun.

"I think most people have left." Elijah bounded down the steps after unplugging and plugging in cords, microphones, amps, and Liv didn't know what else.

She knew plenty about music, but little about the tech equipment that bands and churches used. Orchestral instruments usually didn't plug into anything the way a bass or electric guitar or a keyboard did.

She knew larger orchestras often employed strategic use of microphones, but it had never been any of her concern how that was done.

Actually, it's pretty impressive. Being a worship leader meant having a good knowledge of tech as well as music. And recruiting volunteers, and taking feedback, and trying to please a diverse audience... People going to an opera all wanted the same thing, or a musical theater production, or a performance of Handel's *Messiah.* But unlike specific productions and performances, no one knew exactly what a church service would be like. And every churchgoer had a different idea of what that "performance" should be.

Liv stood, trying not to clutch her bag too nervously. "It does seem to have cleared out. Do you think we can use the instruments now?"

"I have everything plugged into local amps, so we won't be blasting music through the entire sanctuary. I think we should be fine." He glanced at one group of a few older ladies still chatting near the doors and shrugged. "I think we could wait all day if we want everyone to be gone. There's always someone at a church this big. Besides, the VBS crew will be descending soon for last minute tweaks." He fiddled with his earpiece. Was he nervous too?

Worst case scenario, they hate it. She took a deep breath and pulled out her folder of sheet music. "Let's go see what they think."

Liv and Elijah joined Derek and Charlize onstage. "Did you know I can play the recorder with my nose?" Derek was saying. He twirled a drumstick and caught it before holding it under his nose and wiggling his fingers in an impression of recorder-playing.

Charlize recoiled. "That's disgusting."

"All right, guys." Elijah grabbed the neck of his guitar and slung the strap over his head. "We have a couple of songs to show you and see what you think."

Liv opened her folder and pulled out the packets labelled "Finding Harmony 1" and "Finding Harmony 2." She owed Caroline ink money for the printer. "I made two potential arrangements of the same song."

She passed out a copy of each to every band member. "Elijah and I worked on them the other day, and we want your opinions. The score is a little rough, since I threw it into the computer pretty fast, and it's nothing final, but...yeah."

Derek flipped through the pages. "'Floating, falling,' yeah, I've felt that sort of thing that one time when I—"

"Let's get started," Charlize interrupted. "Do you and Elijah want to play it for us, to give us a sense of what you're thinking?"

"Sure." Liv sat at the keyboard and positioned the music and her notes on the stand. "Elijah, you got lead vocals?"

"Yep." He adjusted his guitar and shot her an encouraging smile.

"Right." She turned to the keys, took a deep breath, and began to play.

They played Liv's original version first. She'd tweaked it some, and she was much happier with the counterpoint. The multiple voices wove together well, flowing in the piano, with Elijah's guitar strumming filling out the sound.

Elijah sang, and Liv accompanied. They hadn't practiced this part, but she knew Elijah could keep the melody line of a song with backup vocals harmonizing, so she trusted him to sing his part as she sang hers.

Her words and melody danced around his, the lyrics a counterpoint as well as the melody. His eyes widened, but he kept singing. "Am I chosen—"

"*I have chosen you—*"

"Forsaken?"

"*Never forsaken you.*"

They reached the ending of the song, all voices and parts coming together in a dynamic, harmonious close.

As the last notes faded away, Liv lifted her fingers from the keys and cleared her throat. "Well. That's version one."

Charlize's eyes were wide, and Derek's mouth hung open. Before they could say anything, Liv asked Elijah, "Version two?"

He blinked but nodded.

They launched into version two. Liv banged out upbeat, standard chords and offered basic backup "ohs" to Elijah as he strummed and sang to the bouncy tune.

Liv cringed while playing. The music seemed to stifle Elijah's lyrics, and in this version, there wasn't nearly as much time to expand on verses when they had to sing the peppy chorus and "ohs" so many times.

After they finished, Liv and Elijah turned to the others. "Well?" he asked. "Thoughts?"

Derek scratched behind his ear. "Lyrics are good, dude. No complaints."

"Solid." Charlize nodded.

Liv forced herself not to fidget. "There will be bass and drums too, of course, rounding out the sound."

"Nah, they're great. It's good stuff. It's just..." Derek scrunched his nose. "They barely seem like the same song."

Liv thought she saw a bead of sweat form on Elijah's temple. "Which one do you like more?" he asked. "Do you think either one is festival-worthy?"

"Number two," Charlize said. "It's a bop. Sounds like winners from past years."

Liv's heart plummeted.

"Yeah. Don't get me wrong." Derek started twirling his drumstick. "First one? I'm more of a screaming-and-electric-guitars kind of guy, but even I could tell that was a work of art, you know? Felt like I was in one of those symphony performances my mom used to take me to as a kid. But like, those things aren't popular anymore, you know?" He scratched his chest. *Does the guy have fleas?* "People don't win awards for that."

People don't win awards for that. As usual, her music didn't fit. Maybe constraints and time limits and lack of instruments weren't the problem. Maybe all along, she was.

"You can't ever repeat this, but I agree with Derek." Charlize tossed him a withering look. "That first piece was really impressive. I got chills, honestly. But I'm a musician. We all are. We can recognize the work and artistry that went into something like that. I can tell you put a lot of time into the different voices." Liv nodded affirmation, and Charlize went on, "But people at a festival, or listening to the radio? People just want something with a beat. Something simple they can sing along with." She huffed and blew a piece of hair out of her face. "It's the same thing with movies, books, anything—people don't really care about craft. They want to be entertained."

Liv felt like she'd been punched in the gut. She opened her mouth to say something, she didn't know what. Maybe "sorry," maybe "version two it is, then."

Elijah beat her to it. "We'll keep working on it."

As Liv collected her sheet music from the keyboard, Elijah watched her lips sag. She hadn't handled the band's reaction to the two versions of Finding Harmony well either, it seemed.

Elijah glanced over his shoulder to make sure Derek and Charlize had ventured out of earshot. Derek was busy making the guitar chords sound like snakes with elongated s's. Charlize rolled her eyes.

Good, they couldn't hear him from their position.

"They'll turn around, Liv." Elijah curved his mouth upward. "They loved the first version. It always takes a few tries to make someone go with something riskier."

She banged the papers against the keyboard. Then she set them inside a green folder she'd brought labeled "Songs."

"For sure." She didn't sound so certain.

When Liv had gone to return her earbuds to the tech team in the back, Elijah scooped up the keyboard. Cold, dank darkness greeted him as he set down the instrument in the storage room. Doubt prickled his mind like a billion needles.

Why was he adamant about the original version? They probably couldn't even get an honorable mention with that.

The other day, after learning some more VBS song moves, he'd headed over to YouTube to watch the other top placers at the festival the previous year. The second-place team, a group of people who loved eyeliner too much called 'Alpha Particles,' played a song that sounded like a near copy of the first-place winners.

Except this one decided to go for "oh, oh" instead of "yeah, yeah."

If they wanted to win the twenty grand, why dig in their heels now?

He exited storage and squinted at the bright sanctuary lights. His vision adjusted, and he saw Liv slinging her bag over her shoulder.

"Hey, Liv." His voice snagged. Why did she have to look extra beautiful today? What was it? The large silver earrings?

She turned, eyes wide, perhaps surprised. "Yes?"

"Usually the band grabs lunch after cleanup. You always leave so fast that we never have a chance to invite you. Want to come? We go to this fun 50s-themed diner and." And what? He couldn't say, "I'd love to have you there with me." That sounded way too forward. "And the cheeseburgers have great prices. Mmm." He rubbed his stomach. "Cheddar."

Liv scrunched her nose and stifled a laugh with her knuckle. Then her features darkened. She bit her lip.

"Umm." She checked her phone, perhaps to scrutinize the time. "Umm. I mean, it sounds fun." Her weight shifted from one leg to the next, and her face scrunched. Was she trying to say she didn't have time for it?

"Liv, you know it's fine to say 'no.' I know your schedule's crazy."

"Are you sure?" She gripped her bare wrist in an automatic motion. Liv must've forgotten to put on bangles or bracelets today. "I could rearrange a few things. It's just with being signed up to volunteer for VBS and all—"

"Wait, you're on the VBS team?"

"They said they needed two music leaders. One to show motions and one to corral the kids, since the classroom leaders get their break time during the music class."

Well, they certainly hadn't informed him of that. He hoped Liv had some expertise on all things corralling, because he couldn't even make Peaches jump off his bed most mornings.

Elijah chuckled. "You know you could've told them no to VBS too."

She hugged her folder to her chest and shrugged. "I don't mind. I like children."

Good to know for the future. He shook the thought away before it could dissolve into a picture of Liv's beautiful offspring in a homeschool van. "Well, I guess I'll be seeing you tomorrow. We'll have plenty of time to grab food in between music sessions with the kids." He nodded at the door. "Don't worry about the diner."

She lingered in the center aisle.

Finally, she cleared her throat. "Are you sure?"

"Yes." The word came out a little harsher than he'd intended. He softened his voice. "Trust me, Derek likes to make towers with his fries. You're not missing much."

Derek had moved on from snake imitations to enclosing Charlize's bass into her guitar case. He presented it with a flourish when he'd finished snapping the locks. "Madame."

Charlize turned up her nose and reached for the handle. "Same place for lunch, Lij?"

"Yep. Just got to check with Pastor Smith if he needs anything else for teardown. I'll meet you guys there."

Derek and Charlize exited stage left and Elijah dropped his earbuds off at the tech booth in the back. He meandered down the winding halls until he reached a hallway full of offices. The first door on the left led him inside a large room, filled with bookcases.

Pastor Smith sat behind a huge wooden desk. He clacked on a computer keyboard, unaware of Elijah's presence.

Elijah cleared his throat. The pastor glanced up at him.

"Hey, Pastor. We've done teardown. Anything else you need us to get set up for VBS tomorrow?"

Pastor Smith cocked his head and thought for a few seconds. Strong lemon air freshener punched Elijah in the nostrils. The pastor did like to disinfect surfaces often.

"Not that I can think of." The pastor decided finally. "Long as you and the others show up at eight a.m. tomorrow to help with setup, we should be good to go. I think the volunteers have finished most of the decorations, so it shouldn't take long."

So many vines and moss decorations had coated the sanctuary that Elijah had heard one or two members, during communion, remark about how they felt as though they'd entered a forest. Elijah and the rest of the band sat in the pews during the service and sneaked onto the stage during Pastor's final prayer to play the rest of their songs.

Relief flooded Elijah and dropped his shoulders two inches. At last, one Sunday he'd gone into Pastor's office without a comment about Don.

"One more thing." Pastor Smith's eyes stuck to his computer screen. Brightness illuminated the dark circles underneath his eyes. "Don's getting more people riled up. Someone was grumbling about how the lights on stage are too bright and flashy. I noticed they approached me right after they talked with Don."

Spoken too soon.

And Elijah could do absolutely nothing about the spotlights and illuminations used during the service. The tech team decided that.

This is getting ridiculous. I'm losing sleep at night trying to make the worship set perfect.

His mind flashed back to Liv in the sanctuary. He'd convinced her to dig in her heels. Now was his turn.

"Pastor Smith, my apartment mate was talking to me about church discipline the other day." Elijah sunk into a soft chair stationed in front of the desk. "I'm not as familiar with that portion of Scripture, but shouldn't we be stepping in at this point?"

All of Pastor Smith slumped. He'd anticipated this question, Elijah bet.

Then the lanky man swiveled in his chair and faced a shelf full of dusty hardbacks. "Don's a special case. His wife was a huge reason he came to church in the first place, and people deal with grief differently. Because his wife was so connected to music, he struggles to sit through worship without her."

Guilt gnawed Elijah's gut. He didn't handle his grandmother's death all that well either, did he?

"True," Elijah admitted. He cinched his fingers together and set them on his lap. "But at what point do we say that he's taken this too far?"

Pastor Smith hesitated. Then he nudged a book with a cloth cover out of the shelf and flipped through the pages. Almondy scents from the old papers caught Elijah's senses.

"This book was from my late father. He would read it to us every Sunday from the pulpit." Gilded letters flashed the title, *Book of Common Prayer*. Pastor Smith released a sigh and placed the book back on the shelf. "That was one of my few good memories from that church."

"What happened?"

"Politics, turmoil, wolves in sheep's clothing." Pastor Smith wiped a sheen of sweat off his forehead. "My father was a big fan of passages on judgment and wrath, and he exercised both on the congregation. I can't count the number of church members he pressured to leave."

This confirmed Elijah's suspicions. The Vine was Pastor Smith's antithesis of his father's church.

"Don is..." The pastor stopped speaking for a moment. Clenched his jaw. Then his eyes lit up, and it appeared he found the right words. "Don is a lost sheep. A disgruntled, cranky lamb, for certain. But still a part of our pasture, nonetheless. I'd like to do what we can to love on him and show him a Christlike attitude."

Most times, Elijah could get on board with this mentality. But something caused burning coals to sear in his stomach. He clutched his abdomen and winced.

The flames felt like the same sear of heat that plagued his brain at night. A question that would not let him go, like a fire that clung to a stick.

"Pastor Smith." He halted. Then pressed on. "Was Don the reason the former worship leader retired?"

The other man didn't answer him. Instead he sighed and reached for his hat on the coat rack behind the desk. "Just a few more weeks, then we can make a decision about what to do about him."

Elijah didn't know if he could last that long.

Chapter Twelve

LIV DONNED HER GARISH BRIGHT-ORANGE volunteer shirt. There would be no doubt who the adults were with this eye-melting color.

Her bedside clock read 7:20. She planned to be on the road by 7:40 at the latest—she wanted to get there even earlier than early, just in case. VBS for the kids started at nine, but volunteers had been asked to show up at eight.

After lacing up her Converse to go with her jeans and t-shirt, she put her hair in a high ponytail and slid a few fun chunky bracelets onto her wrists. She put in orange tassel earrings—might as well try to accessorize to make the outfit a little less atrocious. And she definitely wasn't dressing it up because of a certain long-haired worship leader. No, that would be silly.

Her thoughts turned to yesterday and Elijah. He'd noticed her hesitance about joining the band for lunch, and instead of pressuring her, assured her "no" was an acceptable answer.

And she'd believed him.

Few people noticed when she seemed overwhelmed, but he had. She couldn't help the warm feeling in her chest at that. Usually when people said she could say no, she got the feeling that if she did, they would be upset or annoyed. They said it to be polite, but they didn't expect her to *actually* deny them.

She stepped into the kitchen to find Caroline making eggs with spinach. *At least it isn't kale. She's branching out.* "Hey, girl."

Caroline spun on her toes, light gray slacks swishing around dark gray low heels. Immaculately professional, as usual. Caroline whistled. "Liv. How do you make even horrible VBS t-shirts look good?"

Liv's face warmed. "Accessories," she declared, reaching for the cereal. "You can solve anything with accessories."

"Well, you have fun. I don't envy you." Caroline turned off the burner and slid her eggs onto a plate. "I've grown to love the kids at the Hope Club, but...still not my thing."

"I love kids." She dumped sugary cereal into a bowl.

"I know you want a bevy of your own someday." Caroline shuddered.

Liv laughed. "Girl, don't you and Andy want kids?"

Caroline squeaked. "We're nowhere near that yet." Her face turned bright red as she sat at the table. "Although...he does like the idea of doing art from home...with kids...someday."

Andy as a stay-at-home dad. From what Liv had seen, he would be wonderful. And Caroline would go nuts if she couldn't work off all that ambitious steam. "You two really are a great match."

Caroline's expression turned dreamy. "Yeah. We're nowhere near perfect, but God somehow worked it out so we make up for each other's weak points with our strong points." She pinched the tiniest bit of salt onto her eggs. "He takes the imperfect and makes it perfect."

Liv considered her cereal bowl with more attention than the contents warranted, mulling over Caroline's words. Like two melody lines that felt hollow, incomplete without each other. Together, they made a beautiful harmony. The way her voice harmonized with Elijah's.

No, Liv. Stop it. You don't even have time to think about those sorts of things.

Twenty minutes later, Liv ducked under hanging "vines" to reach Cathy. "What do you want me to do?"

Cathy looked up from her clipboard, hair frizzing in frazzlement. "Liv! We already have some volunteers' kids here—can you watch them while their parents get to their stations?"

"For sure."

"Good, good, and then when the other kids start coming in, can you show them to their areas? It's all color-coded by age."

"I got it." Liv gave her a thumbs up. "You're doing great."

Cathy offered a small smile in return. "Thanks, Liv. You're a godsend."

Liv went to join a wide-eyed young teen trying to corral a gaggle of kids who seemed to be aged three to ten.

One might think kids of volunteers would be better behaved than the average camper, but that didn't appear to be the case. Two boys held a toy over a crying girl's head, a younger child wailed for his mother, and a boy of about seven engaged in the violent destruction of a fallen vine, ripping it to shreds. Meanwhile, a few more kids ran in circles yelling or throwing things at each other.

"Hey, guys, can you please stop?" the teen girl pleaded. "Could you sit down?"

Poor girl. Kids couldn't be expected to sit quietly—without a direction for their energy, they often channeled it into less-than-optimal behavior. Liv whistled and clapped her hands. "One, two, three, eyes on me."

The squirming mass halted their activity.

She knew she had less than three seconds to keep the attention she had captured. "Who wants to learn some of the motions to the songs early? You can impress your friends."

The kids huddled around.

Thank goodness. Without music, Liv sang the first line and demonstrated the moves. "Now your turn."

The kids repeated the line with varying degrees of accuracy.

"Well done. Okay, here's the next one."

She kept them occupied with learning the songs until new kids began trickling in. Then she left them playing Simon Says under the instruction of the teen leader as she went to herd children to their correct groups.

"Hey, buddy." Liv greeted a curly-headed little boy bounding through the door. "What color are you?"

"Green!" He proudly held his nametag aloft.

"Green? Wow, that's an awesome color. Can I help you find it?"

"Yeah!" He bounced along behind her. "G-R-E-E-N spells green."

"Wow, good job, bud." Liv held up a hand, and he gave her a high-five. "You're so smart."

He grinned and ran off toward one of his friends in the green group.

As she turned toward the doors to the sanctuary to retrieve another child, her gaze happened upon Elijah and she suppressed a laugh.

He sat cross-legged on the floor, perfectly still, with three little girls surrounding him and giggling as they added more and more plastic flowers to his hair.

One held up a flower for him to "smell." He sucked a giant breath in, then his face screwed up. "Ah...ah...ah-CHOO!"

He fake-sneezed so violently, shaking his head like a dog, that flowers scattered from his hair, flying everywhere. The girls screeched with laughter, and he laughed with them. "Whew. I guess I'm allergic to pollen."

The girls picked up the flowers and started putting them in his hair again, giggling in anticipation. Liv got the impression that this sneezing-flowers-everywhere game had repeated more than once.

Her heart warmed. Dad would do something like that. He had let Liv decorate his hair with barrettes and do his "makeup" as a customer in her beauty salon as a child, even let her put him in tiaras and capes so he could be the "Evil Queen" to her princess.

As she watched Elijah patiently allow a couple more children to add leaves to the elaborate hairdo, she mused, *Connor would never have done that.* He'd always been kind and attentive, but forever cognizant of appearances. He wouldn't have wanted anyone to get the wrong idea from flowers in his hair.

Not long afterward, after Liv had guided a few dozen kids to their groups, Cathy stepped onto the stage with a microphone. "Who's ready for VBS this week?"

The sanctuary echoed with cheers. Cathy grinned out at the group. "What do you think, should we start off by praising and worshipping God?"

The answering roar of approval seemed to shake the walls.

"Worship team, take it away!"

Liv's job, along with another girl, was to keep any overly enthusiastic children from diving onto the stage. They flanked the stairs, standing on ground level, and did the motions along with the team on stage, ready to catch rogue toddlers or sneaky ten-year-olds who might send plants and decorations crashing. But though Liv had seen such disasters occur before, they needn't have worried this time.

The kids jumped up and down, imitating the motions on stage. The kids who could read picked up the words from the screen quickly, while the younger students chimed in for the chorus. Some learned the motions in seconds, while others mixed up their hands and missed half the actions. Many of the youngest kids forewent attempting the motions at all, instead flapping their arms, jumping, and giggling with joy.

As upbeat, tinny music blasted through the speakers and a packed sanctuary roiled with jubilant dance and voice before her, goosebumps rose on Liv's arms.

A boy a few feet from her stumbled over the words, laughed, and instead shouted, "Yay, Jesus!" to the beat.

This. This churning mass of abandoned dance and cacophonous song, with little coordination or skill, had more heart, more soul than anything Liv had ever seen from the congregation at The Vine. The kids didn't care if someone messed up the motions, or the tune, or even the words. They didn't care about sound quality or song selection. They were at VBS, and they were ready to worship their hearts out, no matter what.

Liv threw more gusto into her own singing and dancing, and joined them in praising the Lord.

"Wow." Elijah slumped into a chair in the designated "break room" for VBS volunteers. The usual classroom for men's Bible studies had been transformed into a haven full of snacks. Blankets covered the rectangle window on the door to prevent children from peeping inside.

Elijah watched Liv sit beside him on a squashy green bean bag and swirl a stir straw in her drink. Hot chocolate and coffee, the well-known elixir that kept all the volunteers going during VBS week. Elijah had a cup of it in his own hands.

She blew on the cup and raised her eyebrows at him. "That was something, wasn't it?"

"Wow," Elijah repeated and ran his fingers through his hair. "Our church really could use that energy on Sunday. Imagine if people let loose like that. Worshipping without giving a care about what you sound or look like. David did dance in the town square like that, in Scripture."

"I just think it's a testament that everyone can worship differently." Liv pressed the cup to her lips. Sipped. "And that everything doesn't have to be perfect."

Best of luck convincing Pastor Smith of that. Since Elijah's meeting in his office the other day, he'd messaged Elijah this morning with an email that iced Elijah's blood.

Elijah,

It seems that Don has not only withdrawn funding, but he's emailed the church secretary about a new worship leader candidate. He says he'll start giving again if we institute his singer to take your place.

To make matters worse, he says that this worship leader wannabe is willing to do everything for free.

I'll keep you in the loop, but I had no idea he'd take it this far. Seems like we need to push up the church discipline we talked about. I'll formulate a plan this week and get back to you.

For now, try your best to accommodate what the congregation is asking for.

Pressing onward,
Pastor Smith

Although the pastor sounded reassuring in the email, how much time would pass before Don's deal sounded sweeter? The church could save twenty grand a year if they slashed the worship leader salary. Plus, Don would start his giving again.

Elijah often wondered if Don had a saving faith. Most Christians Elijah knew would never pull something like this. Pastor Smith had mentioned Don didn't go to church before his wife attended.

Maybe...

Elijah tipped back a water bottle from a nearby snack table and swigged. He hadn't realized how much he'd shouted this morning until the cool water touched the scratches in his throat.

"Doing okay, Lij?" Liv set her cup on the carpet and sank into her seat. Leather fabric swallowed half of her.

He faked a grin. "Dandy."

The door to the break room swung open, and Brooklyn burst in. Something wet stained the front of her orange VBS instructor t-shirt. Elijah recalled one of the classroom leaders mentioning a water balloon toss as one of the activities the kids did outside.

Brooklyn jabbed a finger at Elijah. "I need you for the skit." Her gaze stopped on Liv. "Both of you."

When VBS started, the kids filed into the sanctuary and watched the first part of that day's play. The skit had left them on a cliffhanger where High King Yeter got lost in battle and needed the aid of Prince Raspian.

Each day, the children would go to their classrooms, learn a Bible story, participate in a craft, eat a snack, do an outdoor activity, and return back to the sanctuary to watch the conclusion of the stage play.

"Me. Act?" Elijah sputtered and spilled droplets of water on the carpet. "Brooklyn, be very happy you did not watch me in The Wizard of Oz in sixth grade. Apparently, those tree costumes are easy to trip in."

And the girl who played Dorothy didn't move out of the way fast enough when he'd shouted, "Timber!"

Brooklyn shut the door behind her. "Not much time to explain. Our original Prince Raspian decided to go play on the bouncy houses outside and twisted his ankle. And his trusty wife, playing his love interest Millandi, is refusing to leave his side on the way to the hospital." She stuck out her tongue. "Romance. Doesn't it just make you sick?"

Elijah shared a glance with Liv and his heart kicked his ribcage. Not exactly...

"Anyway." Brooklyn nabbed a bag of Cheetos off the snack table and tore open the top. "Hadassah needs replacements, and now. I figured since you two finished teaching the kids the music motions today that you'd have time. The skit starts in fifteen, and you have about five minutes to practice."

Liv winced. Then her expression softened, and she looked at Elijah expectantly. He understood. How could they say no?

They followed Brooklyn to the stage. By the time they'd reached it, Brooklyn had emptied the chip bag. She crumpled the plastic in her hands, saluted them, and dashed off. Most likely to return to her understaffed classroom.

Hadassah, stationed at the front of the stage with a director's script, relaxed her shoulders when she spotted them. She blew out a long breath.

"Thank the Lord, she found a replacement." She bent down and held up a prop shield. "Elijah, I have the lines for Prince Raspian on the back of this. Just do your best to read them during the skit in your loudest stage voice."

He scooped the shield into his arms. Yellow highlighter illuminated his lines for the show. Yeesh, he had to talk a lot in this.

"And, Liv, you don't have any lines this time around. Just stand by Elijah and act like you are madly in love with him."

Elijah could very much get on board with this skit.

Hadassah clapped her hands and smoothed down her floor-length brown skirt. "I usually would give you two blocking—stage directions and actions," she clarified, "but we don't have much time. Elijah, I just need you to swing your sword at Robert at the line, 'Have at thee.'" She motioned at a young boy who wore plastic knight's armor.

Wait, how young was he? Some middle schoolers had volunteered to help with VBS, as fifth grade was the cutoff for attending VBS as a camper. But the kid's small frame and boyish haircut didn't help with aging him up.

Robert nodded at Elijah. Then, in a shy manner, he glanced at his knee-high black boots.

"I think we have five minutes to run through this." Hadassah pinched her nose and squeezed her eyes shut. "Then we need to get you two into costumes and mics."

Run it they did.

Elijah stared at his shield so much one would've thought someone had taped his favorite candy bars to the back of his prop.

"Angle yourself to your left, Elijah, so the audience can't see the lines." Hadassah shouted this in the middle of Elijah declaring to Robert about his crimes against Barnia.

He edged himself over a little and bumped into Liv. From the redness on her face and the fist pressed against her mouth, it looked like she had to try desperately hard not to laugh.

"Thou, King Smiraz, shall face the wrath of my sword. Have at thee."

Elijah swung his foam blade so fast that he almost knocked Robert over. Fast reflexes took over, and Robert collapsed onto the floor.

"Boy," said a girl playing Bucy. She had her back facing the audience. "I sure am glad we befriended this Prince Raspian. Aren't you, Dusan?"

"Dusan," an adult volunteer with a withering hairline, tried to help "Bucy" turn back to the sanctuary pews. "I sure am, Bucy. I discovered that we can trust Raspian. What else did you learn, Bucy?"

Bucy paused, mouth wide open. She glanced at Dusan. Dusan leaned down and whispered something in her ear, probably a line.

"Oh." Bucy spreadeagled her arms. "I also learned that you can trust Jesus."

Elijah cringed. They really needed Griffith to write these skits. He'd heard Griffith had done so in previous years, but the summer play took up most of his time.

"That'll have to do." Hadassah's bright expression had grayed. She motioned to Robert. "Rob, can you show Elijah and his friend where the costumes are?"

Robert didn't say anything, but he nodded, then disappeared stage right. Elijah and Liv followed, and he led them to a rack full of cheap medieval costumes. Fabric frayed at the edges of most of them. Elijah pinched the thin cotton of a tunic. Yeah, he'd have to wear this over his outfit.

"Rob," Elijah said, pulling off a "knight" outfit with a red cross on it. "You did pretty good up there. You sound like a natural."

Unlike the other actors, Rob hadn't forgotten his lines, said every word crisply, and his believable expressions had transformed his innocent face into one twisted with evil.

"Thanks." Unlike his stage voice, this time, Rob's timbre came out soft and almost indiscernible. Then his eyes lit up. "I'm actually in a play at the local theater. We're performing soon."

"With Griffith?"

Elijah grinned when Robert nodded.

"Well, that's great. He's fortunate to have someone like you."

"Yeah." Robert's expression darkened. Then again, they were backstage where they had minimal lighting. "My dad doesn't think so. He thinks plays take too much time out of my schedule. I don't know what to do. He says after this summer..." Robert sniffled and glanced away. "That I need to focus on more important stuff."

Elijah's stomach dropped.

Liv fluffed a white dress. Dust particles spun in the air. "What could be more important than doing theater, which you love?"

Robert knuckled his nose and blinked a glaze away. "Singing."

Realization punched Elijah in the gut. This was Don's kid.

Chapter Thirteen

LIV PLOPPED INTO HER BUG IN the parking lot of She Brews and laid her head against the seat back. She took a deep breath, then exhaled, relaxing her shoulders. Finally, an evening with nothing at all.

She worked at She Brews Monday night, went to cooking class yesterday, and today, after three long days of VBS, she had an evening off.

Even better, Griffith showed up to his shift early and told her to head out. So here she was, off work early, with the entire evening before her. She might even beat Caroline home.

That gave her an idea. Maybe she could make her roommate a meal, to show what she'd learned in class.

She started the Bug and headed for the grocery store instead of home. Yesterday, Boris had taught them how to create homemade pizza. Together, under Boris's eagle eye, she and Elijah had concocted a chicken bacon ranch pizza with bits of tomato and spinach that tasted like it dropped straight from pizza heaven. She just had to pick up a few ingredients, and she could make it for dinner tonight.

"Is sooner than I want, but was ill last week," Boris explained to them. "Much vomiting. But no food poisoning. Boris knows food." He gave them a piercing stare, as if daring them to suggest such a thing. "We skip lesson on cooking chicken, we make pizza. Americans love pizza."

Liv couldn't argue with that.

In the grocery store, Liv picked out a tomato, spinach, raw chicken, bacon, and ranch. At class, the tomato had already been somehow cooked or prepared, and the bacon had been pre-cooked, but how hard could it be?

She gathered the last of her items and headed to the checkout.

Wow, this many ingredients for one meal is expensive. She hadn't really thought that through.

On her way home, her mind turned back to Robert, Don's son. He was a gifted actor—what a shame his father wanted him to give it up.

Don seemed to be causing problems for everyone—someone needed to stand up to him.

She snorted to herself. Bold words. She'd never stood up to anyone in her life.

Back at home, she laid out her ingredients on the counter, washed her hands, and began pulling out pots and pans.

She stood with her hands on her hips, surveying the scene. She didn't remember what they had made first, but the dough was on the bottom, so probably that, right?

"Okay, yeast, water, flour, oil, salt, sugar..." No way could she remember the exact measurements Boris had them use, but she looked up a recipe that seemed similar on her phone. She mixed the ingredients together as instructed, and the dough looked like what they had made in class. *Success.* Then she read the next line. "Let rise for ninety minutes."

Whoops. They must have used a different recipe with Boris. Maybe? She didn't know. But it probably wouldn't matter if the dough didn't rise for that long. It would just be a little flat.

She pulled a chicken breast out of a packet and slapped it in a pan. Then she cut open the bacon and started laying strips in another pan. Thank goodness for four burners on the stove.

She turned to the other toppings and diced up the tomatoes. She frowned at them. They had seemed less...juicy at cooking class. Maybe they had been pre-cooked?

She tossed them in a pot—she'd run out of pans—and glanced at the bacon. The strips writhed and splattered grease onto the stovetop. She poked them with tongs, but they still seemed wiggly. Bacon was supposed to be crunchy. It must need to cook a while longer.

"Well, you're probably ready enough." She pulled the dough out of the bowl and plopped it onto a baking sheet. She spread it out, then stuck the flattened circle in the oven to let it cook a bit before adding the toppings.

The chicken still appeared completely raw on top, so she left it going. The bacon was starting to look harder, so she pulled it out and set it on a plate. She stared at the amount of grease now filling the pan. She couldn't let Caroline see that, or her roommate would never eat this pizza.

The tomatoes. She peeked into the pot. Juice sizzled on the bottom, and the diced tomatoes themselves looked squishy. Not at all like in cooking class. *They must need longer.*

In the meantime, she could get rid of this grease. She grabbed the pan and poured the liquid fat down the drain before setting the pan in the sink.

She pulled the pizza dough out of the oven and bit her lip when she realized she'd forgotten to turn the oven on. She glanced at the clock. Thirty minutes until Caroline got home. No time to set it going again.

"It's fine. Everything can cook at the same time."

She turned on the oven, then slathered the raw dough with a layer of ranch. She topped that with cheese, then…

The chicken.

She flipped the breast over to reveal one side blackened, the other still raw.

Oh, well. She could cut off the black part.

While she waited for the chicken to finish, she reached for the bacon, only to find it rock-hard.

Too late now. She tossed the strips in a plastic bag and beat them with a rolling pin until the pieces were small enough.

She spread the bacon, then added the soggy tomatoes. Maybe they would dry out in the oven. She threw some spinach leaves on top before checking the chicken again.

This time, it had cooked all the way through. She transferred the breast to her cutting board. Tomato juice stained the meat pink as she sawed through dry, blackened chicken. She sliced off as much of the black as she could and spread pieces of stringy meat on top of the pizza. She drizzled ranch one more time, then popped the entire thing in the oven.

Liv collapsed in one of the kitchen chairs. It had been a lot easier with Elijah at her side and half the ingredients prepped by Boris, but she'd done it.

Her gaze traveled over the mess of ingredients, pots, pans, bowls, and measuring utensils, and she cringed. The rule might be "I cook, you clean," but she felt bad making Caroline tidy up such a mess.

She put her extra ingredients away first, then scrubbed the bacon pan. As she washed the pots and pans one by one, she started singing to herself.

"When I'm in limbo, you're still holding me
When I'm in limbo, finding harmony."

The sink started to fill. She squinted at the dirty water. Maybe she was washing too much at once? Hopefully it would go down when she was done.

By the time she had finished scrubbing, her shirt was soaked with splattered water, mixed with the flour she'd gotten all over herself making the dough. She headed to her room to change.

She put on her pajamas—why not?—and had just walked out when Caroline opened the front door. "Hey, girl."

"Hey, Liv." Caroline held up a bag. "I got home late tonight, so I picked up some salad bowls from that new soup and salad place."

"Oh." Liv clasped her hands behind her back and gave a sly smile. If Caroline's dinner idea was just leaves, thank goodness she'd picked tonight to show off her new skills. "Actually, I made something for us."

Caroline's eyebrows rose. "Oh! Putting that new cooking-class knowledge to use, huh?" She grinned. "I'm excited to see it."

Liv led the way into the kitchen. Caroline dropped her purse and set her salad bag down on the table, inhaling deeply. Liv saw her try to hide the expression as her nose wrinkled. Probably from the burnt bacon smell. "What did you make, Liv?"

"Chicken bacon ranch pizza," Liv announced. Her gaze traveled to the over timer. "It should be done..." She trailed off.

She'd forgotten to set the timer.

"Uh, let me actually check it right now."

She pulled open the oven. A blast of hot air tinged with a burning smell greeted her.

The edges of the pizza were dark brown, the stringy chicken falling apart even more with new blackened tips. The tomatoes had oozed red circles that looked like a pizza massacre.

But it probably *tasted* fine.

"It's done." Liv grabbed oven mitts and lifted the pizza out of the oven. She set her creation on the stove. "Ta-da!"

Caroline's wide grin seemed forced. "Fantastic. Let me wash my hands."

She stepped to the sink, reached for the knob, and paused. "Is the drain plugged?"

Liv peered over Caroline's shoulder. The water level still reached a quarter of the way up the sink. "Uh. I guess so. It started doing that while I was washing dishes."

"Weird." Caroline cocked her head. Then her eyes widened, and she bit her lip. "Did you make that bacon yourself?"

"Uh...yes." Where was she going with this?

"What did you do with the grease?"

Liv fiddled with a bracelet. "It wasn't *much* grease. I know you don't like greasy food..."

"You put it down the drain, didn't you." It was more a resigned statement than a question.

"Yes. Why?"

Caroline sighed. "I'll call maintenance after dinner. You can't put grease down the drain. It hardens and clogs the pipes."

"Oh." Liv wanted to melt into a puddle on the floor. How could she not know such simple things?

Her mother had passed before she'd had a chance to teach Liv cooking, and Dad's prowess stopped at scrambled eggs and toaster waffles.

"It's okay. You didn't know." Caroline put a hand on her arm. "Let's just eat, okay? I'm excited to try it."

It turned out, the dough was burnt on the outside and raw in the middle. Baking did nothing for the chicken or bacon. After Caroline tried to take a third polite bite, Liv shook her head, struggling against tears. "Don't. I don't know if it's even edible."

"Aw." Caroline patted her hand. "Don't worry about it. It was a great first try. You took on something really complicated." She sat back. "Honestly, I'm not sure I would have attempted the dish myself. Each of the steps seems easy, but when you put that many together, it's hard to keep track or do any of them right."

"And no matter how hard you try, the finished product is a mess," Liv muttered. The tears really pricked her eyes now.

Caroline's head tilted. "This isn't about pizza, is it?"

Liv took a deep breath. "I'm trying to keep up. I'm doing so many things. But in the meantime...I feel like I'm falling apart."

"Oh, Liv." Caroline looked down at her hands. "And I've made it worse, haven't I? Signing you up for that cooking class? I should have known you wouldn't say no. You were afraid to hurt my feelings when I thought I was doing something nice, weren't you?"

She bit her lip and nodded.

"You don't have to do everything for everyone." Caroline poked at her slice of pizza. "If you let everyone give you tasks without ever saying no, you'll end up, a, well..."

"Simultaneously burnt and raw mess?" Liv offered, lips twitching.

Caroline laughed. "Something like that." She grew serious. "I'm sorry I added to your stress. I was so wrapped up in my life that I didn't notice you were drowning. And I think that's how it is for a lot of people. I think if you say no, they'll understand." She shrugged. "And if they don't, I don't think they're the sort of people you want to keep around anyway."

This time, a tear did escape. "Thanks, girl."

Caroline put her arms out. "Bring it in."

Liv went in for the hug.

"And if you want to drop out of cooking class, it won't hurt my feelings."

Liv pulled back and considered. Between Boris's shenanigans and cracking jokes with Elijah... "You know, I kind of like cooking class. I think I'll stick with it for now."

"Cool." Caroline held up her takeout bag. "Until then, let's have some salad."

"I'll come back for you." Elijah caressed the head of a red electric guitar. No Strings Attached, his favorite instrument shop, held hundreds of guitars on suspended racks.

But this one in particular, with a $2000 white price tag hanging from the neck on a string, had enticed him for months. Of course, with paying rent and student loan bills, he'd have years to wait until he could make this purchase.

A girl sitting in a wicker chair strummed the tune of "Smoke on the Water," one of the first songs Elijah learned to play on an acoustic. She squeezed her eyelids tight and got lost in the melody.

The scene sent warmth throughout Elijah's chest, even though No Strings Attached had blasted the AC at full volume.

The kids at VBS had gotten engulfed in the music as well. It didn't matter if they couldn't match the key or stay on rhythm. If only the rest of the congregation could find a way to worship like that.

He passed by racks of guitar straps and shelves full of pedalboards. Ukuleles and banjos hung above his head, threatening to drop and bonk him at any minute.

Elijah nodded to the worker behind a glass display case, who parroted the greeting, a smile tucked into his mustache.

A vibration in Elijah's jeans pocket caused him to clap his hand on his leg. He dug out the phone and saw the Facetime call from his sister Miriam. Oh boy. Those conversations always ended in either condescension or a guilt trip. He stepped out of the shop into a bath of warm sunshine and slid open the green button on his device. The sound of a bell tinkling on the door followed him along the street of the town shops and toward a bench.

"Hey, Bud!"

He squinted in the wash of sunlight and spotted Miriam's wide grin. She wore a lacy swimsuit cover up. Seagulls swamped the cerulean skies behind her, and Elijah could hear the waves crashing through the phone speaker.

"We just got back from the beach." Sand stuck in the roots of Miriam's hair confirmed this. So did the dews of seawater on her forehead, and the rosy sunburn that covered her cheeks. "So I figured we'd let you see everyone, since you're not on vacation this year and all."

Elijah collapsed on the bench and grimaced. "That's great."

Miriam had a good heart. But with everything happening with the church—and the fact their band couldn't make a decision about what song to play—he didn't need another reminder about the annual beach trip he had to miss.

His sister led him through the beach house, which boasted of seashell and starfish decor. Elijah even thought he spotted a fisherman's net hanging over one of the walls.

He spotted many couples on the couch. They shared snacks for the afternoon—cheese and crackers. A pang bore into his stomach when he watched them glance into each other's eyes. How he longed for something like that.

Perhaps with a girl like Liv…but she seemed cold and distant at times. Maybe she'd experienced some bad relationships in the past. After all, it took Caroline a while to warm up to Andy.

"Anyway." Miriam turned the camera back to herself. Behind her, through a large window, families walked toward the beach, carrying towels and foldable chairs. "Thought we'd check in. Is everything going all right?"

Elijah winced so much that his cheeks obscured his vision. Hand-holding couples on the sidewalk gave him a wide berth. "Everything's going fine."

How could he tell her that he had to miss this year and could end up quitting his job because of a certain congregation member who didn't like how he played?

"Glad to hear it, Bud. I need to go. There's a Euchre tournament on, and I need to crush some people's spirits. See you!"

Before he had a chance to wave, Miriam hung up. Elijah leaned back and rested his head against the toasty brick building behind him. Could he ever *enjoy* this summer?

A family emerged from a few shops down. One kid clutched an ice cream cone in his fist. Green liquid from the mint chocolate chip ran down the rivets of the cone and onto his hands, but he didn't appear to care.

Besides the meals the worship team had after service, he didn't have many chances to explore downtown with someone. Everyone was far too busy to do the usual summer activities.

His phone buzzed in his lap. He wiped the perspiration on his palms onto his jeans and swiped open the text from Andy.

Andy: Hey, totally forgot if I mentioned this to you or not. But I got four tickets for Griffith's play tomorrow. For me, you, Caroline, and Maisie.

Maisie worked in Andy's church library. Last spring, she'd helped him to reach his goal of one thousand preorders for his children's book.

Andy: Problem is, Maisie forgot she'd double booked the night with her book club. And she simply MUST talk to their group about the book they're reading, *Runaway Romance*. If you know anyone who wants to watch a play, we have a ticket for them.

Huh, he hadn't remembered Andy mentioning Maisie would've originally joined them at the play. Granted, with the amount of stress he had to deal with at church, perhaps his roommate had mentioned it, and he hadn't heard.

He'd scheduled the rehearsal tonight, instead of their usual Thursday morning meetings. Sarah had a conflict in the morning.

Much as Elijah enjoyed meeting Maisie at an Easter potluck— man, could that woman make a mean casserole—relief flooded him when he read she couldn't make it to the play. How awkward…Caroline and Andy clasping hands…with Elijah and the church librarian right next to them.

A name popped into Elijah's head about who to ask, faster than he could say, "e minor."

He clicked out of the text to Andy and pulled up Liv's contact information. After he rattled out the text, he proofread the words at least seven times.

Elijah: Hi, Liv! Had so much fun at VBS with you. Andy has an extra ticket for Griffith's play. I figure it would be weird for me to third wheel with Caroline and him, so would you want to come?

He sent the message. Then ice froze his chest. He typed another one quickly.

Elijah: To support Griffith, of course.

In case the prospect of a date freaked her out.

Three dots appeared under his speech bubble. Oh no. She'd read it and was already responding. Elijah's heart drummed so hard in his chest, he thought it would break his ribcage.

Her response appeared.

Liv: I believe I'm off work tomorrow night. Sounds like a plan.

Then another message followed.

Liv: To support Griffith, of course :)

Elijah's arms collapsed at his sides. A nearby pigeon, who had scavenged for breadcrumbs near his feet, took flight. She said yes. Maybe if this date went well, he could invite her to one *without* Caroline and Andy.

And maybe I can convince Liv to sit somewhere away from those two.

He lifted himself from the bench when he spotted an older couple hobbling down the sidewalk. The man thanked him, and they supplanted the seat. As Elijah made his way back to No Strings, his phone buzzed again.

Ugh, he needed to put this device on Do Not Disturb. That way, he could have a day downtown in peace.

An email from Pastor Smith illuminated the screen. Oh no, not today. Elijah sighed, propped himself against the brick building, and opened the notification.

Hi Elijah,

I know you're not in office at the moment, so I figured email might be better. I had a chance to talk with Don today.

Ringing filled Elijah's ears. All the pleasant sounds of summer— the children giggling in the local fountain, the buzz of the cicadas—had evaporated.

He and I reached a compromise, I think. He says that if you can meet the following guidelines for the next few Sundays, he'll back off. In fact, he mentioned he'll double his tithing and encourage others to do the same.

I know it's not ideal, but I figure, we can roll up our sleeves and grit our teeth for the next few weeks. Below I've compiled some of the points he mentioned:

- *At least two hymns in the lineup of songs. And <u>no more</u> than four songs.*
- *Allowing the congregation to sit in between each song. He says they stand too much.*
- *No fancy harmonies or what he calls "ad libbing." He says that Liv—I believe that's her name?—experiments too much. Any way you can have Sarah in the lineup this week?*
- *No repeating the bridge of the song too often. He says to sing it once, and that's it.*

Please let me know if this works, and I'll inform Don. Thanks for being so flexible, and hopefully we'll be at the end of this soon.

In Christ,
Pastor Smith

Great. Although he had already put Sarah on rotation for this week, these demands knocked the breath out of him. They were doable. But they would suck the life out of the music. Just like it had at youth group, before he let the Spirit guide him.

He pinched the bridge of his nose. "Guess I have to change everything before tonight's practice." So much for that beautiful red guitar.

Chapter Fourteen

AFTER A LONG, THOUGH ENJOYABLE MORNING at VBS and a shift at She Brews, Liv collapsed into one of the comfy chairs by the fireplace. She intended to relish her break before her second shift of the day started.

Elijah seemed to have mastered the motions for all the songs, now that it was day four, and so had the kids. They seemed to get more excited every day.

Luckily, she and Elijah hadn't had to do any more acting—more capable actors had been found—but she had enjoyed watching young Robert shine. The kids loved to boo the evil King Smiraz that Robert played so well.

Two minutes into her break, Liv's phone buzzed.

Elijah: Hi, Liv! Had so much fun at VBS with you. Andy has an extra ticket for Griffith's play. I figure it would be weird for me to third wheel with Caroline and him, so would you want to come?

Griffith's play, the one Robert was in. What a coincidence—of course she wanted to go. She even had Friday evening off.

She began to type a reply, when another text from Elijah came in.

Elijah: To support Griffith, of course.

Her thumbs paused. What did that mean? Not to support Robert? Or…

Her eyes widened. Or because Elijah was trying to make it clear this wasn't a date.

But why? Did he not want to go on a date with her? Not that it mattered—she hadn't expected a date. Had she given indication that she liked him? She'd tried not to.

Her mind whirled. She didn't know what to say, so she hit send on her original message.

Liv: I believe I'm off work tomorrow night. Sounds like a plan.

She stared at the text. Was it innocuous enough? Did it convey that she wasn't offended not to be on a date? She shot off a second text.

Liv: To support Griffith, of course :)

When she slipped behind the counter and donned her apron once more, her confusion must have still shown on her face. Reina placed a hand on her hip, slinging a towel over her shoulder. "What's eating you?"

Liv laughed. "That obvious?"

She recounted the contents of the text messages she'd received. "So, I'm not sure if he *wants* it to be a date, or if he's making sure I don't think so, or..." The bell above the door jangled and a few customers entered. "Hold that thought."

After the customers had been taken care of, Reina pursed her lips. "Well, he didn't use the word 'friends.' In my experience, when someone is trying to make it clear something isn't a date, they'll say something like 'I thought I'd ask a friend,' or 'just as friends.' He didn't, so I'd be inclined to think he's hoping for at least something that will lead to a date."

Liv's heart beat faster. "Oh."

Reina's head tilted. "Do you want to date him?"

Liv distracted herself by washing the cup for milk frothing. "Yes. No." She sighed. "That's the problem. I *want* to. But...relationships are messy." And she hated confrontation or conflict.

When she found out before the other girls that Connor had been cheating, she hadn't said anything. She didn't want to stir things up—she'd hoped she could distance herself from him, until maybe he forgot about her in favor of the other girls. Maybe he would break up with her instead, so she wouldn't have to do it.

Reina shrugged. "They can be. But they're also worth it—especially when a person can cook."

Liv snorted, and Reina laughed. "Okay, no more relationship stuff. Let's make coffee."

The next morning, Liv didn't get a chance to even speak to Elijah. The last day of VBS with prizes and water games and cleanup had her running from one end of the church to the other. When she finally left the building late afternoon after helping tear down, she wanted to plop on the couch for an hour or two before the play. Unfortunately, she had too many lessons to plan, too many scores to write, too many hymns to transpose.

By the time she stepped out of her Bug in the parking lot of the theater, she didn't have the energy to be nervous or worry about what was or wasn't a date. She just hoped she could stay awake during the play.

Cool air rushed over her as she entered the foyer. She scanned the crowd. Caroline had driven directly from work, and she assumed Andy and Elijah might have come together.

She spotted the three of them hanging out near the wall on the right. Caroline and Andy were making eyes at each other while Elijah stood awkwardly scrolling on his phone nearby. *He really did mean third wheeling.*

Liv strode toward them, long skirt swishing around her ankles. She'd opted for a lightweight, flowy fabric that would be breathable outside, but help her not to freeze if the theater were cold. "Hey, guys."

Elijah looked up, and relief washed over his face. "Hey, Liv. Why don't we all go in and find seats?"

Andy and Caroline led the way.

Liv fell into step next to Elijah. "Quite the day today at VBS."

He rubbed his neck. "Tell me about it. I left the church an hour ago, and they're still pulling down vines." He smiled. "All worth it, though. The kids had a blast and learned a lot."

Andy handed four tickets to the usher, who gave each of them a program before they entered the theater. Velvet seats flowed down toward a large stage hung with red curtains.

"Wow." Liv raised her eyebrows. "This is a big venue. Is that an orchestra pit?"

"The youth theater is apparently a really big deal around here. People come in from surrounding towns to watch." Elijah gestured toward the rows. "It's open seating. Where would you like to sit?"

Liv fiddled with a bangle. "Oh, anywhere is fine with me."

"Any preference? Front, back, middle…"

Did he want to sit by themselves? Was this a date then? Or was she choosing a seat for all four of them? Andy and Caroline were looking back at her. Her pulse spiked. "Uh, wherever Caroline wants to sit."

Her roommate gave her an odd look, but she pointed toward the middle. "Dead center. Let's get the best view possible."

Andy shuffled in first, then Caroline, with Liv following and Elijah taking up the rear. They settled into their seats, and Andy and Caroline immediately launched into a conversation about their next book project.

Caroline gave Liv a nudge with her elbow without breaking eye contact with Andy. *What was that for?*

"So." Elijah cleared his throat. "Should we see if we recognize any of the other kids in the cast?"

They opened their programs and paged through the bios and headshots. "Oh, look." Liv pointed. "Robert isn't just *in* the play. He has one of the lead roles."

Elijah grinned. "Talented and modest. He's a great kid." His expression clouded. "I wonder how he's holding up at home."

Before Liv could answer, she heard Caroline groan. She turned toward her roommate, who grimaced and gestured in front of her. "Of course, a tall guy just sat in front of me," she whispered to Liv. "I can't see a thing."

The lights began to dim, and opening notes from the orchestra sounded. They had seconds before the show started.

"Oh, switch me." Liv stood. "I'm a lot taller than you."

Caroline made a shooing motion. "No, Liv, don't worry about it."

"It's fine, just switch me." Liv shuffled over.

"Liv…"

The couple behind them glared. Caroline winced, got up, and slid into Liv's seat.

Liv plopped down next to Andy. Sure enough, she could see just fine.

Andy bit his lip. "Uh, Liv, I could have swapped with her."

"Oh, that's okay, I didn't mind."

The orchestra sprang into full motion, and the curtains swung open. Liv turned to the stage.

And realized her mistake.

She resisted the urge to smack her forehead. Clearly, Andy and Caroline would have wanted to sit together. She'd separated a couple on a date in the name of trying to be helpful.

Her cheeks burned through at least half of the first act.

When the lights turned on for intermission, she suppressed a yawn. The kids' acting was near professional level, but her exhaustion had begun to catch up. She checked her phone for the time.

A text appeared on her screen.

Dad: Something wrong with my back. No movement in legs. Susan's taking me to hospital. I'll be fine, just letting you know.

She read it again. *"I'll be fine"?* What kind of text was that?

She mumbled an excuse about needing the bathroom and headed for the foyer to make a call.

Noise from the crowd echoed in the tiled room, so she wove her way through the theatergoers and outside, where the sky had darkened.

She dialed Dad's number. It rang for a while before a female voice answered, "Hello?"

"Susan?"

"Yes, that's right. I'm here with your dad."

Liv bunched her skirt in her free hand. "Is he okay?"

"Not in pain, honey. We're just confused about what's going on. The doctor is talking to him right now, but your dad wanted me to answer so you wouldn't get worried. We'll let you know as soon as we know anything, I promise."

Liv paced. "But he's okay? Should I come right now?"

"Let me ask him." Susan must have put her hand over the speaker, because Liv only heard muffled sound. Then she returned. "He says he'd rather you didn't drive all the way here in the dark. And he says not to worry. Nothing life threatening." She paused for a moment as a garbled male voice said something. "And he's joking that at least it won't hurt if he stubs his toe. Ha ha, very funny, Mark." Susan snorted. "Always joking away his problems, that one."

"That's what he does." Liv gave a faint smile.

Susan's tone softened. "But please don't worry, hon. I'll give you a call if anything happens, but we're just here for answers, not for an emergency."

"Thanks, Susan." Liv took a deep breath. "Take good care of him."

After hanging up, Liv weighed her options. She could leave the play now, but she would have to explain to her friends, and that would put a damper on their evening as they worried over her. She might as well put her phone on vibrate for any calls and watch the second half of the production. It would do no good pacing and worrying.

But as she headed back inside, she determined that she would leave and call to check in again the moment the play finished.

Why didn't she want to sit with me?

Applause followed the actors as they filed backstage. Two large scarlet curtains closed over the empty stage. The clapping ceased, and the audience members lifted themselves from the dusty, squeaky seats.

Maybe she'd be willing to switch seats for the second half. Then again, she swapped with Caroline because Caroline couldn't see over the tall man and…well, Elijah didn't want to stir up any awkwardness.

In case Liv *really* didn't want to sit with him.

Andy stretched his back and grinned across at Caroline.

"They did a pretty good job, eh?"

Caroline nodded and tucked her playbill into her bag. "I hear we can congratulate the cast members after the show." She gestured at the doors in the back of the auditorium. "Let's go talk to Griffith if we can."

With impressive speed, Liv bolted out of the row and advanced up the slant that led to the exit. A pit dug into Elijah's stomach. Not only did she refuse to sit with him, and spent the entire intermission in the restroom, but now she wanted to dash away from him as fast as possible?

Did I do something wrong?

He *had* texted her about the play at the last minute. Maybe she would've said no but was too nice to indicate otherwise.

Elijah followed Caroline up the carpeted ramp while ushers and the stage crew scanned the aisles for orphaned programs and food wrappers from the concessions stand.

Andy stepped in front of Elijah and banded his arm around Caroline. No doubt, he didn't appreciate the arrangement of Caroline sitting between Elijah and Liv either.

They entered the main foyer area where parents and friends crowded around cast members. Flower bouquets filled the arms of beaming children. One, in a Pippi Longstocking-style wig, had received so many that rose petals littered her feet.

The group weaved their way toward Griffith. All except for Liv, who seemed to have disappeared.

Elijah stood on his tiptoes and found her…exiting out the doors and toward the parking lot.

Great, he'd blown it.

A cluster of people gathered around Robert near the door. Elijah averted his gaze in case, by any chance, Don had shown tonight. After the slew of demands Pastor had sent him on Wednesday, he hoped to avoid that man until Sunday.

Griffith's loud voice drew Elijah back to the conversation Andy and Griffith appeared to be having. "Yeah, I was really proud of the kiddos tonight. I don't know if the theater has ever had this big of a crowd, so a lot of them were nervous."

Griffith motioned, best he could in the compact bubble of space he had, to the crowd that filled the room. Heat prickled Elijah's cheeks from the body temperature of everyone around him.

"That's great, Griff." Andy pulled Caroline closer to him, and she leaned her head on his shoulder. An even wider hole drilled in Elijah's gut. "I bet your parents are real proud."

Shadows formed underneath Griffith's eyes. He palmed his neck. "Yeah. Deep down, I'm sure."

Elijah matched Griffith's wince. "They don't approve?" He meant to add an "either" at the end of the statement but decided to leave the word off at the last minute. But he knew that crestfallen stance from anywhere. Stooped neck, hunched shoulders, like a caveman.

"I come from a family of missionaries, so when I told them I wanted to pursue theater...they didn't outright say they were disappointed. But you could see it on their faces."

Elijah had always admired Griffith for sticking with playwriting and directing, even when the barista gig paid most of the bills.

Caroline cleared her throat and reached into her bag to fan herself with the program. "Well, we think you did a great job. We can't wait to see what you come up with next."

Arms and legs from the crowd swiped this way and that. Elijah scooted closer to Andy for a shield. Caroline noticed and backed out of Andy's arms and toward the wall of the foyer. To make room for the audience, Elijah bet.

Andy grimaced and patted his pockets. "Hey, Lij, I think I left my playbill in the auditorium. Any chance you could grab it for me?"

Elijah scanned over his shoulder and spotted a heap of programs on a countertop, where the usher had originally given Andy his ticket at Will Call. He tossed Andy a squinty-eyed expression, but Andy jerked his chin toward Caroline. Then he raised his eyebrows.

Understood. The two of them wanted some space away from the third wheel.

"Great job, man." Elijah clapped Griffith on the shoulder and dodged around bodies to go back into the auditorium. Blasts of cool air hit his forehead when he entered.

He retraced his steps back to the row. Light had flooded the space, unlike when they first entered and had to squint to find their seats. Elijah found the program stuck between the arm rests of two chairs.

An usher, five spaces down, scooped up an empty popcorn container. She thrust the contents into a garbage bag.

Wait, not an usher, Zinnia. She'd pressed her hair into a tight ponytail and wore all black. He'd spotted the crew all sporting this color in their outfits. Caroline had mentioned something about the history of theater and ninjas during intermission.

Probably should've paid more attention to that conversation.

Zinnia halted when she glanced at another pair of feet in the aisle. She met his gaze and waved.

"Elijah from cooking class."

"You're the Carrot-Cutting Master, right?"

Boris, during Egg Week, had created a nameplate for Zinnia with that moniker. He'd made it out of cardstock and purple marker.

Her expression melted. She snorted and slumped into a seat and wiped her forehead with the back of her hand. "Boris is certainly something else."

Memories surged from cooking class back into Elijah's brain. Zinnia did mention she would help with the stage crew for Griffith's play.

He parked a few spaces away from her. Tension, held in his shoulders the whole night, melted into the seat that wafted a sticky smell. Soda someone had guzzled during a past performance, perhaps?

"You all did wonderful, tonight, Zinnia. I've only been to a few plays in my life—"

Apart from his sister's opera performances. But he didn't count those. She spoke Italian in them most of the time, and he had to read synopses during intermission to figure out why the heck people were wailing and distraught all the time in those shows.

"—but it seems like you all worked really hard with those kids."

Her glossy lips twitched. She leaned an arm on the back of the chair. "Yeah, I used to do theater here as a kid. Before Griffith—" She grinned and stared at the carpet. Did she have a thing for this play director? "—before he came, the last director liked to do these garish spectacles. They drew in a lot of money, of course, but there was no …" Her nose lifted to the high ceiling, as though sniffing out the right word. "Depth."

"He took a risk, doing something more quiet. He might've gotten a small audience or disappointed fans who wanted *Oklahoma!* or something."

Zinnia fiddled with the straps on the garbage bag.

At last, she dropped them and spoke. "One we're happy he took."

That smile appeared and vanished again.

"Are you two…?" Elijah clasped his fingers together, to indicate "a couple."

A flush shot up her neck. She bolted up from her seat. The cushion sent dust motes swirling in the air. "Oh, no. Griffith and I went out for coffee a few times, but we didn't click. I've been on enough dates to know quickly if it'll work out or not."

Elijah didn't have much of a track record with perceiving how dates went. After the taco debacle back in college, he could never exercise complete certainty.

Zinnia settled back down in her chair and scavenged the floor around her. Moments later, she spied a gum wrapper. Into the bag it went.

"You ever gone on a date to a play?" Elijah asked. He chewed on his tongue a moment later. Shouldn't ask personal questions. But embarrassment would seize him later if he had to explain to Andy how Liv bolted out of the theater with a faster speed than the stage crew during scene changes.

Might as well discuss this with a near-stranger who he wouldn't see again after cooking classes.

"Sure, been to see a few with guys." An edge to her voice made the last word sound like a question. As if to query, why do you need to know?

"If someone makes someone sit between you and leaves without saying goodbye...would you say that a second date *definitely* won't happen?"

Her facial features sagged. Eyes widened all pitiful and doe-like.

"Did that happen to you tonight?" Zinnia asked.

That meant "yes."

He should've seen this coming. Liv bolted after every worship set, and if Caroline hadn't showed tonight, he bet neither would she.

Zinnia reached forward and clapped his shoulder. "Don't worry, friend, I'm sure you'll have other chances. Most girls are a lot more forgiving than me. I've gotten picky over the years because there have been a lot of awful guys."

Elijah grimaced at her and budged away from her touch.

"Yeah, I'm sure it'll be fine."

It won't.

Chapter Fifteen

"LIV, WHAT HAPPENED BACK THERE?"

Liv paused her pacing and glanced for the millionth time at her phone. Nothing. She looked back up at her roommate.

Caroline stood in the doorway to their apartment, head tilted and a hand on her hip. She'd gotten home from the play about half an hour after Liv.

She glanced at her phone again. "What do you mean?"

"You ran off before I could ask you why you were acting weird." Caroline shut the door and set her bag on the entry table. "Are you okay?"

Liv fiddled with a bracelet. She hadn't bothered to change after the play, but despite her pacing and worrying and praying, she'd only received one quick text from Susan confirming that nothing had changed.

"Some stuff with my dad. Susan the neighbor lady is with him at the hospital."

"Liv! Why didn't you tell us?" Caroline wrapped her in a hug. "No wonder you seemed off. Is there anything I can do?"

Liv hugged her back, then pulled away. "It's not that big a deal, just back complications again, probably. I didn't want to put a damper on the evening."

Caroline rolled her eyes. "Well, it obviously put a damper on *your* evening, so we want to know about it. That's what friends are for. To support you."

"I guess." Liv rubbed her arm.

"So are you going to see him?"

She sighed. "He doesn't want me to drive there in the dark. I'll leave early tomorrow morning."

"Poor thing. You should get to bed, then, and get some rest before your drive." Caroline frowned and muttered, almost to herself, "And poor Elijah…"

"What?" What did Elijah have to do with anything? Was there an obligation Saturday she'd forgotten about?

Caroline blinked. "Uh, Liv, he asked you on a date and you *switched spots* with me."

A date. "Did he say it was a date?"

"He didn't have to." Caroline leaned against the wall and shook her head. "I'd never dated anyone before Andy, and even I could tell."

Her stomach sank. A date. And between switching seats with Caroline, spending intermission in the "bathroom," and running off without saying goodbye, what must he have thought?

She gave herself a shake. "I'll have to deal with that later. Right now, I'm focused on my dad."

That night, she couldn't sleep. Before bed, she called to check on Dad, but they didn't have answers at the small local hospital, so they were transferring him to the regional one where his previous surgeries had taken place. They would call with any updates.

Which left her tossing and turning, worried she would miss the call.

The next morning, she headed out before Caroline even awoke. On the drive, her mind spun with possibilities, but kept coming back to one thought, like a wave slapping again and again against the shore.

How would they pay for all the hospital bills?

The music festival was a long shot, a futile effort. They would never win. Now more than ever, she needed to focus on earning money for Dad. No more practice sessions, no more worship band, no more taking time to help with VBS or transposing for little old ladies.

She didn't have the heart to play music during her long drive, so she sat in silence. As the sun rose higher, so did the temperature. She rolled down the windows to avoid becoming Liv Soup.

At the hospital, she found a spot in the parking garage. She shut off the ignition and took a deep breath. Let it out. In. Out.

She'd been in the hospital plenty of times with Dad, but it still triggered a panicked fluttering in her chest, a repressed sense of desperation that had brought her here twice.

Once had been with Dad after his accident.

The first had been when they lost her mother.

She had been so young, she didn't remember much besides the sounds, the smells, the impression of white walls.

She'd blocked most of it out of her memory, but the horrible facts remained. When her pregnant mother was rushed to the hospital three months early, neither Mom nor Liv's unborn sibling made it.

Her clearer memories consisted of the faces of so many church ladies clucking "the poor man" and "the poor dear."

"You be good for your father, you understand?" one of them told her. "It's going to be hard for him. You'll need to be a good girl, daddy's big helper."

Liv's hand went slack on the steering wheel. Was that where it all started? This trying to help everyone, the inability to say no?

Not the time. She shoved open the car door, stepped out, and slammed it behind her, shutting out the memories.

She followed the signs to the entrance and checked in. She waited at the desk for only a moment before Susan hustled toward her, gray hair bouncing and gait the same as it was every day she power-walked by their house.

Susan smiled up at Liv, who had at least half a foot on the petite woman. "I'm so glad you made it, and so good to see you again in person. I missed you last time you came around."

Liv gave her a hug. She even smelled nice, like fresh-baked bread and a sunny day. "How's Dad?"

"Oh, I think he made pals with one of the nurses. The young man is going to be a father soon, so Mark is teaching him a few of his best 'dad jokes.'"

Despite the nauseating smell of antiseptic and the ominous beeps that filled the air, Liv cracked a smile. "Oh, no. That's not a legacy that should be passed on."

Susan led her down the hall to a door that stood half-open. The older woman gestured for Liv to enter first.

As Liv stepped inside, she heard her father say, "And of course, there's the classic, 'Hi, Hungry, I'm Dad.' Gets an eye roll every time."

Dad sat propped up in the hospital bed, chatting while the young male nurse took down his vitals on a tablet. The nurse gave a good-natured groan. "I may not have had a dad, but my mom did use that one."

"She called herself 'dad'?" Liv's father queried.

"Goodness sake." Liv strode across the room, trying to maintain a severe expression. "Dad. Leave the poor man alone."

He chuckled. "And there is the ungrateful recipient of all my best jokes. Good to see you too, Livy."

She stepped to the side of the bed and kissed the top of his head. "Take a break from tormenting the hospital staff and tell me how you're feeling."

The nurse saluted. "I have my readings. Thanks for the advice, Newly Adopted Old Man. I'll come by for some more later."

"Whoa, hey there, who are you calling an old man?"

The nurse left chuckling, and Dad leaned back, pleased with himself. "See? He liked it."

Liv had no doubt Dad was one of the highlights of the young nurse's day, but she had bigger things on her mind. "So. Lay it on me."

On the other side of the bed, Susan raised her eyebrows at him in a clear directive.

He sighed. "Okay, get ready for some medical mumbo jumbo."

As Dad explained, with Susan adding details he missed, a rock grew in Liv's stomach. After they finished, Liv said, "So basically, if they don't operate soon, they're afraid the loss of movement—or at least, some loss of motor function—will be permanent?"

"That's what they're saying. Of course, it's not guaranteed that this will fix it." Dad grimaced. "Maybe I can learn to just...roll around the house?" He patted his tummy. "I am getting a bit more barrel-shaped these days."

"No," Liv and Susan said simultaneously.

"Well, you two are no fun at all then." His expression grew serious as he turned to Liv. "I don't want you to worry, okay?"

Liv snorted. "That's my job. Your job is to heal, mine is to worry."

"Really, Livy. I don't want you to worry about me, or the money, or anything. It's the parent's job to worry."

Liv bit her lip. She wouldn't argue with him. But nothing he said would stop her. Especially without any ability to do even his consulting work while going through surgery, he needed all the money she could get.

"I think you're both wrong." Susan put her hands on her slim hips. "It's no one's job to worry and all of our job to pray. We'll get through this."

Liv saw the promise in her eyes. It really was a *we* for Susan. Deeper feelings had grown between the two of them than Liv had realized.

Suddenly, it became even more important that Dad could one day stand on his own at the end of an aisle.

"So we'll pray," Liv confirmed.

And she would work like her life depended on it.

Cement filled Elijah's arms.

Indeed, so heavy, he could hardly lift his coffee cup to his lips backstage. The caffeine-infused liquid burned the back of his throat. But it would do no good.

Not after he spent a total of two hours asleep last night, and the night before. Thoughts about where he went wrong with Liv consumed the rest of his time. Had he trained his stare on her a little too long in the practice room when they created both versions of "Finding

Harmony"? Did she feel uncomfortable that Hadassah made her the love interest to him in the VBS skit?

Or had she wanted to dodge him this whole time and didn't have the courage to say anything?

Charlize clenched her teeth, holding her guitar pick in between her incisors. She used both hands to adjust the bobby pins in her hair. Even in a pixie cut, she always had a few flyaways that got in the way of her nose.

"Lij, you certain about how you want us to play today?" She dropped her arms and pinched the pick between her thumb and forefinger.

He set the coffee cup down on a table where Pastor Smith liked to keep his sermon notes. Elijah's gaze zoomed past the curtain to the congregation members filling the pews. Soon the worship band would traverse the stage and give the most pitiful performance he'd ever witnessed—at least, that's how it felt in practice.

With no harmony, Sarah taking the vocals, and even with a last-minute note he sent about Derek "needing to cool it" with the drums, all the band members felt stifled. At the end of worship practice, Charlize had flung her guitar strap over her shoulder so fast, Elijah thought she would snap the fabric in half.

"This is ridiculous," was all she said before she slammed her instrument shut into its case.

Elijah winced and blotted some coffee on the corner of his lips with his sleeve. "I know it's not ideal."

She crossed her arms. "It's like the music lessons Mom made me do back in high school. And why I *quit* piano and bought a bass guitar to teach myself. Because I hated all the rules."

"Hopefully Don will relent after today."

A sharp breath shot from Charlize's nostrils. "Yeah. Right."

When Pastor finished the announcements about the number of VBS attendees who gave their lives to Christ and the amount of money the children raised for orphanages in the Dominican Republic, he invited the worship team to join them on stage.

What felt like a robotic arm propelled Elijah forward. He barely heard the words, "Good morning, Vine. Please stand and worship with us," slip out of his mouth before his pick strummed his strings.

So the next two songs went. The congregation members sat between each number, and all the notes blurred in Elijah's ears. Like someone had thrust him underwater, and he could make out a dreary melody.

Sarah, beside him, took hold of the vocals. The notes drifted at least a half-step flat, but they continued to play how Don asked.

Charlize has a point, he thought while adjusting his fingers from one chord to the next.

Yearning to add in some harmony or at least a drum solo from Derek, Elijah felt his body grow weaker and weaker when he denied it the satisfaction of any musical variations. When he glanced over his shoulder at the plexiglass cage, Derek tapped the tom-toms with padded mallets, to stifle the sound.

All the usual vivacious color in the drummer's cheeks had drained.

At the end of service, they finished with an older hymn that used quite a few "thou"s and verbs ending in "st." Elijah had never heard the tune before—neither had the band during their practice on Wednesday—but supposedly Don loved the song. In fact, the man put in a request a week in the suggestion box at the back of the sanctuary for the song with far too many verses.

Five in total.

They concluded with a high note that Sarah did *not* nail and the congregation filed out of the pews. As Elijah put away his instruments and began his usual un-plug fest with the chords, he spotted a larger figure advancing in his periphery.

Great, here comes Don.

Maybe this time Don would tell them he hated the performance, and they could go back to how they used to play.

He craned his chin over his shoulder and beamed at the man. "Happy Sunday."

Don grinned, an actual dimple-boring *grin*. "I appreciated the work you did this week."

"You did?"

Yeesh, Don needed a hearing aid or something.

"It was simple, with nothing flashy. Keep it up the next few weeks, and I'll lay off the complaints to Pastor Smith." One of Don's eyes squinted in a near-wink. "And double my giving, like I promised."

Don didn't let Elijah respond. Instead, with what Elijah swore was a skip, he bounded up the center aisle of the sanctuary.

Perfect. Now they'd have to play like this for at least a few more weeks.

A groan sounded from Elijah's side from Charlize. She threw him a withering glare and then returned to clicking the metal latches shut on her case. She'd overheard.

"Lij, we *cannot* do another set like this. I'll go crazy. I'd rather go out to coffee with Derek than have to be like a robot again."

"If that's the case." Derek emerged from his cage, twirling his mallet around his finger. "Elijah, let's do worship *exactly* like that next week." The wool head of the stick bonked him on the forehead. "Oof. But honestly, I'd give up a coffee date with the beautiful madame if we could play music like normal people again." He paused. "Or maybe abnormal people. After all I—"

"I'm assuming Pastor Smith didn't really confront Don," Charlize cut off Derek. Probably a good thing.

"He 'compromised.'"

"Meaning, he bent to Don's will and made you take the heat for it."

"Well, that is what compromise tends to mean in a boss and employee relationship."

The same occurrences slammed his insurance agency until they let Elijah go. Customers would complain, and the bosses would "compromise" by making those under them do more overtime work to make them happy.

Elijah finished some of the last-minute cleanup, and the group headed toward the large hill of grass behind the church. Sarah had evacuated after the last song, mentioning something about an Elvis-themed festival. No questions asked, as Elijah didn't wish to know.

They wound their way toward some gingham-covered furniture. Every year, during the weekend after VBS, the church threw a potluck. Elijah let Charlize go in front of him and then picked up a Styrofoam plate.

Sweet potato casserole covered in brown sugar and roasted corn on the cob filled the dish before him. On his way back to a picnic table, he almost dropped his plate from the sheer amount of food he'd piled on.

Charlize slid across from him and propped her legs on the bench so Derek would have to find a spot next to Elijah instead of her. "So, I'm assuming that's a no to playing worship how the Spirit leads us—rather than what Don wants us to do."

Elijah dug a fork into his pulled pork. Spicy barbeque covered his tongue. He swallowed. "I—I don't know. I felt so drained up there. Like it was—"

"A job?" Charlize suggested and raised an eyebrow. She swirled the clinking ice in a red cup and drained some of the orange soda.

"Yeah, that."

He'd gotten into worship to get out of something that sucked out his soul. And now...picking up angry calls from customers about deductibles sounded more appealing.

Derek shrugged. "Maybe if we win the contest," he pointed a spoon at Elijah, flinging mashed potatoes onto his lap, "you don't have to worry about working something that feels like a chore. You could make indie music your thing. At least, your split of the money could last a few month's rent payments to help you figure out what's next."

True, but without Liv on stage today, they already were a day behind on practices. He set his plastic cutlery on his plate and pulled out his phone to send her a message.

Elijah: Had a lot of fun at the play on Friday. Was wondering if you'd be able to do a few practices this week. To polish and get ready for the festival.

A read receipt appeared on the screen. Perfect, she often responded right after she saw his messages.

Minutes flew by. No response from Liv. Elijah distracted the thoughts that buzzed in his brain and stung him like bees by challenging Derek to a game of cornhole. 21–7 later, Derek losing big time, Elijah returned to his seat. Wasps swarmed the tangerine liquid that Charlize had left behind on the table.

Liv still hadn't replied.

He tucked the device back into his pocket and watched children in their VBS t-shirts chase each other around with bubble wands. Iridescent foam followed behind them. His lips sagged as he thought about how Liv directed the kids, days before, in the songs.

Elijah checked his phone one last time, hope buoying in his chest. Nothing.

I wish you could tell me what I did wrong.

Chapter Sixteen

LIV LEANED AGAINST HER CAR AS gasoline flowed into the tank. An echoey voice from above announced something about a two for one deal on whatever drinks this gas station offered, but she stared down at her phone.

Elijah: Had a lot of fun at the play on Friday. Was wondering if you'd be able to do a few practices this week. To polish and get ready for the festival.

She had no idea of her schedule. Everything had flown from her head over the past—twenty-four hours? more?—at the hospital.

She had left Dad in Susan's capable care only because she had a Sunday evening shift at She Brews. The shop was closed Sunday mornings, but opened again in the afternoon.

Dad's surgery couldn't be scheduled until Monday, when the right surgeons were available, so he and Susan would be hanging out in the hospital for the day, giving Liv nothing useful to do by being there anyway.

Susan squeezed Liv's hand as she left. "You're not alone in this, honey. Please ask for help if you need it."

Until that point, Liv had felt strong, pushing through. But Susan's words brought to light the weight on her shoulders, the responsibility she felt for their little family of two. Liv blinked tears from her eyes. "I will."

The gas clicked off, and Liv removed the nozzle. She would respond to Elijah's text later, once she was home and could look at her planner.

She slid behind the wheel of the Bug and had been cruising toward home for less than five minutes when her phone began ringing.

She glanced down at the Caller ID, which read "Jen Etmann."

Jen? Why would she be calling? Maybe Claire or one of the other kids had some questions on their assignments.

Liv pressed the green button and put the phone on speaker. "Hello?"

"Hey, Liv. I had a quick question for you."

A semi-truck pulled in front of her, and Liv put on her turn signal to change lanes. "Sure, go for it."

"I know you're a music instructor, but do you ever babysit on the side?"

Did the Etmann kids need a babysitter? Liv would think the older kids would care for their younger siblings, but maybe with moving stresses, Jen needed more help. "For sure. I haven't done it in a while, but I love kiddos."

"Oh, good. I know this is a little out of the blue, but my friend Beth Ann just had her fourth a few weeks ago, and she needs help with her other three, all under five. She's had a part-time nanny helping her out, but the girl needs to be in Florida this week for her grandfather's funeral." Jen sighed. "Usually I would help, but with moving…"

Liv had always thought she wanted to have multiple kids, so her children could experience siblings in a way she never had the chance to, but these moms with so many young kids so close in age were nothing short of superhuman. "Of course, I'd love to, but I have to work around my schedule for lessons and at the coffee shop."

"Beth Ann is pretty flexible—the poor thing just needs a break from time to time and some help around the house. I can put you in touch. She'll pay the same rate she would the nanny."

Was this an answer to prayer? It wasn't much, and only a week, but this extra gig would provide at least some to help. "Please do. Thanks, Jen."

"No, thank *you*." Something clattered in the background. "I better go. I think the boys are doing something they shouldn't, based on that noise. I'll send her your info."

After Jen hung up, Liv took a deep breath and let it out. One thing at a time. First, get home. Next, get to She Brews.

Instead, her phone rang again ten minutes later.

"Hello?"

Liv heard a child screaming before a female voice asked, "Hi, is this Liv Wilson?"

"It is. Are you Beth Ann?"

"That's me. Did the kid screaming tip you off?" The woman chuckled. "I would be so blessed if you could help me out."

"Sure. When do you need me?"

"I know it's a little soon, but the baby has a doctor's appointment tomorrow morning. I'd love if you could take care of the other three so I don't have to bring the whole brood."

Liv mentally pictured her schedule. Monday morning, before her lesson or shift at She Brews. "Absolutely."

By the time Liv had worked out the details with Beth Ann and hung up, she had reached home. She took a deep breath, clutching the steering wheel, then relaxing her grip. She could do this. A few more jobs, a lot more prayer, and somehow, she would make it through.

Caroline wasn't around when Liv entered the apartment— probably out for Sunday dinner—so Liv got ready for She Brews alone. She tried not to allow negative feelings to drag her down, but she wished Caroline, someone, was there to tell her everything would be okay.

That's your own fault, Liv. You haven't told anyone but your roommate about your situation.

At the last moment, Caroline came crashing through the door. "Liv. I missed your text earlier that you were coming home. I drove as fast as I could to catch you before She Brews, but I wasn't sure if I'd catch you, and... How are you?"

Liv couldn't help the smile that rose to her lips at Caroline's breathless explanation. Her heart warmed at the thought of Caroline's "mad dash" driving—which probably consisted of a mile or two over the speed limit.

"I'm doing okay. Susan being with him makes me feel a lot better."

Caroline tossed aside her purse and wrapped Liv in a hug. "I've been praying for you all day. And night. And day. Well, ever since you left."

Liv's heart warmed further. She blinked as tears threatened. "Thanks, Caroline."

"Always. Here." Caroline pulled away, reached into her oversized purse, and thrust a paper bag into Liv's hands. "I got you a sandwich from the cafe. You should eat."

Food, one of Caroline's love languages—ironic, considering what a health nut she could be. Feeling that love, Liv accepted the bag and inhaled the smell of a warm sandwich. "Thank you. I'll eat this on the way."

She shared a shift with a teen coworker she didn't know well, so she kept up her customer service smile and managed not to worry too much. After checking in with Dad and Susan after work—no updates— Liv drove home in the dark, hoping to sleep at least a bit instead of staying up all night worrying.

She fell into bed exhausted, barely remembering to set her alarm. As she drifted off, the thought crossed her mind, *I never responded to Elijah.*

The day passed in a blur. Liv bounced from babysitting to her lesson, trying not to glance at the time too often, counting down when Dad would get out of surgery.

Finally, the text came from Susan.

Susan: They said everything went well. He's waking up, and I'll get to see him soon. I'll keep you posted.

Liv let out a sigh of relief before heading off to her shift at She Brews.

That night, Dad was still loopy on pain meds, but Liv got all the details from Susan—the surgery had gone well, Dad had been cracking jokes until the moment he went under, and they would be in the hospital a few more days, assuming nothing unexpected came up.

She crashed into bed again—and remembered she'd forgotten to text Elijah.

I will. In the morning.

The next day found her in another cycle of She Brews and lessons and babysitting. She even skipped cooking class to help Beth Ann, since her husband had to work overtime and wouldn't be home until after the kids were in bed.

She stumbled through the door Tuesday night, ready to collapse directly into bed. Well, maybe she would take off this t-shirt with spit-up on it. Then she'd crash.

Caroline met her halfway to her room. "Whoa, girl. You look like death."

Liv raised an eyebrow. "Thanks."

"Sorry." Caroline tilted her head. "You know, there's an accounting job opening up at Helping Hope. It's full time." She hesitated. "I can put in a good word for you. I know you wanted to keep doing music, but...maybe you can teach on the weekends or something?"

Liv looked down at her bag full of music books that she hadn't had a chance to bring home in between jobs. The lessons, working with music with the kids, were the bright spot in her days. If only she could do that all day, every day...

And if only money fell from the sky so she could pay hospital bills.

"Yeah." Liv looked up and repeated with more surety, "Yeah. How do I apply?"

"Guys, we need to focus." Elijah gripped his microphone and held back an eye roll as Derek showed off his newest souvenir from Michigan's Adventure.

A giant, neon green squid hat. Lights dazzled in the fabric tentacles when Derek flipped on a switch. Charlize hoisted a hand on her hip and then made her way to the stage in the sanctuary. "Yes, Derek. Very nice."

Didn't help that Derek arrived five minutes late and had to bolt back to his car to show them his newest purchase from the amusement park. Pastor Smith had already graciously let them use the sanctuary for the indie music festival practices. And Elijah didn't want to take advantage by wasting half the time looking at cephalopod headwear.

Charlize hopped onto the stage and looped her bass strap around her shoulders.

Once more, Elijah's gaze flicked over the back doors. Then he glimpsed his watch. Fifteen after, why hadn't Liv showed yet?

She'd also not made an appearance at their cooking class yesterday. A shame because she missed Boris nicknaming Elijah "Mr. Jumping Soup'" when Elijah managed to get his tomato concoction in his hair. When he returned home, Andy said he had a similar problem when he and Caroline served at a soup kitchen last spring.

Apparently, they were the Jumping Soup brothers now.

Derek wiggled the tentacles in a spooky fashion. "Ooooh, Charlize, Mr. Squid is gonna eat you."

"Oh, the horror," she said in a deadpan, tilting her head back to take a sip from her water bottle.

"Guys," Elijah repeated, pinching his pick until his knuckles whitened. "We need to focus."

Derek didn't appear to listen. Instead, he snapped his fingers. "Ooh, I have one more item I need to get. One moment." Carpet skid under his heel when he zoomed up the center aisle, tentacles flying with reckless abandon.

"At least he didn't go for the turkey-shaped hats they sell at Cedar Point," Charlize muttered. "Then again, a turkey somehow seems more fitting for him."

Elijah blinked away visions of Derek sporting tail feathers.

Charlize clapped her hands. Metallic rings on her fingers clicked. "Lij. I was thinking that maybe we could play the slower version of your song. The non-radio one."

He frowned and placed his mic back on his stand. Derek wouldn't return any time soon.

"I thought you all were dead set on the one that'll help us win."

"Yeah." She scrunched her nose, the earring obscured by the flare in her nostril. "But that was until we acted like robots this past Sunday. And it got me thinking—"

She placed a thumb in the crook of her chin.

"—if we win, and get that record deal, they'll want more tunes like the one we played. Do you really want to create songs you hate for the rest of your life?"

He licked his lip, neck hunched toward the black stage. No.

Musician friends of his, who had signed with small record labels, talked about how it took them years before they could branch out and do what they wanted. Even then, some places severed contracts with them, and they had to go full indie.

"Derek has been texting me, and apparently he's been practicing the slower song." Charlize chewed on her lip. "And actually, I have been too."

They had?

"Speaking of Derek," Derek's voice announced from backstage. Why didn't Derek enter the doors at the top of the sanctuary?

A popping sound erupted from Elijah's left side. Followed by a sting in his cheek. He clapped a hand to his face.

His eyes darted to the source of the noise. Derek held a Nerf gun and appeared to be doubled over and pink from laughter. In his other hand, he gripped a larger rifle.

"Charlize, I brought you this from the youth center." Derek held the blaster above his head. "What say we pummel Elijah with foam bullets, since he's been super strict lately?"

They didn't have time for this. The festival, which ran from

Monday to Friday of next week, started in five days. Although Elijah encouraged them to practice every night on their own, they'd only met a few times to go over the music.

Thankfully Charlize had signed them up for the last day, so they had more time to prep. But if practices continued to operate like this …

"I will gladly take a man down today, Derek."

Charlize strode over to Derek and took the plastic gun from his hands. Then she pointed the barrel at him and fired several rounds at Derek's stomach.

Derek collapsed on the ground, and it was hard to tell whether the sounds that emerged from him were laughter or groans.

"Guys." Elijah waved at them, but Charlize continued to fire foam bullets. A smile crept up her cheek. "Guys."

"You will die today, Derek." Charlize's skin had gone pink from laughter too.

"No," Derek wailed. "Alas, I doth see a light."

Elijah slapped his hands together. "Guys."

Sound ceased. They both glanced at him, the grins withering into thin lines. Rosy cheeks now white.

"I don't know about you two, but I'd really like that twenty thousand dollars. That means we play the radio song," he jabbed a finger at Charlize, who bent her neck, "and we stop fooling around." He glared at Derek, who had busied himself with collecting the foam darts into his t-shirt.

Both of his band mates glued their eyes to the floor. "Sorry," they said.

"We just." Charlize sighed and dropped her blaster on the stage. "We just wanted music to be fun again…to experience life again."

Regret punctured Elijah's stomach like a needle. Charlize's words from earlier bounced around his skull. If they got a record deal for the radio-style song, would every practice look like this? Where Elijah had to confiscate nerf guns and squid hats from Derek?

Where he'd suck out the joy from music like so many professors at his university?

He clapped a hand on his neck. "Sorry, that was harsh."

Doors to the sanctuary opened. Elijah's heart catapulted into his throat until he thought he was choking on a hummingbird. Liv?

The bird settled back into his chest again when a middle-aged man entered instead. "Who wants any pizza?"

Elijah cocked his head. "Pizza?"

"Yeah." The man took a napkin out of his pocket and dabbed a grease stain on his oxford shirt. "Our men's Bible study just got out, and we have tons of leftovers. Classroom 126, if you're interested. Get it before it goes cold."

"We should probably focus on practice." Charlize's stomach, as if on cue, imitated a whale. She clasped her palm over her abdomen.

Elijah slipped his guitar strap over his shoulder. "We should eat. Liv isn't coming anyway, so there's no use practicing."

While they packed up their supplies, and Derek shoved nerf bullets into his pockets, Elijah felt a buzz in his own. He dug the phone out and his heart once again sank. The message hadn't come from Liv. Instead, from Sarah.

Sarah: Hey, got food poisoning at the Elvis Festival. Apparently, bananas that have been sitting out in the sun all day do wonders on the intestinal tract. Anyway, it's pretty bad. I can't come to practice tomorrow. Can you find a replacement for me? Thx.

So much for meeting all of Don's demands. He preferred Sarah on stage instead of Liv who, as he put it in a recent email to Pastor Smith, "always liked to do all those frilly, nonsense harmonies."

But they needed a female singer to hit some of those higher notes in the song lineup.

He clicked Liv's contact number and sent her a text.

Elijah: Missed you at rehearsal. Sorry about this, but Sarah canceled for this week. Would you please be able to make it to tomorrow's practice? We need you on rotation for this week.

Liv didn't reply.

They headed to classroom 126 and found three half-filled pizza boxes left on a round table.

Derek slid a large slice of pepperoni onto a plate. "If we *do* win, what'll you all use your prize money for? I know my answer."

Charlize grabbed a plate and picked off sausages on her pizza. "Do I even want to know, Derek?"

"One word. Bacon."

"Great," Charlize cut in before Derek could elaborate further. "I don't know what I'd do with mine. I may end up giving it to Liv."

As Elijah reached for a meat lover's slice, he glimpsed his phone he'd placed on the table. No text from Liv illuminated the screen. "Why's that?"

"She doesn't talk about it much, but I'd overheard her dad's been having a lot of health issues. I bet she could really use the money right now."

Elijah slumped into a chair. Grease dribbled over his fingertips from the quick motion, but he hardly noticed. How could he, moments earlier, demand Liv show up at practice?

No wonder she hadn't answered his messages.

"I didn't realize."

Charlize waved her hand. "She doesn't bring it up. Probably too worried we'll make a big fuss over her. So, Lij. What would you do with your prize money?"

He recalled how the shadows had fallen over Liv's face in the practice room. Hadn't she mentioned something about wanting to finish college? Did her dad's health problems prevent her from achieving her dream?

"I think you have the right idea, Char. If we win this, we do it for Liv."

Even if they had to play that awful radio-style song. And even if every Sunday he'd have to robot his way through the worship for Don. She probably needed that money more than any of them.

This makes sense why she's always busy. She'd mentioned doing a bunch of freelance teaching jobs. If he knew anything from Andy during the spring, she was counting pennies.

Most freelancers he knew were doing that, whether they had a loved one in the hospital or not.

"Bacon can wait." Derek swallowed a large wad of pizza and went in for another heaping bite. "Although I do want to keep five bucks to buy another squid hat." He winked at Charlize. "Mr. Squid needs a friend."

Chapter Seventeen

LIV FILLED OUT THE FINAL LINE on the Helping Hope application. She shifted in her seat at the kitchen table, rear end aching and eyes starting to go buggy from concentrating so intensely on her computer screen. An hour and a half of pretending to be passionate about accounting later, she could finally hit submit.

Her finger hesitated over the button. Did she really want to do this? *You don't even know if they'll hire you yet.* But from what Caroline said, they were pretty desperate, and Caroline had already mentioned Liv to her boss.

She remembered her conversation with Caroline after her pizza-making failure. Just like with the pizza, she was trying to do too many things at once. Changes needed to be made, and things had to be cut.

Like cooking class. And the indie music festival.

Elijah and the band would be fine without her. She hadn't worked up the nerve yet to tell them she planned to drop out, but the odds of winning were so slim, it would only be a waste of time she could be spending on actual jobs. Besides, what did she really add to the band? A lack of pop music knowledge? Classical twists no one wanted?

She clicked the button.

According to the clock on her laptop, she had another ten minutes before she needed to leave for She Brews. But she couldn't make herself stand up.

Accounting. She hated math. The worst part of composing was figuring out time signatures and how the notes fit into measures. She avoided math at all costs.

Except at the cost of a job that could help Dad, and maybe, just maybe, save their house.

Although she'd begun to give up on the house part. She couldn't bear to think about the fact that her childhood home would most likely soon be sold off by the bank.

She stood, redid her bun, and reached for her bag. As she did, her phone buzzed. She held up the device, and her gut twisted at the name on the screen.

Elijah, who she still hadn't responded to, even though it was now Wednesday.

Elijah: Missed you at rehearsal. Sorry about this, but Sarah canceled for this week. Would you please be able to make it to tomorrow's practice? We need you on rotation for this week.

She pursed her lips. One more thing she didn't have time for—worship band. Especially since she had been planning to offer her services to Beth Ann during their practice time.

Tears pricked her eyes. All the things she enjoyed—music lessons, playing with the band, worship team, even cooking class—were being stripped away and replaced with long shifts, screaming children, and soon, a job that revolved around her high school nemesis, math.

All the opportunities popping up seemed like Godsends, but could this really be what He wanted for her? Was the price of making it in life giving up everything that made it feel like living instead of surviving?

While pondering what she would say to Elijah, she headed out to her car. She weighed her options all the way to She Brews. Maybe it would be better to tell them in person that she couldn't do the music festival.

So you can see the disappointment in their eyes firsthand? That would be even worse.

Right before going into the coffee shop, she rattled off a text to Elijah.

Liv: Sorry I've been MIA. I'll be there.

The next day, Liv's heart raced before practice. What could she say for herself? How could she explain five days of not responding to texts? Would the band be upset with her? Technically she had only missed one meeting, but she'd been ghosting Elijah for longer.

She clutched her bag as she walked into the church, trying to convince herself that her hands trembling came from the chilly AC, not from nerves.

Elijah sat on a stool, tuning his guitar. He'd pulled his hair back in a messy ponytail, and strands had fallen out around his face as he looked down at the guitar, plucking the strings and adjusting the tuning pegs. He didn't seem to notice her approach. Maybe she'd have enough time to think of what to say.

Liv hesitated too long. He looked up and broke into a wide smile, but it receded into uncertainty. "Hey, Liv."

"Hey, Lij." She fiddled with a bracelet. "I...I'm sorry for not responding to your message. I had a lot going on."

"I'm just glad you made it." He gestured to the stage. "The others aren't here yet, but I can give you a rundown on what's happened since you were last here. We received some, ah, instructions on how and what to play. Here."

While Liv ascended the steps, he shuffled through a binder, slid out a pile of papers, and held them out to her.

She took the music and scanned the pages. Then she looked up, brows furrowed. "What *is* this?"

"Don is holding his giving over our heads. As long as we play the way he wants, he tithes." Elijah shrugged. "We did this last Sunday, and he was pretty happy."

Liv's stomach clenched in horror. Don had strongarmed the worship team into doing things his way by refusing to tithe? Tithing was about being faithful to God, not about controlling others.

But as she saw the defeated look on Elijah's face, she didn't protest. Maybe if they appeased Don for a while, he would leave Elijah alone. Liv sensed more was on the line than just an unhappy parishioner—she feared the worship leader could lose his job.

"You haven't had this job for very long, right?"

"Not long at all." He sat back down on his stool, and Liv perched on the piano bench. "After I got laid off from my insurance job, I didn't know what I'd do. But then this job showed up. Part time, crazy hours, sure, but at least I'm doing what I love." He grimaced. "Sometimes I have to remind myself of that with things like...this." He held up the papers.

Insurance? That seemed as far removed from music as accounting. "Did you like being in insurance?"

He chuckled and shook hair out of his face. "No, I couldn't stand it. But my siblings were all so successful, I felt like I needed to have a 'real job.' When I got laid off, I think it was a blessing, even if it didn't feel like it at the time. It gave me an opportunity to go in a different direction." He strummed a chord, then tilted his head in thought. "You know, I wish someone had told me before I took that job that I didn't have to do what would make other people happy. I could have been doing what God called me to do—music—all along."

Liv bit her lip. "It's scary, though. Sometimes your passions aren't exactly...stable. Sometimes they seem impossible, or like a waste of time."

"Yeah." Elijah strummed another chord. "That's something I've been learning from my roommate, though. If God gave you a passion, it isn't a waste of time."

Conviction stirred in Liv's gut. In her attempt to do it all, was she throwing out the baby instead of the bathwater?

Was God instead calling her to trust Him?

"Heyyyyy, it's Liv."

She turned to see Derek swaggering up the aisle. He grinned. "Ready to make some super exciting music?" He glanced at Elijah. "We're still playing the Don-approved stuff, right?"

"That's right." Elijah stood and held papers out to Derek. "Try not to go too hard on the drums. More like...light taps."

Derek rolled his eyes. "Wouldn't want to scare Downer Don with too much drums." He winked at Liv. "Don't worry, I can still rock a sick solo in practice."

"We actually have a lot to cover…" Elijah began.

"Charlize." Derek waved past him.

The bassist, who had slipped in a side door, gave a half-hearted wave. "Did I hear we're playing some more Don songs?"

"Our favorite," Derek confirmed.

Charlize joined the other three on stage and set down her case. She frowned. "Still?"

Elijah nodded. "We need to appease him for now."

"I don't know." She fiddled with the clasps on her case, snapping them open to reveal her bass guitar. "I feel like if Don had his way, we'd be playing like this for the rest of our lives."

Liv watched Elijah's shoulders sag and stepped in. "For now, let's just practice the songs so we know what we're up against."

Elijah shot her a grateful smile. "Okay, all, how about we start with that first selection?"

The band finished practice with a long note of a hymn Don requested.

Elijah blinked the sleep out of his eyes. Liv lifted her hands from her keyboard and caught a yawn. Perhaps she'd gotten even less sleep than Elijah had these past few nights.

Fires burned in Elijah's gut.

He shouldn't have asked her to play worship this week. Not with all the medical problems with her dad that Charlize mentioned yesterday.

Speaking of, before Liv had attended their church regularly, Elijah often substituted Charlize on harmony certain Sundays when the other vocalists couldn't show.

Not ideal, as Charlize's vocals held a darker, more gravel-filled tone. And she couldn't stretch her notes beyond a certain range—which male worship writers inevitably made females sing. But should he have asked her to ditch the bass guitar this week and substitute for Sarah?

Vibrations from Derek's cymbals ceased. He stared at his mallets and his shoulders slumped in a sigh.

Elijah knew that expression. The great, we-have-to-make-Don-happy-again look.

Releasing his grip from his microphone, he turned and addressed the group.

"I want to start." He exhaled and avoided Liv's gaze. "By apologizing for these past few practices—both worship and for the indie festival. I know I've been a stickler, and you're all here on a voluntary basis. And…music should never be something you *have* to do."

Charlize smirked and slid her pick into her guitar strings. "We appreciate it, Lij. But we also know the amount of pressure you're under."

Aches filled his knees from standing. How long had they been at practice? He eased himself onto the stage floor and sat. One by one the other band members followed him, with Derek emerging from his cage to park close to Charlize.

Liv let out a groan when her knees cracked. They all needed a break.

Elijah waited until they'd settled into comfortable positions.

"I've been thinking about what you said, Charlize. About having to play this way the rest of our lives and…Don's going to keep dangling this over my head forever, isn't he?"

Charlize chewed on her lip. Nodded.

A sigh deflated Elijah's chest. He should've seen this coming.

Back in college, he had a professor who promised him a lead role in the student opera. Wanting to emulate his sister, Elijah agreed to go out for the part. But during the audition, the director kept critiquing the way Elijah would deliver lines, would tell him to quit using the mellismas Elijah liked to add while singing notes. At the end of auditions, Elijah delivered everything in a monotone, with no expression. Everything he hated about music balled into thirty-two measures.

All life had drained from him.

"Perfect," The director had said. "Now, even less energy."

Right then and there, Elijah walked out of auditions. No way he could dedicate hundreds of hours to something that the director would keep making him change. Something that didn't even sound like him anymore.

Derek drumming his fingertips on the wooden platforms of the stage drew Elijah back to the sanctuary.

"If Don's never going to give this up, then I don't see a point in doing what he wants every Sunday." Elijah fiddled with a loose shoelace on his sneakers. "We can't make everyone happy."

The last statement exploded within him like a jar of fireflies. Had he needed to hear these words all along, even if they came from himself?

"If that's the case." Liv shifted a bracelet down that had crawled up to her elbow. "What would the perfect worship set look like for you?"

Elijah shut his eyelids and scanned his memories. Images from the circle back in Brooklyn's youth group tore through his mind first.

He set the scene for the other three. Discussing how even a girl who hid herself in a corner found her way into the circle.

"I don't think there's a 'perfect' worship experience." He tossed up air quotes. "PowerPoint lyrics get misspelled, and you might have a tone-deaf neighbor. But I think the best worship happens when we come as we are and hold nothing back."

Liv's lips twitched.

A flush crawled up Elijah's neck and he flicked his glance away. He hadn't realized he'd stared at *only* her the whole time he talked about youth group.

In his periphery, he watched Liv lift a finger. "I have an idea. Everyone follow me to my car. It's going to be a bit of a squeeze."

Somewhat dazed, and legs wobbly from sitting for so long, they stumbled toward the parking lot with Liv. She clicked the keys for her Bug and motioned for them to get in.

"Shall we sit together, madame?" Derek waggled his eyebrows at Charlize and bowed, presenting the door of the passenger side to Charlize. They'd have to shimmy their way into the back, as the car had no backdoors.

Charlize's jaw sunk, as if to launch a protest against this whole idea. But then she clamped her mouth shut and eyed Liv and Elijah. Back and forth.

"Sounds like a plan. Elijah should take shotgun."

She dove into the backseat before Elijah could register that would mean he and Liv would sit side by side.

Clammy humidity stuck to his t-shirt on the drive. Liv apologized about the lack of AC and handed her Aux cord to Charlize. She shuffled some Christian rock band songs, and they listened to the throbbing bass…all the way through curtains of trees and to a national park.

Liv pulled into a parking spot and had to jerry-rig her car door to open it. They stepped out, and sunshine warmed their backs.

"It's nice," Charlize offered. "Why are we here, Liv?"

"Sometimes it helps to get away and walk in the trees for a little while. Most artists turn to creation when they need inspiration."

She spread-eagled her arms to the spectrum of verdant leaves that decorated the trees. Something about this place comforted Elijah. Like he could spend days here and never worry about deadlines or Don's demands.

"I know it's weird to have an impromptu hike." Liv re-fastened her shoelaces. "But I figure we're all wearing tanks and tees."

True, worship practice often called for a more casual look. With all of them in shorts and tennis shoes, they could've gone for a marathon run had they so desired. Liv beckoned them to follow her. Charlize and Derek hung back several yards behind them.

Weird, Elijah thought. Charlize had mentioned in past practices about how she used to do cross country. Shouldn't she be up here with the tall people who had longer strides?

On the way to wherever-in-the-world Liv would take them, Liv stopped from time to time to point out winding creeks or beautiful views over cliff faces. Cyclists and runners would pass by on their left with a ding of a bell or a pant.

"Liv, I..." Elijah palmed his neck and skirted a patch of poison ivy near the rocky path. "I'm sorry for putting you on rotation this week. Charlize mentioned your dad's having a lot of health complications. I should've been more aware about that."

She didn't answer for a moment. Instead, she pulled out the white wildflower she'd placed in her hair and let the plant fall on the path.

"Honestly, Lij, I should be the one who's apologizing. My roommate told me to trim the fat, and so I thought that meant cutting out cooking class and the indie festival."

"Well, Boris did make us use leaner meats." Elijah waggled a finger and tried his best to imitate Boris's thick accent. "'No fat. You get to be like Boris. Look at Boris's tummy. Boris eat too much fat.'"

Liv giggled into her fist full of wildflowers. Then her expression slackened. "But I do need music. I don't care if it doesn't bring in much money or is considered fat...I need time to just play."

Elijah nodded. Andy did, after all, paint for fun, even if none of those artworks would reap a profit.

They wound past large, slippery boulders until the sound of rushing water filled Elijah's ears. Michigan certainly boasted of many beautiful natural wonders, but seldom did they have a chance to witness a waterfall.

Sure enough, a large one that cascaded over a shield of rocks greeted them when they turned left. Liv had them stop several meters before it and they settled on a large rock. Misty water tickled Elijah's ankles. Everything smelled like sunshine, like green, like cool fog.

"So, Lij, you mentioned having the perfect worship experience. Why don't we do so out here?"

In an automatic motion, he reached for his shoulder, where his guitar strap often rested. "With no instruments?"

"God gave you a voice, didn't he?" Liv sat, cross legged. The others followed.

Derek found two beefy sticks and drummed a steady rhythm onto the rock.

Then Liv started the first chorus to a well-known song from Elijah's high school years. He joined in with a lower harmony, and Charlize, moments later, with a higher one. One song blended into another. Like the lake's waves lapping over and disappearing back into the water.

Notes carried Elijah away until he felt as though someone had placed him in a kayak on a smooth, bobbing river. How much he missed this.

This went on for some time until Derek snapped one of his sticks in half from drumming with too much fervor.

"Now that," Liv said with a smile, "is music."

Chapter Eighteen

RAIN SPLATTERED THE SIDEWALK AND HAMMERED Liv's umbrella as she scurried toward the church.

She ducked underneath the overhang near the doors, folded her umbrella, and shook it out before stepping into the foyer. A few ushers and staff members huddled in the entrance, hanging up wet raincoats and umbrellas before hurrying off to their tasks. Unfortunately, she didn't recognize any of them, so she headed toward the sanctuary on her own.

She'd skipped out on cooking class on Friday in favor of work so she could spend Saturday with Dad on his first day back home from the hospital. As a result, she hadn't seen Elijah since their nature walk as a band. That also meant she hadn't told him about the developments on the accounting job.

Helping Hope must have been desperate, because Friday morning, they called her in for an interview. Even though her experience working with money was limited to the cash register at She Brews and her own personal finances, and she didn't have a college degree, they seemed strangely impressed by the amount of math that went into composing. Apparently, getting A's in high school math also counted to them. They said they would contact her early next week with their decision.

Early next week. Desperate indeed not to spend a couple weeks looking for the most qualified candidates.

Her footsteps echoed down the aisle of the empty sanctuary. Elijah knelt onstage, plugging in instruments and adjusting pedal boards. He looked up at her approach. "Hey." He stood and brushed his hands on his dress pants, which matched his blue oxford shirt nicely. It looked like he had put in extra effort today—probably to placate Don.

"Hey. Anything I can help with?" Liv had opted for wedges instead of sandals, navy dress pants with a white pinstripe, and a buttoned shirt with a layered necklace in an attempt to seem a bit dressier and less...free-spirited. She'd even left her hair down and curled the ends in a classic church-or-office-friendly style instead of a wisping or braided messy bun or ponytail. She'd started to regret that last choice as humidity did its work. But maybe the congregation would appreciate it if she didn't look like she'd come from "a dance in the forest with elves," as Caroline had described it that morning.

"A *what*?" Liv had asked while Caroline fussed with the curling iron.

"You know, like a traveling bardess who may be part fae, who dances in the moonlight with fairies and brings tales of legend to your village while strumming a lute and twirling." Caroline's eyes grew dreamy.

Liv burst out laughing. "I love it. Do all of us have roles in your imagination? Please do Andy next."

Caroline burned bright red. "I think your curls are done." She set down the iron and fled.

In the present, Elijah cleared his throat, and Liv realized he'd been blinking at her for a moment, taking in her new look. "Uh, well, you can make sure the keyboard is all set up."

"Sure." She ascended the steps to the stage.

He rubbed the back of his neck. "You look nice today. I mean, you look nice every day." He scrambled for words. "I like your usual style. You just look different today." Panic spread across his face. "A good different. Not that it was bad, they're just...both good..."

Liv saved him from his stammering with a smile. "Thanks, Lij. You look nice too."

She set down her purse and turned on the keyboard, checking the plugs and amps. He began fiddling with the mics.

A few minutes later, Derek sauntered down the aisle, Charlize not far behind. He looked slightly less greasy than usual, though considerably wetter. Liv wouldn't be surprised if his method of avoiding the rain involved dashing inside as quickly as possible instead of using an umbrella.

"Ready to not-rock and roll," Derek said, pulling drumsticks out of his back pocket.

Elijah pressed his lips together.

Charlize flicked Derek in the back of the head. "Remember how we talked about having a good attitude?"

"Ow." He glared at her, then the glare morphed into waggling eyebrows. "Aww, Charlize, I think that's the first time we've ever made physical contact. That's like a hug from you. I think we're making progress."

Liv snorted, and a smile flitted across Elijah's face. "Okay, guys, we don't have long to practice before people start rolling in for the first service. Let's get into position."

Practice passed without incident. Noise levels rose in the foyer as members of the congregation began to arrive, so the band took a break to grab pre-service donuts and coffee.

The first service passed as a monotone as Liv had feared. Derek's eyes glazed over behind his plexiglass, and Liv's fingers longed to explore the keyboard beyond the chords she played. After the service, Don gave a single nod before walking out.

As congregants filed out in a rustle of raincoats and umbrellas and Derek scooted off to find yet more donuts, Elijah slumped into a seat at the front of the church, looking down at his hands clasped between his knees.

Liv's heart ached. Lightning flashed outside the windows, the pouring rain accenting her dreary mood.

Charlize took a swig from her water bottle and frowned. "He's probably taking it the hardest of all of us, even if he doesn't complain."

Liv made her way toward Elijah and slid into the pew next to him. "Hey."

He looked up, straightened, and mustered a smile. "Hey. You did well, keeping it simple."

"Thanks." She hesitated, then put a hand on his shoulder. "You're doing the best you can with what you've been given. The rest of the band gets that." She bit her lip. "I have to believe God is going to work this out somehow."

His attention fixed on her hand touching his shoulder, then he pulled his gaze away and met her eyes, his expression softening. "Thanks, Liv. I know His hand is in it somewhere. Sometimes it's just hard to see what He's doing."

When Liv and the rest of the band took their places onstage for the final service of the day, thunder crashed so loudly the building shook. Elijah glanced at them with a small shrug and led them into the first song.

Lightning cracked and thunder boomed again, drowning out the music. The lights flickered, then with a pop, went out.

In the dim light of the sanctuary, a few people squeaked in surprise, while a rumbling rose from the congregation as heads turned, taking in the blank projector screens that usually displayed lyrics, the lack of stage lights, and Liv and Elijah's voices that had suddenly cut out.

Elijah glanced at the rest of the band, eyes wide. Derek shrugged, and Charlize held up her bass helplessly. Liv clunked the keys of the keyboard. Nothing.

A head poked over the top of the tech booth as the operator shook his head and slashed a hand across his neck. No power.

Liv watched the panic in Elijah's eyes harden into resolve. He raised his voice. "Okay, Vine, it looks like our power is out for now, but that doesn't mean we can't still worship the Lord." He stepped forward to the front of the stage. "We don't have any lyrics on the screens, so how about some old favorites?"

He hesitated, and Liv could tell that though his quick thinking had suggested this solution, he hadn't thought far enough ahead to choose a song.

Her mind latched on a classic from childhood, "Here I Am to Worship." She lifted her voice and sang, "Light of the world…"

"You stepped down into darkness," Elijah joined.

Slowly, members of the congregation began adding their voices to the mix. Charlize stepped up next to Elijah, bass useless, but her raspy voice a supplement to his. Derek drummed softly, perhaps for the first time in his life, providing a steady beat beneath.

Liv made her way to the front of the stage, where the piano sat, lid closed. Usually, the team used the keyboard, since it could be plugged into the speakers, but the piano remained for smaller gatherings.

Liv slid open the lid and placed her fingers on the keys, gently coaxing chords from the old upright.

As the first song faded away, Elijah launched into another. "Amazing Grace, how sweet the sound…"

Voices soared toward the ceiling, distinct yet flowing together, not masked by a few people on microphones, but a great host of voices deep and high, small and loud. Liv watched smiles bloom, hands raise, as voices lifted unobstructed to the Lord.

Hymns, contemporary classics, even a rendition of "Jesus Loves Me"—every time one song trailed off, someone launched into another.

Goosebumps rose on Liv's arms as she sang and played. She could feel the Spirit sweeping the room, making His presence known.

This music wasn't for Don, or for the band, or even for the congregation.

It was for God.

Pastor Smith concluded his sermon by reading a passage from Colossians.

"Let the peace of Christ rule in your hearts, since as members of one body you were called to peace. And be thankful. Let the message of Christ dwell among you richly as you teach and admonish one another with all wisdom through psalms, hymns, and songs from the Spirit, singing to God with gratitude in your hearts."

For the first time since Elijah had heard any of his sermons, the pastor didn't use movie clips to illustrate his point. Pastor Smith closed his Bible and gestured for the congregation to close their eyes in prayer.

Just before Elijah did so, he noticed Pastor Smith looking right at him and pointing to his wrist.

Elijah glanced at his own watch. The service had gone fifteen minutes longer than usual. Got it, they couldn't go up on stage at the end of service to play a few more songs, like they often did. He met Pastor's eyes, nodded, and then shut his own.

"Father, may we remember when things are out of our control, you are in control."

Buzzing had not stopped in Elijah's chest. Never before had he felt the Spirit burning so bright within him during worship.

Wish a power outage would happen every week at church.

"—and may we remember to be thankful in all circumstances, even when things don't go according to plan."

Elijah wondered if the pastor added that last part for any congregation members who would complain about the lack of electricity during the sermon and worship. When Pastor Smith concluded with an Amen, Elijah's eyelids flew open. People stumbled their way up the aisles in the beams of the emergency exit lights.

He glanced over his shoulder and tried to probe the shadows for Don, who sometimes had a habit of coming to multiple services a week to see how the performance of the band differed. No luck.

Someone behind him clapped his shoulder. An older woman. "Young man, that was beautiful this morning."

Hope catapulted into his throat. "You didn't mind about the power?"

"It was so nice to hear everyone's voices. Often those amps can drown out my neighbors." Something glittered in her eyes. Tears? "I know you can't do worship like that on normal Sundays, but I wouldn't mind asking God for more thunderstorms if we can see more of this."

Speaking of storms, the rain had ceased its heavy drumming on the roof.

No longer did the skies growl and shake the walls of the church.

A few more people ambled to Elijah's row to express how much they enjoyed that morning's music. Too bad the power went out during the last service of the day—he'd have loved to do it all again for the next group of people who filed into the sanctuary.

Once the sanctuary had emptied, the band jumped onto the stage to finish cleanup.

"I could play like that forever."

Charlize's gravelly voice sounded behind Elijah on the left. She bent down to place her bass guitar into her case.

During the electric-less worship, Charlize had added a third harmony whenever she could. Even Derek, at times, dropped his sticks and joined into the singing.

"Too bad we can't practice for the festival today." Elijah, by habit, clicked the off button on his microphone. Not that it would do any good now. "It starts tomorrow, and we only have until Friday before we perform."

Even with them practicing at home alone, it was never quite the same. When Elijah talked with Griffith about it at She Brews, Griffith nodded, while scrubbing down a glass counter with a spotted rag.

"Same works in the world of theater. You can do your lines at home all you want, but stage chemistry is a whole other ballgame."

What Elijah wouldn't give for more music sessions with Liv.

Chemistry, indeed.

Like all those science experiments he did back in his classes in college. Where various liquids of dubious colors would fizz and spew out of beakers and test tubes.

That's how he felt around her. Like every part of him wanted to explode in effervescence.

"Who says we need electricity to practice?" Liv's silhouette moved to help Charlize, since Liv had minimal cleanup today. "Why don't we head to the national park again, to give Finding Harmony a go?"

"Mmm, I don't know. Doesn't Charlize need a bass to play? You kind of need that to be plugged into an amp." Derek leapt off the stage.

"I can bring an acoustic." Charlize said. "It won't be the same, but power isn't coming on in here anytime soon."

They settled the plan. They'd go home to get changed into hiking clothes and return to the national park. Elijah and Charlize, with acoustics. Derek promised to find loads of meaty sticks on the trail, since he had a tendency to snap them in half.

When Elijah arrived at his apartment, he tore off his dress oxford and reached for a gray t-shirt, then traded his nice slacks for basketball shorts. His weather app threatened a high of almost ninety degrees today. Moments later, Andy knocked on his door.

"Did the power outage hit your church?" Andy gestured over his shoulder. "Seems to have got the apartment. Just finished resetting all the clocks."

"Ours went out, as well. But actually, I'm glad it did."

Elijah recounted worship. How tears had streamed from his eyes when he watched most of the congregation lift their hands. How every voice, tone-deaf to operatic, surged into one.

"That sounds amazing." Andy leaned against the door and folded his arms. "Better than our service. Pastor sort of freaked out, so Maisie just read from Hosea. She says she finished a recent book based on it."

"Sorry to hear about that. I think our congregation actually liked the change of pace."

Andy lifted his eyebrows. "Even Don?"

Hot wax dripped onto Elijah's gut. He'd almost forgotten about Don after service and on the drive home. No way that man could've enjoyed service, with none of his demands met. Liv and Charlize *both* dove into what Don would call "frilly" harmonies. And Derek, caught up in the spirit, laid hard into the drums.

Even though they had a number of hymns, Elijah cringed when he counted the number of modern worship songs they played too.

"One bridge at a time, I guess."

Andy shrugged and lifted himself off the door. "Maybe Don'll give you a break. It's not *your* fault the power went out."

Elijah finished getting changed, slipping on a pair of tennis shoes. Dressed and ready to sweat in this humidity, he headed to his car and drove to the national park with his windows down. His car AC had a mind of its own and wouldn't work on most days, including today.

He found the group waiting for him near the wooden sign that advertised some Eagle Scout who'd built a nearby pavilion.

Families picnicked under the ramada and had spread gingham blankets on the wooden tables.

"Speaking of." Liv held up a picnic basket. "Caroline said her church had a lot of leftovers from their church's potluck. Don't worry," she added to Elijah with a wink. "She didn't pollute any of these with kale."

They settled in the pavilion. Shade cooled Elijah's sunburned arms. He'd spent a lot of time outside lately, compared with past weeks. Maybe he'd get that tan he often did at the beach, even without the vacation this year.

He grabbed a slice of watermelon and bit into the fruit. Watermelon juice exploded on his chin. He'd been so hungry he forgot to grab a dish, or silverware. Liv passed around paper plates and plastic utensils.

Man, Caroline's church threw great potlucks. Liv pulled out the rest of the Tupperware containers full of barbeque pork and mac and cheese. Supposedly she'd heated the food before she came, so steam still managed to wisp off it by the time they ate.

Food finished, they headed for the trail.

Turned out they couldn't make it to the waterfall. Muddy patches blocked them from going all the way. Plus, Elijah had volunteered to carry both acoustics, and by the time they'd gone halfway down the path, he'd soaked his shirt in sweat.

They settled on a large rock near a gnarled tree.

Sparrows chirped on a nest, in the crook of a branch.

"Let's try the radio version first," Liv suggested.

Try was a good word for it. Without her bass guitar, Charlize struggled to strum constant notes on her acoustic at a fast pace. And Derek had splintered all but four sticks by the time they got through the second verse.

Liv waved her arms to get them to stop.

"Slower one, this time?"

They all nodded, and Elijah strummed the first chord. The group didn't venture into the song at first, as though soaking in the note. It seemed to harmonize with the birdsong above.

> *"Am I falling,*
> *Floating?"*

Just like church, everyone shut their eyes. And disappeared. Charlize managed to keep up with the pace this time.

Liv entered with the harmony, and goosebumps rippled up Elijah's arms. Then came the counterpoint, and the chorus, and Derek's steady beat growing louder, louder.

> *"When I'm in limbo, you're still holding me*
> *When I'm in limbo, finding harmony."*

The song had finished, but it took several moments for Elijah's spirit to fall back into his chest. For gravity to take hold of him again. During the song, he felt as though someone had pulled him higher and higher toward the cerulean sky.

Did heaven feel like this? Sound like this?

"I really wish we could play that one." Charlize rested her head on her bent knee.

Everyone nodded but said little else. If they wanted to get the money for Liv's dad, they needed to play the radio version. Elijah hadn't let Liv know about this plan, but he could see it. In her lip quiver, in her forlorn expression, in the cracks of her voice. She needed the funds, badly.

And Elijah would get it for her, no matter what the cost.

Chapter Nineteen

"I'LL CHECK IN WITH YOU TWO LATER. Try to behave yourselves."

Dad's chuckle carried through the phone. "Fine, fine, if you insist."

Liv hung up and slid into her Bug, breathing a sigh of relief.

The surgery still seemed to have gone well. Dad had movement in his lower body, and he was home with Susan helping him out. *Thank you, Lord, for Susan.* Otherwise, Liv would have had to be with him, not working, or they would have had to hire a caretaker—another expense they couldn't afford.

Susan had mentioned some redness around the incision, before Dad butted in to tell Liv about the squirrel drama he'd been missing while gone and what had happened with the backyard squirrels Hamlet and Ophelia.

Liv tried not to worry about infection. Redness didn't necessarily mean anything—it was a surgical site, after all.

Her Bug puttered along, splashing through puddles left by yesterday's storm. The power had returned to most places in Roseville, but the sky remained cloudy, helping to keep the rising temperatures at bay. Liv hoped it wouldn't rain out their day checking out the festival.

She parked in a field that had been converted into an overflow parking lot. In the distance, tents, poles, and rides rose from the county fair, the venue of the music festival. Voices and music drifted across the expanse of cars.

Liv's stomach tightened. What would the other musicians be like? The first bands would be performing today, so she and Elijah would be scoping out the competition. Strangely, Charlize and Derek weren't coming, though she hadn't been told why.

Maybe they had to work. She supposed that was one good thing about not having heard from Helping Hope yet about the accounting job. Her schedule, though erratic, had slots like this open for a bit of reconnaissance.

"Liv!" a gravelly voice called.

She turned and saw a familiar pink-haired barista waving at her from a group of black-clad, chain-wearing punk rockers.

"Hey, Reina." Liv stopped and waited for Reina and her band to catch up. "Are you playing today?"

"We sure are." Reina grinned, lips filled in with black lipstick parting to reveal a radiant smile. She waved a leather-and spike-bedecked arm toward her group. "This is Gary, Sue, Molly, and Bob."

A thin, spectacled man with a video camera and a huge grin strode toward them from the direction of the fairgrounds, waving.

Reina waved back. "And that's my husband, Tim. He was scouting out the best place to record." She leaned toward Liv and whispered, "I told him people record on their phones these days, but he wants every one of our big performances on tape." She straightened and smiled at her husband.

Liv watched the affection in Reina's eyes, and her heart warmed at the man in khakis and a button-up staking out the best spot to record his punk rock wife. *What a pair.*

"Good luck to you guys," Liv said. "I'll pray today's judges are rock lovers."

"Sometimes it's more fun when they aren't, just to watch the looks on their faces." The man named Gary ran another coat of eyeliner under his eyelids and checked his spiky gray hair in a compact mirror. "We're not here to win, we're here for a good time."

Sue winked. Or was Sue the green-haired one and Molly the one with red hair? Liv had lost track. "We like surprising people, expanding their idea of who can play what music. A bunch of old people like us, in a rock band? Sure. We play the music we love."

"I'm not *that* old," Reina complained, laughing.

Liv wished she and the band had that ability. But with the prize money looming…

She spotted a familiar long-haired worship leader weaving through cars. "Ah, there's my band leader. I better go find him, but I'll try to catch your performance later."

Bob saluted. "I'll throw in an extra guitar riff just for you."

"No!" the entire band shouted, then broke down laughing.

Reina clutched her stomach, guffawing. "Ah, inside joke. Have fun, Liv."

Liv waved and made her way toward Elijah, who seemed to be scanning the cars for her Bug. She could have texted him when she arrived, but she'd been distracted by Reina. The easy camaraderie of that many years playing together...would she ever be in a band like that?

Elijah spotted her and waved. They met near the entrance to the fairgrounds.

"Ready to do some spying?" Liv circled her fingers around her eyes like binoculars.

Elijah chuckled and held up his own "binoculars." "Agent Peterson, reporting for duty."

After passing through the ticket counter, they followed the sound of music toward the stage. The clamor of carnival hawkers, kids shouting, friends calling to one another, and tinny music from booths almost drowned out the voices of singers and the strumming of guitars playing over loudspeakers near the stage.

Liv inhaled the scents of fried food, popcorn, someone selling scented candles, barbeque smoke, sweaty children, wet earth. It smelled like childhood, when her dad would take her to fairs and carnivals and they would ride the questionable-looking rides, eat way too much junk food, and take it upon themselves to judge the livestock competitions, trying to guess which animals would win, even though neither of them knew the first thing about farm animals.

Elijah's voice brought her back to the present. "Water?" He held out a plastic bottle and pulled another from the deep pocket of his cargo shorts. "I brought two."

"Thanks." Liv accepted the drink, surprised to find it still cool. She twisted off the cap and took a sip. "Impressively prepared."

He shrugged, cheeks tinged pink. "Didn't want anyone to get dehydrated."

They found a seat on one of the long benches set up near the stage. On the platform, a bearded man sang bluegrass while another played the banjo and one plucked an enormous, weathered upright bass.

"Imagine if Charlize had one of those instead," Liv joked.

Elijah laughed. "It's bigger than she is."

Bass in a band setting and one in an orchestra setting meant two very different things. Charlize's bass was a type of guitar, while the basses Liv was used to were the larger cousins of cellos.

The bluegrass band left the stage to a smattering of applause. Elijah leaned back on his hands, smiling at the stage. For a rare moment, the lines of tension smoothed from his face.

Liv wished she could banish that furrowed brow and tense jaw forever. Elijah was always handsome, but with the slight smile on his lips, the breeze teasing back locks of hair...

No. Bad Liv. No thinking about guys when your dad is in poor health and your finances are in shambles and... Her heart rate picked up again. *Aaaaand now I'm stressed again.*

"Hey, you okay?" Elijah cocked his head, focusing on her.

She looked away, realizing she had been staring. "Yeah, sorry."

His attention remained on her as the next band took the stage. Now she wondered if he knew *he* was staring. But instead of distressed, his expression seemed...tender.

Oh, no. Did he *like* her? Like *that*?

What if he did? What would she do? *I'm not ready for a relationship with all of the crazy going on in my life.* If she told him about all of her problems, would he run for the hills? He already had enough stress without *her* stress on top of it. That is, if he actually *did* like her. Maybe he didn't, and she had read too much into the situation.

She swiveled to face the band on stage as they took their places. A group of boys with shaggy hair and no instruments struck broody poses, mics affixed over their ears. Oh, dear. "Lij. I think we're about to witness some aspiring K-pop artists."

They tried to maintain straight faces as the teens lip-synched what was obviously a pre-recorded version of their song and attempted to swagger and smolder while dancing off-beat.

Liv leaned toward Elijah. "You know, I had a guilty pleasure of K-pop in high school and college."

Elijah's brows shot up. "Classical and K-pop?"

"It's great to rock out with. And the dancing is impressive." Liv nodded toward the boys on stage. "Um, not like that." Unlike these boys, the Korean pop stars had usually trained together for years, all the way since childhood, with a dedication that she found both impressive and a bit concerning.

"You'll have to show me some later."

Her cheeks warmed. That would involve hanging out in situations that weren't practicing or playing. "Yeah." She wouldn't admit quite yet that she had an entire playlist.

The boys hopped around rather than bowing, and a few people in the audience offered confused clapping.

She glanced back at Elijah. She didn't know what they would do for the competition, or how she would pay for medical bills, or whether she would get the job with Helping Hope. But for right now, she would enjoy this moment, and the man who had unwittingly agreed to a full education in K-pop.

The festival had enough fried food to give an elephant a heart attack.

According to the man at the ticket counter, who stamped Elijah and Liv's hands when they entered, Roseville decided to host the county fair and music festival at the same time.

"In years past, they had them as separate events. But most people don't want to see a bunch of nobodies. Then we brought in funnel cakes. And boom. Instant crowd."

Speaking of funnel cakes, Elijah stood in line with Liv to get one while a band with a steel drum ensemble played on the stage behind them. Elijah got so lost in the music, he almost forgot to keep following the queue. A large gap of space formed between him and the customer in front. Liv ordered elephant ears and Elijah slipped the cashier a five-dollar bill before Liv could reach into her purse.

A flush covered her cheeks and she thanked him. She took the plate of fried dough covered in cinnamon sugar.

She tore off a piece and offered him the plate. He held up a hand to indicate she could eat the whole thing by herself.

"Wonder why Charlize and Derek couldn't make it," she said, after she swallowed the chunk of the "ear." "After all, we all agreed at our last rehearsal that it would be good to scope out the event to get our bearings."

Elijah, too, pondered that very thing. Charlize and Derek's texts didn't make a whole lot of sense either.

Charlize: I have...to fix a string on my bass. That seems like a valid reason for me not to show up, right? Okay, anyway, see you at band practice tomorrow.
Derek: Whatever Charlize is doing, I'm probably doing.

Often, when Charlize and Derek needed to ditch, they had far better excuses than this. Did they *purposely* leave Liv and Elijah alone to scope out the music festival?

That would make sense. Charlize suffered Derek's company on the hike to give Elijah and Liv space to walk alone.

The steel drum band finished on stage, followed by some enthusiastic clapping from the front row of the audience. Probably the family of the group. Elijah's eyes roamed the crowd and dead-stopped when they landed on Brooklyn and a gaggle of the youth group teens.

Signs obscured the faces of most of them.

He motioned with his hand for Liv to stay put. "Just want to say hi to a friend." He weaved his way through the haphazard lawn chairs placed in front of the stage.

"Brooklyn?"

The youth leader whirled around. A large headband held back her flyaway hairs. "Lij? What are you doing here?"

"Was about to ask you the same thing. I have a band scheduled for Friday. How about you?"

Brooklyn tapped her sign that had the name "Parker" etched in glittery pink cursive. "One of our teens is playing later today. You might remember her—the redhead who was hiding in the corner."

She played? No wonder she opened up so much during their worship time. Music spoke to her like a second language, just like it did for him.

"I'll pray it goes well." He gestured over his shoulder at Liv, who brushed cinnamon crumbs off the corners of her lips. "Should get back to my friend, but let me know how it goes."

"Will do." Brooklyn saluted him. "We'll make sure to come Friday to cheer you on then too. Text me the time slot."

He did so, then rushed back to Liv. She'd finished the contents on her plate and dumped the Styrofoam vessel into a nearby trash can. Bees circled around the receptacle's hole.

"One of the youth groupers is playing," Elijah explained as the two of them zigzagged through the crowd, scanning the various booths and wares. *Why in the world is someone selling bathtubs here?* "Cool to see so many people from the town participate."

"Reina, a fellow barista, is also signed up."

Liv paused and gestured at a stall with various bracelets. She admired a silver one with elephants etched into a swirly pattern. Then she set the jewelry back down on the table.

"She says she probably won't win. But she just loves the feeling of doing music." Liv spread-eagled her arms, and almost whacked a father, who wore a large cowboy hat. "Sounds freeing."

That it did.

But freeing doesn't get you twenty thousand dollars.

"Mr. Jumping Soup?"

Elijah halted at the sound of this nickname and turned to his left, in time to watch Boris do his best impression of broth leaping from a pot. Boris giggled and patted his cooking classes booth. "Get my email earlier?"

Indeed he had.

Boris canceled cooking classes for this week, on account that he'd have to man a station at the fair. Photographs from past years decorated the front of his table. On the surface of the stand, Boris had several sample dishes prepared, to show what students would learn.

No doubt, in this mid-afternoon heat, all the meat had spoiled. Hopefully no one would eat the contents and get food poisoning.

"You two lovely couple." Boris winked at them.

"Oh, we're not—" Elijah started, but Boris waved down a family with a brochure, no longer paying attention to Elijah or Liv.

Needing something to do, to distract himself from the fire burning in his cheeks, Elijah cinched the flannel tied around his waist tighter. The summer heat would make the long sleeve clothing way too hot to wear. Liv played with the bracelet on her arm.

"So." Liv cleared her throat. "What are your thoughts on Reina doing music for the fun of it?"

Elijah dodged around a kid's inflatable squid she'd won in a carnival game. "It sounds amazing. Like a dream, really. But not practical."

Light died in Liv's eyes. "So you think we should do the radio version."

Should he tell her that he wanted to give her all the prize money? So she could help her dad and finish college?

A wad of pink cotton candy, carried by a distracted mother, about bonked him in the nose. "I know there are a lot of people in our band who could use that prize money. Do you think it's wise to risk that and play something we enjoy, but the crowd might not?"

"Hmm." She cocked her head to the side.

Noise from the electric guitars strumming on stage and a man nearby hitting a carnival game with a mallet filled the silence between them.

Liv cleared her throat. "It is risky. But the way I figure it, God already knows who is going to win. If we play with all our heart, soul, mind, and strength, then what does it matter what version we choose?"

Huh, why hadn't he considered that before?

The radio version stole away his heart, his soul, his strength...did that mean he ought not do it?

An "ooh" from Liv followed by a finger-point interrupted his thoughts. She gestured to a Ferris wheel. "My dad and I loved going on those when I was a kid. Can we?"

Elijah nodded, and they stepped into a winding line. Faint but grungy guitar and vocals sounded from behind them. Liv perked up at this, while Elijah paid for two tickets.

"I think that's Reina."

Elijah squinted at the stage. Someone with pink hair tore her guitar pick up and down her strings with fervor. No doubt, Reina loved an edgy, rock style.

They slid onto the white Ferris wheel seat. Their cart creaked and wobbled back and forth. Yikes, Roseville did not value safety as much as they should. Liv, jolted by the motion, scooted closer to him. Perhaps to ground herself.

In that case...who needed safety?

He fought the urge to wrap his arm around her shoulder. Especially with her head inches away from his.

The wheel jolted, and they wound toward the sky. Neither spoke for a while, both absorbed in Reina's music.

They reached the top, and Elijah surveyed the layout of the whole fair. Striped tents covered every corner, and 4-H barns dotted the spaces between booths and the large stage. Elijah reminded himself to check out some of the prize animals and foods later. Back in the day, one of his siblings joined a 4-H club, so he could soak in the nostalgia.

A high screeching note from Reina drew his attention back to the stage.

Yes, most audience members wouldn't like this sort of thing. Reina sounded like she gargled glass on a daily basis. And her drummer drowned out most of the other instruments on stage.

But even from a distance he could spot the wide smile on Reina's face. Liv, beside him, mimicked the expression.

Not until their cart reached the bottom did Elijah realize his lips had also curved upward.

Chapter Twenty

LIV STARED AT THE EMAIL.

Dear Ms. Wilson,
We are pleased to offer you the position of Accounting Assistant at Helping Hope Publishing and Charities.

She'd been hoping and praying for this. So why did she feel so empty?

She skimmed the rest of the email—background check, pay, benefits, all the usual. If everything went through, she would start next week.

Today felt like a far cry from the fun of the fair two days ago with Elijah. Having just gotten home from work, she rushed to her room to check her email—to check for *this* email. The competition, Elijah, and all else had taken a back seat to a busy day and stress about Helping Hope.

She tapped her fingers on her desk. No cooking class, no shift at She Brews...she actually had an evening off. She could procrastinate on responding to the email until later tonight. It was the end of the workday anyway—Caroline would be home any minute. They wouldn't see her response until tomorrow.

Her hand drifted to her phone. Before she quite registered what she was doing, she'd typed out a message to Elijah.

Liv: Missed seeing you—and Boris—with no cooking class yesterday. Doing anything fun and exciting with your evening?

She turned back to her computer and pinched her eyes shut.

"Doing anything fun and exciting?" That sounded like an invitation, didn't it? Would he take that as flirting? Did she, perhaps, want him to take it that way?

Her phone buzzed.

Elijah: Nothing as exciting as naming eggs or wearing vegetable hats, unfortunately. I'm thinking about taking the dogs to the park, but Andy's busy, and it's hard for one person to handle both of them when they get too excited about squirrels. What about you?

Liv searched her memory for the names of the dogs. Caroline talked about them all the time and had convinced Andy to adopt the smaller one that spring. Sandy? No, Sammy. Sammy and...something to do with a fruit. Peaches.

Odd that it's difficult to handle both at the park. What about when they go on their daily walks around the apartment complex?

She blinked as understanding dawned. Wait. Was that meant to be a hint that he didn't want to go alone? Was *he* flirting with *her*?

Time to find out.

Liv: I find myself with an unexpected evening off with no plans. Maybe petting Caroline's hamster, which I'm sure isn't as fun as hanging out with Sammy and Peaches.

Her heart beat faster than the situation warranted. She fiddled with a pen.

When the phone buzzed again, she swiped open the message instantly.

Elijah: If you'd like, you could join us at the park. They both love belly rubs from new people.

"There it is." She glanced toward the window. The Midwest

summer sun stayed out late into the evening. They had plenty of time before it would be dark.

Liv: Lucky for them, I love giving belly rubs. What park?

Twenty minutes later, Liv strolled along a path with trees branching overhead toward an open, grassy area where a group of kids played a game of pickup soccer, moms sat on picnic blankets, and at the far end, children clambered over a jungle gym. One little girl seemed about to take flight as her swing soared. She shrieked with delight while a man, presumably her father, grinned and gave her another push.

On the sidewalk ringing the other end of the field, a shaggy golden retriever and his stubby-legged canine companion pulled the man walking them at a brisk pace. Peaches, some sort of corgi mix, seemed to be doing twice the pulling, despite her smaller size. As Liv approached, Peaches bounced at the end of the lead, tongue lolling.

"Hey there, Peaches." Liv squatted to pet the dog. The corgi barreled into Liv, and Sammy nosed her ear and snuffled her neck. Liv laughed and scratched both of their fluffy ruffs. "And hi to you too, Sammy."

Elijah panted, smiling wide. "Wow, they took a long time to warm up, didn't they?"

"They're just a *little* friendly." Peaches rolled over, and Liv rubbed her belly.

"They won't do that for everyone. Dogs can tell when someone is a good person." Elijah cleared his throat. "Although, ever since she came home from the shelter, Peaches has gotten more and more outgoing. She's a terrible guard dog."

Liv stood and held out a hand. "Want me to take one of them?"

"Oh, only if you want to."

Liv raised an eyebrow. "I thought you needed assistance in case of squirrels."

Elijah's cheeks flushed. "Right. Squirrels." He handed her a leash.

"Take Sammy. He's better behaved than Peaches."

Liv fell into step next to him, the dogs snuffling the ground ahead of them. Peaches took a moment to bark at a kite, but Elijah redirected her with a whistle and a pat on his thigh.

"So." Elijah fiddled with the leash. "What, uh, have you been up to today?"

"Oh, you know, work." She hesitated, then blurted, "I got offered the accounting job at Helping Hope."

He took a couple of steps before he asked, "Are you going to take it?"

"Yes. Well. Maybe." She took a deep breath. "My dad has ongoing health issues, and he spent a lot of time in the hospital recently. As much as I would love to keep teaching music lessons, having a steady source of income would be a huge help." She decided not to include the information about the surgery, or the house. No need to make him feel guilty for asking her to do worship team things. Knowing Elijah, that might be his first thought—how he could have better supported her.

Her heart warmed. *And isn't that one of the things you like most about him? His caring heart?* Maybe she should let him in more.

"I'm sorry, Liv. That's hard." He paused and turned toward her, head tilted. "Please, if there's anything I can do, let me know?"

She swallowed the lump in her throat. "Of course. But right now, there's not much to be done."

The path meandered into an area overhung with shade trees. The shouts of children faded into background noise.

Sammy buried his muzzle deep in the leaves on the side of the path, tail wagging. Peaches trotted over to join him, sticking her snout in next to his. Two seconds later, she dashed across the path to sniff a tree, then chased a leaf blowing in the wind. Sammy kept his nose to the ground, following some trail with his tail moving faster than his legs.

Liv realized she was grinning. "They're adorable."

"Dogs make everything better." Elijah patted Sammy's rump.

"Even when this big goof thinks he's a lap dog."

Liv laughed. Elijah watched her with a small smile teasing his lips. For some reason, Liv's cheeks warmed. She turned her attention back to the dogs. "I think what I love about them is how excited they are about everything. No one enjoys God's creation like a dog. They think every day is a gift and adventure."

"Maybe because it is. Sometimes, we just get so stressed and anxious and worried, we forget to see it."

Liv glanced toward him out of the corner of her eye. His gaze was fixed on her, rather than the dogs. Her heart thumped. She couldn't tell who slowed down first, whose hand brushed the other's. Fingers began to weave together, eyes met…

Buzz. Buzz. Buzz.

Liv pulled her hand away and reached into her pocket. She grabbed her phone and saw both a text and a missed call notification. Oh, no. How had she missed a call? She read the text.

Susan: Things took a turn with your dad. Call me.

She looked back up at Elijah. "It's about my dad. I have to go."

"Of course." He took Peaches' leash. "I'll be praying."

Her head still spinning from what had almost happened, what kind of happened—what *did* just happen?—she hit the buttons to call Susan, already power walking toward her car.

A tight feeling in her chest told her this wasn't going to be good.

"Sorry we didn't call much during vacation." Miriam in her stage makeup squinted at Elijah through the screen. "After the jellyfish debacle, we'd been preoccupied for the rest of our time at the beach."

One of Elijah's cousins found it hilarious to launch a dead jellyfish at another cousin's back. Often, on the shore, iridescent blobs once full of life let the waves lap over them.

Problem was, they often still had their stingers attached.

From what Elijah could make out from Miriam's texts the previous week, their family spent a long time in the hospital.

"Okay, who hid my eyeliner again?" A man behind Miriam, with wrinkles drawn onto his forehead, chased another actor off screen.

If Miriam ever had time, she called Elijah from the backstage area. Lights decorated several mirrors. Elijah had, through a screen, spent many hours in this room. Even though he'd never visited in person, he imagined it would have a strong stench of hairspray and cheap makeup.

Miriam rolled her eyes at the chase scene between the actors, who flitted on and off screen. "Anyway, what's up with you, Bud? That's a nice room you're in."

"Just waiting in the church library before worship practice."

One day away from the festival, Elijah needed some time to think. Even though practices had gone well, with the band alternating between the radio and non-radio versions of the song, anxiety buzzed in his skull.

So he sought solitude in the quiet library.

Much of the building layout didn't make sense to Elijah, including this place.

Pastor had decorated everything in Victorian-style wood. Polished bookshelves lined every wall. And a French-style chandelier hung from the ceiling.

Every time Elijah stepped into the room, he swore he'd time-traveled back to the 1800s. Pastor claimed this room reminded him of his time studying abroad in Oxford. Hence why he *had* to include it in the building plans.

"How is worship leading going, by the way?" Miriam adjusted some of the white makeup in the corners of her eyes. Must've smudged. Elijah, for a moment, wondered how she could do this. But then he realized she must've placed her phone against a mirror in the dressing room, so she could go hands-free.

Elijah's spirit sank within him. His family already didn't approve of his career. How could he tell his successful sister about how his position each week relied on the happiness of one congregation member?

But this was Miriam. The sister he'd told about his first crush in middle school.

The one who hugged him when he failed to make the talent show his sophomore year.

Of all the siblings, he could trust her the most.

"Depends on the week. Mom and Dad were right—I should've done something else with my life."

Miriam pursed her lips and grabbed a bottle of hairspray with her free hand. Clouds of translucent liquid sprayed down some stray hairs.

She set the bottle back down on a nearby counter. At least, Elijah assumed that from the clack he heard.

"Lij, did I ever tell you what Mom and Dad said when I told them I wanted to pursue opera?"

He squeezed his eyes shut and scanned through his memories. "No, not that I can recall."

"'Don't go into music. You'll regret it.'" She wagged a finger at the phone, imitating their father's low voice.

What?

Elijah didn't remember this. Why would their family, who breathed music, discourage Miriam from pursuing a career in it?

"And when I was auditioning my heart out after college and couldn't land roles—I really thought I'd made a mistake." She shrugged. Tight shoulder straps on her costume scrunched. "Do you know why they told me not to do it?"

Elijah shook his head and leaned back into a red leather chair.

"Because they had to struggle, to fight in their own music careers. They didn't want to see me do the same." Someone behind Miriam practiced scales. She whirled around and pointed at the phone. "Do you mind?"

The other girl, who wore a hoop skirt that could hide five bodies underneath, shuffled off screen. Her scales sounded moments later, but quieter this time.

"Anyway, I kept at it, and we're here. I know that a lot of people think I simply got a job right out of college and am having a successful opera career. Because I'm posting about all the good stuff on social media."

Sure, all her stories, posts, everything showed her singing on stage, holding large bouquets of roses from adoring fans, signing autographs on playbills.

"They don't see that I still don't land parts in plays. Or that some nights I don't hit the notes correctly and can't bear to show my face to the crowd after in the cast meet-and-greet. No calling is without its hills and valleys."

Elijah's chest warmed.

Maybe he needed to talk with more musicians and artsy people who seemed successful. Would they all tell him the same thing? That they, too, had doubts, insecurities, and rough days?

"Ten minutes to curtain," someone in all-black clothing called behind Miriam.

"Thank you, ten," Miriam said. Supposedly theater people did this as a response to the stage manager's time calls. "Well, Lij, that's my cue to go. We often do a few warm ups before we go on stage. Best of luck, and I'll be praying that you start seeing some hills soon."

The screen went dark.

Elijah sank into the leather chair, neck craned over the cushy back of the seat. He snapped forward, moments later, when he heard the doors to the library creak.

Pastor Smith entered, mouth receding into a thin line.

Although not unusual to spot the pastor in his favorite room in the church, something about that somber expression sent chills down Elijah's back.

"Elijah." Pastor Smith paused, sighed. "I'm afraid Don emailed again."

Gravity took over and forced Elijah deeper into the chair. He'd almost forgotten about the blackout from this past Sunday. Don couldn't blame Elijah for the lack of electricity, could he?

But even so, Elijah could've done his best to meet Don's demands. Instead, he did everything the man hated—harmonies, modern songs, repeating bridges.

"What did he say?" Elijah winced and braced for impact.

A glow stung his eyes. Pastor held up his screen so Elijah could read the email composed in one sentence.

Pastor Smith,
 We need to talk about what happened on Sunday.
 Don

"At first I thought he'd had an issue with my sermon." Pastor Smith clicked off the light on his screen and slid his phone into his pocket. "But he only complains about worship. We can assume he had a problem with the way it was played."

Whatever hope Elijah had left sank like an anchor into his stomach.

He should've known that even though Don didn't confront him after service, he couldn't get away with letting loose.

Worship leaders he'd connected with on Facebook groups had even mentioned tighter restrictions within their own churches. Some posts in those groups included,

"Every song has a timestamp, and we can't play more than fifteen minutes of worship. You play sixteen, you get in trouble."

"We have to submit a report about what went well and what went wrong. If the same 'wrong' stuff keeps happening, we get yelled at."

"We always have a meeting later in the afternoon where we talk about what went wrong. If a bassist hits a wrong note, if the lyrics slides are too slow, we will hear about it."

Elijah'd always counted himself more fortunate that Pastor Smith didn't find these types of meetings necessary.

But now…

"Do you want me to make sure worship fits his demands this week?" The question crackled in the back of Elijah's throat. Like it had fractured on its way out of his mouth.

That's how he felt right now. Broken.

Thank goodness Elijah arrived half an hour early. He could adjust what he'd planned for the group. Sometimes he'd come closer to an hour ahead of time to peruse the nonfiction books on worship and discipleship in the library.

"I think it's best if you take a few weeks off."

Elijah's spine snapped straight so fast, an ache formed in his lower back. "Pastor, I—"

Pastor Smith held up a hand. Then he rubbed his face with it. He looked tired, worn. "I've asked the former worship leader if he'd be willing to do the services for the next few weeks. Just him and his guitar. To tide things over and get Don to cool down."

Did this mean he could still keep his job? Or would Don tell Pastor he preferred the former worship leader, and Pastor would have no choice but to let Elijah go?

"I-I'm—" But what was he? Sorry?

For what? For following the Spirit's lead, and playing with all his heart and soul?

"—disappointed."

"I am too, Elijah." All of Pastor Smith slumped, and the giant of a man shuffled toward the doors to the library. If Elijah hadn't known better, he would've said the pastor shrunk by at least a foot. "Please let your band know that practice is canceled tonight and—"

He reached for the door, held the handle in his beefy palm. Then he turned back to Elijah, eyes glassy.

"Please play your heart out at tomorrow's festival. I'd hate to see such a beautiful gift go to waste."

With that Pastor Smith exited the room, and the door shut. Its bang reverberated throughout the room.

Chapter Twenty-One

LIV RUBBED BLEARY EYES, STRUGGLING TO stay awake.

Susan put a hand on her shoulder. "I know you weren't hungry earlier, but you should really get something to eat. I'll stay here."

Liv nodded and stood, stretching her arms over her head. Her aching back popped. Even though the hospital staff had moved Dad into his own room with a reclining chair for a caretaker, her tailbone didn't like sitting for that long at a time.

Before staggering out of the room, she glanced at Dad, tucked beneath thin hospital blankets and hooked up to beeping machines. In sleep, his furrowed brow belied the pained grimace he wouldn't allow to show while awake. But the steady tempo of the machine's beeps marched on, the first real sleep he'd had in the past twenty-four hours.

Not many people frequented the hospital cafeteria after midnight. The cafe was closed, so Liv purchased a cold sandwich, banana, and bottled iced coffee from the fridge and brought them to the single worker manning the register. She took a seat at one of the tables, not far from a man slowly pushing a mop from one end of the cafeteria to the other, back and forth, back and forth.

Yesterday, Liv's Wednesday evening had flipped from laughing about dogs with Elijah to holding back tears in an instant. After Susan's call, Liv had packed an overnight bag and driven to the hospital as fast as she could.

She met Susan in the waiting room. Circles underlined the older woman's eyes, but when she saw Liv, she offered a warm smile. "I'm so glad you made it."

Liv hugged her. "Thank you so much for calling me." She stepped back, trying to keep her breathing even. "How is he?"

Susan bit her lip. "I'll be honest, not so good. The doctors are pumping antibiotics into his system intravenously, but with how high his fever is..."

"Right. You mentioned the fever." Liv clenched her fists, trying not to yell. None of this was Susan's fault, but she could shake Dad. "He admitted he had a fever for days and just didn't tell anyone?"

Susan rubbed the bridge of her nose. "He claimed he figured he had a little cold."

Liv stared up at the ceiling tiles, trying not to flash back to another waiting room, another anxious person delivering uncertain news.

She looked back down and sighed. "Do they know how bad the infection is?"

"Not yet. We probably won't know more until the doctors come in tomorrow morning."

They'd spent a long, restless night taking turns in a hard chair by Dad's bedside and the recliner. It pained Liv to see his flushed skin, his glassy eyes. She held his sweaty hand and brushed hair from his forehead.

Worst of all, he'd hardly cracked any jokes.

"Hey, Livy." He gave her a wan smile. "Fancy seeing you here."

She squeezed his hand. "I'd rather we saw each other somewhere else. We keep meeting here too often."

"I'm sorry, Liv." He sighed, closing his eyes. "I'm a bit tired. I think I'll take a short nap."

She wondered if he realized the passage of time, that they'd reached the middle of the night. "Get some rest."

Now, peeling her banana in a quiet cafeteria underneath a buzzing fluorescent light, Liv fought the urge to rest her forehead on the table.

The doctors had waffled all day on the necessity of re-opening the surgical site. The infection in the incision seemed to be deep, and that close to the spinal cord...for now, it seemed they would simply keep an eye on the wound.

She bit into her banana—why were the hospital bananas always too green?—and pulled out her phone. Only five percent battery left, and she'd forgotten her charger. She would need to borrow one before she headed back to Roseville. She might need the GPS to get to the festival.

The festival. *Oh no.* They were supposed to practice this evening, hours ago, and she'd missed it.

She rattled off a text to Elijah.

Liv: I'm so sorry I missed practice. My dad's health isn't doing so well. I've been in the hospital with him since last night.

She hesitated, then added a second text.

Liv: I'll be there tomorrow.

As long as Dad continued to stabilize, she could rush down to Roseville tomorrow morning, perform in the festival, and hurry back to the hospital without spending too long away.

Back in the room, Susan snoozed in the chair. She lifted her head when Liv entered.

Liv's heart squeezed. When was the last time Susan had a proper night's rest?

"Hey, you've been here longer than me. Why don't you go home and get some real sleep? We won't hear much more from the doctors until tomorrow morning anyway."

Susan hesitated, sitting forward. She raised a hand to her rumpled hair. "I could use a shower..."

"Go." Liv put a hand on her shoulder. "And thank you." She bit her lip, tears threatening. "So much."

Susan rose and enveloped her in a hug. "I'll always be here. For both of you."

Exhausted, Liv slumped into the chair. She didn't intend to fall asleep, but the next thing she knew, the voices of Dad and the doctor awoke her.

She startled upright, glancing at her phone. Dead. She turned her gaze to the time stamp on one of the many machines—seven-thirty a.m.

Friday morning already? Had she really slept for more than six hours?

"Sorry, Mark." A familiar doctor flipped through papers on her clipboard. Dr. Nevins had been a constant presence throughout Dad's recent health struggles. She tapped her pen against the clipboard and shook her head. "We're going to have to go in there and clean it out."

Liv rubbed her eyes, trying to wake up, and Dr. Nevins turned her way, auburn ponytail swinging. "Good morning, Olivia. Sorry to wake you. You looked so peaceful."

Liv hoisted herself to her feet. "No, I'm glad you did." What sort of daughter was she, conking out while Dad lay in a hospital bed? "What's the situation?"

"My incision just needs a little cleaning." Dad shifted and grimaced. "Nothing too crazy."

Dr. Nevins cleared her throat. "Right." She glanced at Liv. "By that, he means we need to reopen the incision to drain the abscess and use a debriding agent to remove some of the contaminated tissue so we can make sure the muscle tissue is properly—" She trailed off, probably noticing the green tinge Liv was sure had risen to her face. "We need to make it all nice and pretty in there again," the doctor finished. "The infection appears to be deep."

Liv knew she should be used to medical terminology by now, but anything with open wounds gave her the heebie jeebies. "Does that mean surgery?"

"Since this is a more delicate procedure, we will need to use general anesthesia." Dr. Nevins glanced at her watch. "I was talking with the surgeons, and we're thinking we should be able to get you in around late morning. You've already been fasting, so no liquids before then."

Dad faked a grumble. "I guess I'll lay off the Arnold Palmer."

As Dr. Nevins turned to leave, she almost imperceptibly bobbed her head toward the door. Liv caught her meaning and followed into the hall.

The doctor faced her. "I'm not trying to frighten you, but his symptoms indicate possible infection in the cerebrospinal fluid and a potential CSF leak. We're going into this as a simple procedure, but it may last longer." She took a deep breath. "I tried to impress this upon him while you were asleep, but no matter what we find, he needs to be very, very careful with the incision. This isn't something to mess around with."

Liv swallowed. "Thank you. I'll try to hammer it through his thick skull."

After the doctor left, Liv reentered the room, turning her focus to Dad. His eyes seemed a bit clearer today. She clenched her fists. *I can't handle this anymore, Lord. Just when I think he's getting better.*

"Livy." He held out his hand, and she took it. "What thoughts are buzzing around in your head like angry bees?"

She sighed. "I just want you to be all better."

He squeezed her hand. "I'm sorry, Livy. I should have thought more of it. But when Benji, Susan's grandson, came over last week, he ended up having a case of the sniffles the next day. When I felt myself developing a fever, I figured after sharing a plate of cookies and playing Hot Wheels, I probably caught something from him."

"Why didn't you say something?" She let go of his hand, running her fingers through her hair instead. "Maybe someone else would have caught on."

He grimaced, looked away. "I didn't want to make Susan feel bad for bringing him over, so I didn't mention the symptoms. She wasn't too sure she should bring a kid over so soon after my surgery, but my little buddy helps keep me from getting stir crazy."

Liv softened. She'd assumed he'd been acting stubborn. Instead, he hadn't wanted to hurt Susan or his young pal, even if his self-diagnosis had been faulty.

Maybe she got part of her people-pleasing, the nobler elements, from him.

"Are you going to marry her?" she blurted.

His eyes widened, and his cheeks reddened. "Uh, well," he stammered. "I…" He looked down, almost bashful. "I would like to. If you two get along, of course. And if I can do something about the medical stuff, and get back on my feet, and if she would have an old coot like me—"

Liv took his hand and squeezed. "She will." She huffed a laugh. "She's crazy about you, Dad. And I don't think she's particularly concerned about whether you have it 'all together.'"

Moisture gathered in his eyes. "Thank you, Livy." He smiled. "Susan...she's a special woman. I didn't think I'd ever find someone again, but God's full of surprises."

Her mind wandered to Elijah. He and Susan had a lot of similarities—they didn't seem to care whether people had it all together, and they came into her life by surprise. She'd never thought she would want a mother figure. Or that she could trust another musical man. And yet, she'd grown attached to both of them.

"Oh, no. Elijah."

The words slipped out of her mouth before she could stop them. The festival. Their performance. She needed to be there soon. She needed to leave *now*.

Dad raised an eyebrow. "My name is Mark."

But she couldn't. Not with Dad going into surgery. Not with the doctor's warnings. How could she leave him here?

"Who's Elijah?" a female voice asked.

Liv turned to see Susan bustling through the door with a duffel bag. "Shh, I brought snacks and games," she stage-whispered. She dumped the duffel on the ground by the chair and set her hands on her hips. "So? Who is this Elijah?"

"And why is he an oh no?" Dad pointed a finger at her. "The whole truth."

Liv took a deep breath. "So, I kind of joined a band."

"Where is she?"

Charlize looked over Elijah's shoulder at his phone, as though hoping to summon answers as well. Apart from Liv sending a message about her father's health hitting a serious decline, she hadn't texted since.

Even her read receipts showed nothing. Did her phone die?

"She didn't show up to last night's rehearsal." Charlize chewed on her lip and then smudged off a blemish on her bass guitar. "Should we plan for the worst?"

A woman with a clipboard jabbed a blue pen at Elijah's group. "You're on in five."

"Thank you, five," he said by habit, having listened to Miriam do the same thing when she was backstage for shows.

She disappeared around the black curtain that hid their band from the audience next to the stage. Wooden steps led up to the large platform where a group of handbell players now graced the stage.

From what Elijah heard, they didn't actually enter to compete. Various town musicians booked a slot to play for fun, but not for the prize money.

"Lij?" Charize's gruff whisper pulled him back.

He palmed his neck. "We could have you try to sing Liv's part."

Charlize grimaced. "Not sure if that'll go well. I can't hit some of those notes, and I'm bad at multitasking."

When Liv didn't arrive at practice the night before, Elijah had them play both versions of the song with Charlize on the harmony. Whenever she went to sing, she had to stop playing her guitar. Said she had a difficult time focusing on both.

A drumstick whirled on Derek's fingertips. "Maybe we should back out?"

"And lose the prize money?" Charlize shook her head. "We'll just have to play without her."

"We can't." Elijah had to growl this to keep his words at a whisper. The handbell group on stage brought out a rainmaker to play a tune from a popular movie set by the ocean. "The whole point of Finding Harmony is the *harmony*. Without Liv, the whole song falls apart."

He scanned beyond the curtain again, hopeful.

A crowd milled around lemonade stands and booths full of the largest stuffed animals in the world. A heavyset man caught Elijah's eye. He wore a bowling shirt and a pair of khaki shorts. Even in the blaze of sunlight that made Elijah squint, he recognized the man from so many videos he'd watched.

Chris Bethel, the former worship leader at The Vine.

"Wave me over when we start," he told Charlize, and bolted toward Chris before he could hear any protest.

He slowed his pace and approached the man. Chris wiped off powdered sugar on his chin from a funnel cake he held in his other hand. The man's neck straightened when he spotted Elijah advancing in his direction.

Chris pointed a sugar-dusted finger at Elijah. "I've seen pictures of you on the church's social media pages."

Elijah had never met the person in charge of snapping pictures of him and the band during worship on Sundays. But sure enough, about twice a month, images of him with his guitar and microphone, strobed by some stage lights, popped up on his Instagram feed.

"Don give you trouble too?" Chris set his plate down on a nearby wooden table. Then he slumped into the seat.

"How did you know?"

"Pastor called me to fill in for you for a few weeks." Either flush or a sunburn crossed the man's forehead. "I let Pastor Smith have it in his office. For not sticking up for you."

Elijah's heart skipped a beat. "You did?"

"Certainly. Don was the reason I'd left The Vine in the first place. You could never satisfy the man with anything. Even if you didn't play a single note on Sunday, he'd find some reason to complain."

Huh, so this did confirm Elijah's suspicions. That Chris quit before Easter because the stress of Don's demands had gotten to him.

"Surprised I haven't seen him here yet." Chris pinched a piece of his funnel cake and tossed it into his mouth. "I thought he was one of the judges of something. Or at least, he donated a portion of that prize money, so he has a lot of say."

Weights dragged Elijah's heart to his toes.

Even if Liv did show up, Don would make sure they lost. Here was to hoping the other judges would ignore Don's comments.

Elijah parked on the bench across from Chris.

"Thanks for sticking up for me." He clasped his hands, thumbs chasing one another. "It's helpful to know that I'm not the only one Don was after."

Chris laughed and thumped his chest with his hand. "Some powdered sugar got stuck," he explained. "And yeah, Don was always against us doing harmony and those modern worship songs. They reminded him too much of his wife."

If Elijah drove a car right now, he would've screeched the tires to a halt.

He had to settle for his eyes widening. "What?"

"She had the most beautiful soprano voice. Could hit any harmony you asked her to. And was always a fan of introducing new songs into the lineup. Said it would help the congregation to branch out and understand God's word in new ways. So when she passed..." Moisture filled Chris's eyes. He blinked the mist away. "Anything that sounded remotely like her had to go."

Chris shrugged.

"Soon enough, I took the comments personally and decided that I couldn't do anything right. Pastor Smith didn't want to get in the middle of it, so I helped make it easier on him."

"You left."

"Indeed."

Would that mean that Elijah would have to seek employment

elsewhere? In that case, would there be another Don waiting for him at a new church? Or would he have to pick up the insurance gig again and hope for enough music gigs on the side?

Laughter from a girl carrying a large balloon interrupted the silence between them. The handbell choir had entered an intense chorus where they clapped the head of the bells on the foam tables.

Elijah sighed and slapped his palms on the warm table's surface. Splinters threatened to stick into his fingertips. "Well, Chris, if Don is judging or has any sway whatsoever, our band is doomed."

Even if they played the radio-style version, it included some harmonies. Granted, without Liv, they could cut those out.

But the minute Don spotted Elijah on stage, he'd give the band the ol' Roman Emperor thumbs down.

That being that case…maybe we should play the one we love. If we go in with the guarantee we won't win, what'll it matter? Why not do something we love and be proud, knowing we gave it all?

An immense relief washed over him. His shoulders dropped two inches, and in the blazing heat of the sun, he could've melted into a puddle.

"Thanks, Chris." He rose from his seat and angled toward the band. The stage manager had returned and held up two fingers. Liv had two minutes to show, or they'd have to go on without her. "You were helpful."

Chris lifted a brow and swirled a chunk of funnel cake in a patch of powdered sugar. "I thought I'd come off as more of a downer, but I'm glad I could assist in some way." He grinned, white dust coating his mouth.

Elijah gave a thumbs up to the band. He didn't know how they'd play without Liv, but they'd give the slow version of the song a go.

He scanned the audience that crowded around the stage. Youth groupers held up neon signs. Bubble letters declared, "Elijah Never Falls Flat" and "Our Worship Band Is Nothing But Treble." The redheaded girl named Parker flashed a pink sign that said, "Bass-ically, Elijah's Band Is The Best. Deal With It."

Oh boy, they must've Googled all those horrible worship puns.

Joy lit up like summer fireworks within his chest.

They'd come to support him, no matter how much the band would fail in the next five minutes.

His gaze roamed the faces at the judge's stand. No Don. Maybe Don didn't score per se, but as a contributor to the prize money, he'd have a large amount of input.

That didn't seem to be the norm with most contests Elijah knew about. But knowing Don...

Sure enough, when Elijah craned his neck to the right, he recognized Don's form in the front row. Next to him sat Robert, who had busied himself with tying and untying his shoelaces. Theater was far more interesting to this kid than music concerts.

Perhaps one day Don would understand.

Footsteps thumped behind him. He had a scarce second to spin around in time for a runner to crash into him. He hit the grass with a painful thud. Who went jogging at the fair?

Elijah looked up to find Liv apologizing and brushing grass off her skirt.

"Sorry, I saw the stage, and the sun got in my eyes, and—" She held out a hand. Pants filled each breath. She must've sprinted from the parking lot.

"You—you're here."

She waved a hand, as if to indicate they didn't have the time to explain. Then she helped pull Elijah up and they rushed toward the backstage curtain. Derek and Charlize leapt up and down, faces gawking. But no sound came out. After all, the handbell group had finished their last plunk of their bells. Now the stage crew, all clad in black t-shirts, put away the handbell tables with alarming speed.

They'd need to go soon.

"We have a crew member bringing your keyboard on stage," Charlize whispered to Liv.

Liv nodded and brushed a sweaty lock from her forehead. "Which version are we playing?"

Elijah clenched his jaw. Determination coursed through his veins like fire. "The right one."

Chapter Twenty-Two

LIV HAD NEVER RUN SO FAST. She heaved in gulps of air, trying to recover from barreling into Elijah.

Nor had she ever driven so fast. Or quick-changed so fast.

"Go, go, go!" At the hospital, Susan had shooed her out the door. "Go win that competition."

"You're a star, Livy," Dad called after her.

She'd still been half-hopping into her shoes as she dashed into the hospital hallway, wearing her only set of clean clothes she'd brought. Susan had loaned her makeup, and she brushed her hair as best she could in under thirty seconds of prep. "You have to look your best," Susan had said, stuffing a bag full of snacks for the drive.

It had taken less than two minutes of explanation about who Elijah was and about the festival before both Dad and Susan were ready to shove her out the door.

"But what about you?" she'd protested. "You're about to go into surgery."

"Sure, but you're not a surgeon." Dad waved her off. "I won't even be conscious for a few hours. It does no good for you to sit around worrying."

"I agree with him for once." Susan smirked at Dad's protests. "Your band is waiting for you."

"Livy." Dad's expression grew serious. "There's nothing that makes me happier than seeing you happy and pursuing the gifts God has given you. You're so talented, and your eyes light up when you talk about this." He sniffed. "I couldn't be more proud of you. Go. God has given you this opportunity. Don't turn it down."

Liv blinked back tears. "Thanks, Dad." She planted a kiss on his forehead. "I love you."

"Yeah, yeah, enough mushy stuff." But he wore a silly grin. "I love you too, now get out of my sight and go sing your heart out."

She sped the entire way to the fairgrounds—and not Caroline's definition of speeding. Even still, she'd leaped out of the car at a run, sprinting for the stage.

A crew member positioned her keyboard and gave a thumbs up. She smiled in thanks, sitting on the squishy collapsible bench. She adjusted the standing mic to her head level, keeping her mouth turned away as she sucked in deep breaths, let them out. Calming her heart rate. Preparing her lungs.

Her gaze went to the crowd in front of them, and she mused that it might have been a good thing she could only think about sprinting for the stage. She hadn't had time to get nervous, to wonder what the judges would think.

Her eyes roved over the seats as she prayed, *Lord, I don't know what's going to happen here today, or with Dad, or with anything. But I trust you.*

Her gaze stopped, catching on a woman in the front row, holding up a phone, screen toward the stage. Not just any woman—Caroline. What was she doing here? And why would she hold her phone that way?

Caroline waved and pointed at the phone. Liv looked closer and sucked in a breath.

It was hard to see from this distance, but she could swear those two figures were Dad and Susan, watching her performance via video chat. Wasn't he supposed to be in surgery?

She turned to Elijah. His eyes sought hers, and for once, instead of nerves or anxiety, they were filled with peace. She glanced at Charlize and Derek, who gave a wide grin and flipped a drumstick. She found she didn't have an ounce of nervous energy. Only tranquility, knowing that whatever happened, they had followed God's leading.

Win or lose, it was His plan.

Elijah gave the signal, and they broke into music.

Liv's fingers danced over the keys, floating and molding, sinking and soaring. Breath returned to her lungs as her voice wove with Elijah's.

"When I'm in limbo, you're still holding me
When I'm in limbo, finding harmony."

Health, finances, love—what was life but a limbo held together by the words of God singing over her?

The final notes floated away. The sounds of the festival, of fair rides and carnival games, filtered toward the stage.

Then applause.

Audience members rose to their feet. A group of teens with signs bearing terrible puns whooped and cheered. Caroline slapped her leg with one hand while holding the phone aloft in the other.

Liv turned to her band. Elijah blinked out at the crowd as if in shock, while Charlize took a modest bow and Derek flourished his drumsticks.

My band. She liked thinking of them that way.

Before the crew could kick them off the stage to make room for the next act, Liv jumped down from the front of the platform, landing in front of Caroline. "You're supposed to be at work."

"I couldn't miss this." Caroline grinned, handing her the phone. "And some lady named Susan found me on social media and asked if they could tag along."

Susan waved, sitting next to Dad where he reclined in the hospital bed, propped up by pillows. "That's me. I asked Caroline if she was going. Your roommate is lovely."

Liv laughed, her eyes misting. "She's pretty great."

Dad clapped. "That was stunning." He wiped tears from his eyes. "You sound just like your mom."

Now she felt more than mist. She blinked away moisture obscuring her vision.

"Also, Liv." Susan leaned forward. "We have some good news."

The crowd moved around her, and she could hear the next band setting up, but she couldn't tear her eyes from the screen.

Dad nodded. "That's right. They took a look at the incision to get it ready for surgery, and it looks like the antibiotics have been doing their work. The infection isn't as deep as they thought. Barely reaches the muscle." He flashed two thumbs up. "No surgery for me."

Susan patted his shoulder. "He's a *little* excited about that. Dr. Nevins is confused how it happened so fast. She swears it seemed like there were issues with the spinal fluid before." She winked. "But we're not confused."

Thank you, Lord. Liv could hardly keep from bouncing up and down. "That's wonderful."

"Go enjoy your day, Livy." Dad waved. "And tell that young man we say hello. He seems like a nice fellow. Think he might want to come by for some Arnold Palmer?"

"Dad." She rolled her eyes, trying to hide her smile.

"Oh, sure, roll your eyes at your poor old man. Love you, Liv."

"Love you, Dad. Bye, Susan."

Liv clicked off the phone and handed it to Caroline. "Thank you."

"Of course, Liv." Caroline accepted the device. "There are a lot of us rooting for you, you know." She glanced at the time. "I have to get going—this has been an extra-long lunch break—but I'll see you when I get home." She hugged her roommate. "And I'd bet anything you'll be coming home with a blue ribbon."

"Either way, it was worth it."

As Caroline left, Liv turned toward the crowd. Time to find Elijah.

Elijah floated off stage in a daze. That all had gone far too quickly.

It felt as though he'd drifted on top of a cool, calm lake and someone yanked him out. Cheers from the youth group and the collapse of bodies around him in a group hug jarred his senses back to life.

"Lij," Brooklyn said when the tangle of arms released him. "That was amazing. Different from what we've heard from the other bands, but amazing."

Parker kept her distance, with her arms crossed. But she couldn't stop a grin from wriggling up her cheek. "Did you write all those lyrics by yourself?"

"Liv and I collaborated on the music."

"You both will have to teach some of us how to do it." Parker looped her arm with another girl from the youth group. "Some of us have talked about forming a band."

Glad to see she's making some more friends. What he wouldn't have given, back in his youth group days, for some fellow teens who wanted to join in his love for music.

He scanned the crowd and spotted Ryan in the back with his eye planted into the zoom lens of his filming camera. An announcer on stage let the group know that no more bands would be competing and that a local banjo group would take the stage in about fifteen minutes.

Did Charlize sign them up for the last slot?

Maybe she'd hoped they would have the best chance if they stood out freshest in the judges' memories. But with Don having sway over them…

At least the band played something they loved.

Elijah ambled over to Ryan, who lifted his face from his lens. He cracked his neck, and then his back. No doubt he'd hunched over that video camera for hours.

"You looked amazing up there, man." Ryan gestured to the stage. The black-clad crew busied themselves with sweeping the dark surface. "Gonna take me a while to edit all this and upload, but I'll let you know when you can have a first peek at the footage."

Elijah grinned and shook his head. How Ryan managed to film weddings, VBS's, and concerts all in one summer, he couldn't tell.

Doubt niggled in Elijah's gut, while Ryan re-watched some of the band footage. Elijah cringed at how much he closed his eyes in the flicker of images.

"Ryan, you saw all the bands, right?"

"That's what they're paying me to film."

"My friend just said that we sounded way different than the other competing groups. Do you think that means we're automatically out?"

Maybe Chris has gotten the whole intel wrong, and Don didn't actually have any sway over the judges. Had Elijah picked the right song to play?

On stage, it sure felt like it.

All the notes lifted his spirit like the almost-hand hold he and Liv shared that one day.

But now, when they'd announce the winner later that day, sourness filled his stomach. Did they risk everything to do the version they loved?

Ryan paused the footage.

He squinted at his camera for a long time before he turned his gaze to Elijah. "Lij, do you know what films tend to get the awards?"

Elijah frowned and tried to remember his last Oscars party that he and Andy had had at their apartment. They'd split sparkling apple cider and sharp cheddar cheese slices on a charcuterie board.

"The sad ones?"

"No—well, I mean yes, but—" Ryan adjusted his glasses up the bridge of his nose. "The different ones. The movies that experimented with cinematography, with character development, with the story."

Dreaminess filled Ryan's eyes as he spoke. Sparks extinguished in his pupils moments later when reality pulled him back to earth.

"Awards go to those who take risks. Don't be afraid that you're different. Be afraid if you're the same as everyone else."

Elijah stared at the rustling blades of grass and let these words sink in.

With a grunt, Ryan heaved the large camera onto his shoulder. "I should probably film some of the fair attractions before the next group goes on stage. Should get some footage for the intro to the video."

Without so much as a wave goodbye, Ryan ventured toward the carnival games.

"Son, we need to talk."

Elijah whipped his head over his shoulder in time to watch Robert, Pastor Smith...and Don approach. His eyes darted to the left for any restrooms or duck-and-cover shelters he could use.

The nearest porta-potty, situated by a tent full of beta fishes in bowls, had a winding queue that snaked all the way to the food stalls.

No escape. "Hey." Elijah's voice cracked. "What can I do for you?"

Don halted, mere feet away. He wouldn't meet Elijah's eyes. Instead he kept his expression transfixed on a multi-colored super slide in the distance.

"When I first saw you take the stage at The Vine, I thought you were inexperienced. Insincere. I've had"—the toe of Don's shoe dug into a mound of dirt—"some bad experiences at other churches with worship leaders. Where they worried more about looks than the heart."

Don thumped his chest with a fist. Robert, beside him, played a game on his phone.

"I thought the same about you until this past Sunday. When the power went out, I could tell there was something very heartfelt about your performance. I realize now that I should've worded my email to Pastor Smith differently."

Pastor Smith sunk into his shoulders like a tortoise. Perhaps embarrassed about his rash actions, making Elijah take a few-week hiatus from worship.

Wait, did that mean that Don had something positive to say about the worship service during the blackout? Elijah had almost lost his job over that email.

Don grinned. "After a few days of pondering Sunday, I sent that to Pastor Smith. I hoped the curtness of the message would get his attention, so I wouldn't have to wait for a meeting. But I can see how someone may have misconstrued it as angry, given my past track record."

Dings from Robert's phone game mixed with the carnival sounds in the distance.

"I-I don't know what to say." Elijah palmed his sunburnt neck.

He had to check to make sure the earth hadn't adjusted its tilt. Because he may have fallen over at any moment.

"Understandable. I owe you more than an apology, I know. But I also wanted to come over to say that I believe you more than earned that prize money with your performance on stage."

A shock jolted Elijah's ribcage.

"You-you what?" Words tripped over his tongue. Speech refused to work.

"Often I let the judges pick a winner, but considering I am the one who donated the prize money, I do have final say." Don lifted a brow. "Not that you need my help. From what I saw on their score sheets, they were plenty impressed."

Elijah gripped the stand that held Ryan's tripod to keep himself steady.

Did they…did they win?

"Look forward to hearing your song on our car radio." Don tipped a baseball cap rim. Robert glanced up at Elijah and grinned, before returning to the game.

"And," Don added, "I look forward to hearing you play again next Sunday, without any of my previous restrictions."

Don patted Robert's shoulder, and the two of them meandered toward a Fresh Fries stand. Elijah's knees wobbled so much he parked on the grass to stop his legs from shaking. The giant of a pastor loomed over him. Pastor Smith hadn't left yet.

"Elijah." Pastor Smith started, stopped, sighed. "I got quite the chewing out this morning from Chris."

"I'm sorr—"

Pastor Smith held up a hand. "And I deserved it."

Elijah's jaw, which had sunk, clamped shut.

"I'm sure you know that I get my fair share of complaints from the congregation. They can get mad if my sermon goes too long one week or if I don't preach on a topic they like." He fiddled with a watch on his wrist. "I thought I'd let you handle the Don situation, since he was mad about worship specifically."

Glints of sunlight overhead blocked Elijah from reading Pastor Smith's expression.

"But I should've stood up for you. Especially knowing that Don was the reason we lost our last worship leader. For that, I'm sorry."

Elijah pulled himself up into a standing position. Water filled his eyes from the sun's beams.

"Thank you, Pastor Smith. I forgive you."

Pastor Smith's mouth twitched. He nodded once. "Next Sunday, you play. Make sure Liv is on rotation more. You sound lovely together."

Did Pastor Smith just wink at him? Did he, too, know how Elijah felt for Liv?

Is it that obvious?

Question unanswered, Elijah watched Pastor Smith disappear in the vast array of tents. Something tapped Elijah's shoulder. He turned on his heel and found Liv withdrawing her index finger.

"Sorry, was talking with a friend. Want to check out the Ferris wheel again? Line's looking pretty empty."

Elijah froze, memories from the last few moments seizing him. He didn't speak, unable to transfer thoughts to speech.

"Lij?"

"Liv, I think we won."

Her grin formed an O shape, eyes widening. "What?"

"Don stopped by to talk. We won." The last word fractured in his esophagus. It didn't taste real yet.

Liv slapped a hand to her mouth and choked on a sob. Tears glazed her cheeks. She lifted her arm to swipe away the moisture. "Oh, I can't believe it. Does that mean everyone gets five thousand dollars?"

Hope danced in her eyes. And perhaps she saw a medical bill from the hospital she could use that money to pay for. Or a handful of college classes.

Elijah brushed a hand across her shoulder. She, too, shook. "Twenty thousand. Liv, the band decided we want you to have it all."

"What, I couldn't possibl—"

"It's already decided. Your dreams are important, and we want to see you accomplish them."

She collapsed into him in a hug, tears wetting his chest. Liv trembled so much that Elijah had to keep her steady. They stood in limbo, in that hug, for a long while. Until the shaking stopped, and Liv pulled away. She tucked a few flyaway hairs that had stuck to her cheek behind her ears.

"So." She swiped moisture off her nose. "About that Ferris wheel ride." Liv extended a hand, and they weaved their fingers together.

Chapter Twenty-Three

"SEE YOU WEDNESDAY." LIV WAVED TO her classmate as they reached a fork in the sidewalk. "My band leader's picking me up."

The younger woman glanced at the long-haired man leaning against the hood of his car in the parking lot. Her eyebrows shot up. "Girl, is that one your boyfriend? Because if not, I'd like to be introduced."

Liv made eye contact with Elijah across the patch of grass dividing the sidewalk meandering between the academic buildings from the visitor parking lot. He grinned, and her face heated. "Yeah. He is."

"Well let me know if you come across any other cute guys at the studio." The girl flipped her ponytail over her shoulder.

"Ha ha. See you later."

Oh boy. Liv remembered the so-called "freshman frenzy" from her first time in college, when the new students all hoped to meet their perfect match. Going back to college as a twenty-five-year-old freshman, she felt old as dirt.

She strayed off the path and onto the grass, pulling her light jacket closer as a chill autumn breeze picked up, in time for the first official week of fall. At nine in the morning, the sun hadn't had time yet to warm the earth.

Tunes danced through her head from her eight a.m. music composition class. Homework weighed down her bag.

And she wouldn't have it any other way.

After she and the band had been named the winners of the competition, she'd received an unexpected email a week later.

Olivia,

You may recognize my name from The Vine. I'm not ashamed to say that I've been seeking counseling on grief, and one of the ways in which I decided to honor my wife is through a memorial four-year scholarship to award to one student per year.

It isn't quite a full ride, as they say, but I've been talking with the university my wife attended, and they said that a qualified candidate for this grant would probably be eligible for their academic scholarships as well.

Anyway, I saw your flyer advertising music lessons in She Brews and put some things together. The woman with pink hair told me you always wanted to finish college and become a music teacher. She also gave me a demo CD of her band, which I don't believe I'll play.

All this to say, I would like to offer you the first annual Becky Wadsworth Memorial Scholarship for music. Below, you'll find the college information and the scholarship amount.

Let me know if you are interested.

Don Wadsworth

Liv had stared at the screen. Stared at the numbers, at the name of the college only half an hour away.

And then she jumped and shrieked for Caroline to come read this email *immediately.*

Leaves crunched on asphalt as Liv made her way to Elijah.

He pushed off the car and strode toward her. "What are you grinning about?" He struck a pose. "Is it the flannel? I broke it out for fall."

She laughed and slipped her hand into his. "No. I was remembering when I got the email from Don."

"Ah. That is a good thing to be smiling about." He opened the passenger door for her. "Though slightly less exciting than flannel season."

She snorted and slid into the car, placing her bag on her lap. "You ready to make some music?"

"With you?" He leaned on the door and smirked. "Always."

Butterflies danced in her belly, and she giggled like a schoolgirl. But instead of shutting down the bubbly feeling, she let her heart float, the music of happiness filling her soul.

They drove with the windows half down, crisp air filtering into the vehicle. Her phone dinged, and she looked at the screen to see a text from Dad. She opened the message, revealing a poorly angled selfie of Dad posing with pumpkins sitting on his kitchen counter, Susan rolling her eyes in the background.

Dad: Making some fresh pumpkin pie and roasting pumpkin seeds for when you and Elijah visit tomorrow. Have a GOURD time at your recording session. Love, Dad

Liv groaned and read the message to Elijah, who guffawed. "That's a pretty *gourd* one."

Liv slapped a hand to her forehead. "Not you too."

With the prize money, they'd been able to fend off medical bills and keep the house for the time being. Dad felt well enough to continue his consulting, and he'd acquired a larger client. *Might even have enough left over for a ring*, he'd told her bashfully before rushing on to a discussion of the squirrels.

Liv leaned her head back and closed her eyes, gratefulness filling her heart. From college, to Elijah, to Dad's health and recording with the band, the melodies of blessings blended into one big, beautiful harmony that serenaded her soul all the way to the studio.

"That last one sounded perfect," the producer in the control room boomed into the microphone. He cracked one knuckle, released, and used that finger to make a circular motion in the air. "I think that's a wrap, guys."

"Speaking of wraps," Derek said, "Charlize, you wanna grab gyros from that pop-up stand you mentioned you saw at the strip the other day? I think they're only around until the first week in October." Derek tucked a drumstick behind his ear. The stick clattered onto the carpeted floor moments later.

"I have no idea what you're talking about." Her eyes flicked to the ceiling. She waved at Elijah and Liv. "See you all at worship practice on Thursday."

Charlize exited the studio with Derek following inches behind. Perhaps Elijah's imagination decided to play tricks, but he swore he saw them link hands before they disappeared around the corner.

Elijah tore off his headphones.

What a weird process, recording one instrument at a time. And doing a "scratch" recording at the beginning—a sort of rough draft to help the producer get the feel of the song.

Over the past few months, the group had experimented with some of the harmonies. Charlize finally got the knack for singing and playing bass at the same time, so she'd added a second harmony in the counterpoint, going two notes lower than Liv in those parts.

When they stepped into the control room, the producer pushed some mysterious levers up and down. He paused and grinned at them.

"We'll have the audio engineer mix this. Then we'll email you when you can expect to hear your song go live on the radio. We're hoping we can have it premiere in November, just before they start playing the Christmas songs."

Man, had the months flown. Summer had dissolved into autumn faster than Elijah could say, "An' a one, an' a two…"

Elijah didn't realize just how much time it would take for them to finally get in the studio. He half-expected to get an email days after the festival with an invite. Andy explained that perhaps the music industry worked in a similar fashion to publishing.

"Caroline says she gets emails all the time with submissions for Helping Hope. Authors demand to have their books published within months. Really, it takes years."

Songs didn't seem to get produced in that slow of a fashion, but he didn't expect they'd wait to record until September.

They thanked the producer and stepped out of the studio into the darker afternoon light.

Thank goodness Elijah had picked up Liv from her 8 a.m. class after it finished. They'd spent hours in that studio. And with the days growing darker, they didn't have many hours of sunlight left.

Scarlet leaves swirled underfoot in the parking lot. Soon every green tree would fade to deep oranges and yellows within weeks, if not days.

Liv hoisted her nose to the air and breathed in. Elijah parroted the move.

Scents of weak sunshine and sweet earth tickled his nostrils. Who didn't love fall? He untied his flannel from his waist and slipped it over his shoulders.

"Call me crazy." Liv shut her eyes and inhaled again. "But even though we spent hours in there it wasn't enough. Up for more music?"

He grinned.

Ever since they played at the fair, Liv and Elijah found any moment to find harmony. In She Brews, in No Strings, anywhere, one would start a melody and the other would join in.

"I think I know just the place."

They piled into his car.

Windows down, his vehicle sped down backroads. Wind kicked up Liv's hair as she tuned the radio to a worship music station. Hope leapt into his chest as he imagined their song streaming from those same speakers weeks from now.

They pulled into the parking lot of the national park. Hikers with walking sticks dotted the entrance and the sparse rows of vehicles. Not as many people traversed these trails when the weather got colder.

Wet leaves stamped their shoes as Liv and Elijah made their way up the winding, muddy paths.

Couples sporting rings and nice outfits posed on cliff faces and near the most vibrant trees. Ryan had mentioned he often shot the most engagement pictures during autumn, Michigan's most beautiful season.

Elijah had once, in jest, told Andy that he needed to propose to Caroline so he could get in on the photo op. This caused Andy's cheeks to flush to beet red.

Liv and Elijah wove their way past hikers and cross-country runners to the waterfall. To his surprise, no couples waited beside the water to take photos. Mist spit onto his clothes seconds later.

Ah, they wouldn't want to get their nice clothes wet.

Liv, bedecked in jean overalls with holes on the knees, sallied forth and sat on the wet rock by the falls. Roaring waters drowned out Elijah's senses.

"It sounds like music here." Her finger traced the shape of a leaf stuck to the rock. "Feels like music."

"You know what else does?" Elijah reached out his hand and laced his fingers with hers.

"Agreed." Liv squeezed his palm. "There's something else that feels like music."

She scooted closer and placed her head on his shoulder. He wondered if she could sense the vibrations of his heartbeat, that had accelerated to a fortissimo.

His words hitched in his throat for a moment. Instead, he allowed birdsong and the gurgle of the waters to take a few measures. Then he squeezed her palm again, and she looked up at him, eyes dreamy.

"Liv, you want to know what else feels like music?"

Before he could give her a moment to respond, he leaned in and kissed her. Warmth filled his insides, and he wanted to stay suspended in this limbo forever.

They drew apart, and blush lit her cheeks on fire. Her skin matched the maple tree behind her.

Then she puzzle-pieced her head back into his shoulder, sighed.

"Agreed," she said. "That's the best kind."

AUTHOR'S NOTE

To say we're people-pleasers is the ultimate understatement of the year. Alyssa and I met in college and had it drilled into us, "You say yes to every assignment. Every volunteer opportunity. Or someone else will take it and you will fail miserably." So we followed that advice, and it took a very long time to reverse that habit.

In fact, to this day Alyssa and I (Hope) have to call each other and ask, "Is it okay if I turn down this unpaid opportunity? I'm just so worried what they're going to do if I say no."

And the other one of us has to calmly explain that we're going to "smack you" if we add one more commitment to our crazy pile of deadlines.

Our writing at the University became more about attaining that illustrious A+ grade rather than for the pleasure of it, and it took us a while to find our way back to falling in love with our work for the sake of writing itself.

So we wanted to channel some of that journey through the characters of Elijah and Liv. Pushovers who eventually learn to embrace music and worship by its beautiful roots in their lives.

As far as the worship leader aspect goes, I (Hope) would be remiss not to admit that I have complained more than once about worship. As a hymn lover, I have a tendency to get frustrated by the repetitive and sometimes unbiblical nature of some modern worship songs.

That was, until my brother became a worship leader.

He helped to open my (Hope's) eyes to the inner workings of a church—especially a large one like the Vine. Worship leaders and pastors have such a sacrificial heart for their congregation, and it pains me the amount of negative feedback they receive whether on worship, sermons, or anything in-between.

True, no one will agree on the best way to do worship.

Some of us prefer hymns, others, something more contemporary.

But songs like "The Heart of Worship"—seriously, go check out the story behind that song—remind us that worship isn't about us. Rather, we do it to glorify God. Even if our legs ache from standing for too many songs in a row or it seems like the worship leader keeps repeating the bridge one too many times.

This, of course, isn't to wag a finger at the readers and say, "You're a meanie because you complained about church once." We all have our various gripes, some preferential, and some that we should seriously bring to the attention of a pastor.

But rather we encourage you to send a note of encouragement to your pastor or worship leader.

They may not get it perfectly. But a healthy church cares deeply about its congregation.

CPSIA information can be obtained
at www.ICGtesting.com
Printed in the USA
LVHW082008150622
721158LV00003B/4

9 781943 959785